T0124671

Jim Haynes has travelled far and wide to interview the people whose stories make up this book. From his days driving trucks in the bush for his mates, and later as part of the Slim Dusty touring show, Jim has been aware of the special nature of the trucking industry in both rural and urban Australia. 'Every year Slim would do a show to raise money for the truckers' memorial at Tarcutta,' said Jim, 'and those families loved him. It was a privilege to be part of that. I have also done many shows with my bush poet mate Frank Daniel who ran a trucking company for many years and met many great characters from the trucking industry. Their stories inspired this collection.'

Before becoming a professional entertainer, songwriter, verse writer and singer in 1988, Jim Haynes taught writing, literature, history and drama in schools and universities from outback New South Wales to Britain and back again. While teaching he gained two masters degrees in literature, from New England University and the University of Wales. Jim is the author of many great Australian titles including books on railways, aviation and horse racing, and is one of our most successful and prolific Australiana authors.

THE BEST AUSTRALIAN TRUCKING STORIES

JIM HAYNES

ALLEN&UNWIN

This edition published in 2018
First published in 2011

Copyright © Jim Haynes 2011

All rights reserved. No part of this book may be reproduced or transmitted in
any form or by any means, electronic or mechanical, including photocopying,
recording or by any information storage and retrieval system, without prior
permission in writing from the publisher. The Australian *Copyright Act 1968*
(the Act) allows a maximum of one chapter or 10 per cent of this book, whichever
is the greater, to be photocopied by any educational institution for its educational
purposes provided that the educational institution (or body that administers it) has
given a remuneration notice to the Copyright Agency (Australia) under the Act.

Allen & Unwin
83 Alexander Street
Crows Nest NSW 2065
Australia
Phone: (61 2) 8425 0100
Email: info@allenandunwin.com
Web: www.allenandunwin.com

A catalogue record for this
book is available from the
National Library of Australia

ISBN 978 1 76063 332 5

Text design by Bookhouse, Sydney
Set in Versailles by Bookhouse, Sydney
Printed in Australia by McPherson's Printing Group

10 9 8 7 6 5 4 3 2 1

The paper in this book is FSC® certified.
FSC® promotes environmentally responsible,
socially beneficial and economically viable
management of the world's forests.

THIS BOOK IS DEDICATED TO THE
MEMORY OF KEITH BRINDLEY

CONTENTS

ACKNOWLEDGMENTS

I owe a debt of gratitude to Liz Martin, Grant Luhrs, Frank Daniel, Rod Hannifey, Ray Gilleland, Kingsley Foreman, John Elliott, Ron Pullen, Irwin Richter, Sharon Hourn, Jayne Denham, Steve Theobald and Cheryl van der Velden for their contributions and support.

A special mention must be made of the assistance given by the National Road Transport Hall of Fame, Alice Springs.

Thanks to Stuart Neal for suggesting this collection and to Clara Finlay for her invaluable assistance. John Mapps and Lisa Macken did a great job copyediting and proofreading.

Photos appear by courtesy of the National Road Transport Hall of Fame, Ray Gilleland, Ron Pullen, Frank Daniel, Rod Hannifey, Jayne Denham, John Elliott, Kingsley Foreman, Robyn McMillan and Grant Luhrs.

INTRODUCTION

My only claim to fame in the trucking world is that I have held a heavy vehicle driver's licence since I was 21 years old.

As a young single schoolteacher in the bush I boarded with a family who owned a drilling business, and one day the local police sergeant asked me when I was going to get a truck licence.

'Why do I need one of those?' I asked.

'Well,' he said, 'you've been driving those trucks of Kolstad's around for a while now, I thought you might want one.'

'Me ... driving trucks?' I replied nervously. 'No, not me, Sergeant! I don't really need one, do I? I only move the trucks around the yard ... mostly.'

'Look, Jim,' he said seriously, 'stop lying to me. I know why you haven't come in for a truck licence driving test.'

'Oh,' I said, 'why is that?'

'Because,' he sighed, 'if you turned up to get your licence in one of those trucks you've been driving around the bush, I'd probably have to put it off the road for many and varied defects, so just drop into the station tomorrow and I'll GIVE you a bloody truck licence, OK?'

I did . . . and he did . . . and I still have it.

When I was asked to compile, edit and help write this collection of stories, certain of my younger musical friends, who knew nothing of my trucking claim to fame, found it rather amusing. They seemed to think that truckies were rough, tough macho men, strong and independent, practical, physical types of blokes, and that I . . . wasn't. Little did they know that I had spent some time as a truck driver, albeit a very brief period now decades in the distant past.

I also had 'connections'.

Although I had no direct contact at all with trucks or trucking, my first thought was that I knew people involved in the trucking community through my connections with country music. I had toured as part of the Slim Dusty Show and served on the board of the Country Music Association for many years with Slim and Joy McKean. Slim recorded many trucking songs and was universally loved by truckies, and Joy wrote the best trucking song of all time, 'Lights on the Hill'.

I had done shows with Travis Sinclair, who comes from a trucking family, owns and drives a big rig and has had many hits with truck songs.

I was also friends with singers like Jayne Denham and Amber Lawrence, who both had sponsorships with trucking companies. I knew I would find some good trucking stories if I asked around.

I was right.

When I called Slim's daughter, Anne Kirkpatrick, to ask about material for a story, she said, 'Jim, why don't you just call John?!' An old friend of Slim's and mine, photographer and journalist John Elliott was the obvious person to turn to for good stories about Slim and the truckies. John travelled many thousands of kilometres with Slim and was the photographer for many of Slim's albums and books. Thanks to John, I didn't have to strain my memory banks about Slim's connection with trucks.

Luckily for me, two good mates, Grant Luhrs and Frank Daniel, also came to the rescue. I have known Grant for 30 years, since we met performing at the Longyard in Tamworth. I have recorded in his studio in Wagga and we have been partners in crime running opposing shows at the Tamworth Festival for years, as well as travelling to other festivals together.

Grant was also involved in Rig Radio, a radio show for the trucking community, and he put me in touch with Rod Hannifey, who was a terrific help in getting this collection together, providing several great contributions of his own, making many useful suggestions, and sending me the poem by Cheryl van der Velden.

Rod Hannifey was involved in Rig Radio and also runs the 'TRUCKRIGHT Industry Vehicle', a truck in which he takes motoring journalists, politicians and representatives from road authorities for long hauls, so they can see and understand the issues facing the road transport industry. The website www. truckright.com.au gives tips on sharing the road with trucks and welcomes comments and feedback.

Grant has also been involved with the Tarcutta memorial and knew people like Ron Pullen and Irwin Richter, who were part of the driving force behind the memorial. Both Ron and Irwin have a long history of involvement with the road transport industry. Their stories appear here, as does Grant's story about Rig Radio, and their memories and assistance with this collection have been invaluable.

It's odd how things are connected sometimes. Grant arrived at my place one day with some recorded memories of Ron's and said, 'Ron sent this brochure about the Tarcutta memorial, in case it might be useful.' I opened it as we chatted and there was a photo of Slim Dusty doing a fundraising concert for the memorial. Standing right next to Slim on stage was . . . yours truly, Jim Haynes. Neither Grant nor Ron had realised I was featured in the brochure, and I had no idea either.

Frank Daniel always comes good when I need help with a book, whether it's poetry or a yarn or a contact. Frank owned a trucking business for many years and operated a fleet of sixteen vehicles out of his hometown of Canowindra, but I have known him for almost twenty years as a writer and performer of bush verse. We have done a few thousand kilometres and a lot of shows together in that time.

I knew Frank was the man who dumped the load of wheat at Parliament House in 1986 and I figured that would be a good story for this collection, if I could pester him into writing it. I figured he'd have a few more good yarns about his trucking days if I annoyed him enough. He didn't let me down.

I soon came to realise that the trucking community is full of very gracious and helpful people who also happen to be just about the most 'Aussie' characters you can find anywhere. There is a general desire among them for the transport industry to be seen in a positive and realistic light.

Everyone I talked to was enthusiastic about conveying a true picture of the role played by the road transport industry in Australia's development and history. They all felt that truckies had been given a raw deal by the media and suffered from negative perceptions and a stereotyped image. The more I had to do with them, the more I realised they were right.

Everyone I approached for help with this collection was amazingly generous and helpful and enthusiastic about the project. The day I called Liz Martin in Alice Springs and introduced myself was a truly lucky one for me.

Liz Martin OAM has been so helpful in providing stories and contacts and suggestions that it's no wonder she is so admired for her efforts in getting the National Road Transport Hall of Fame to become a reality in Alice Springs. She is an inspirational woman! The website for the Hall of Fame is www. roadtransporthall.com and it's worth the trip to Alice Springs just to visit the hall. Thanks to Liz, I now know a bloody lot more about road transport history than I did twelve months ago!

Meeting the 'Nullarbor Kid', Ray Gilleland, was a genuine thrill for me. I'd read his stories because Jayne Denham had told me I had to and we finally met up while I was working in a show at Twin Towns RSL, on the Gold Coast.

Ray is a larger-than-life character. There is no bullshit in Ray's yarns; what you see is what you get and what you read really happened. They are fantastic stories! Ray's book, *My Way on the Highway,* is still available direct from Ray (nullarborkid@ hotmail.com) for those of you who want more of his stories.

Kingsley Foreman and Sharon Hourn were very gracious in providing their stories and I thank them both sincerely. Kingsley's stories made me laugh out loud and Sharon's story will break the hardest heart. I admire her bravery in telling her story so that others can understand the tragedy that too often comes with the trucking life.

Steve Theobald emailed me after I'd talked about truck stories on 2UE one Sunday. He had a story from his childhood that he allowed me to use, after his dad had added a few details and memories. It's a wonderful heart-warming yarn, too.

Apologies to all those who contacted me with stories and ideas that I didn't get around to including. So many stories came 'out of the woodwork' as the collection was being put together. Jeff Spence, Tony Dyer and Allen Robb were especially helpful, but those stories, like so many others, will have to wait for Volume Two.

Jim Haynes, October 2011

THE AUSSIE TRUCKIE

TRADITIONAL/JIM HAYNES

When the Lord was creating all things, all the elements, plants, creatures and people, he'd made it to the sixth day without tiring, although he'd been on overtime for a couple of days.

Each creature required special care and attention and, when it came to humanity, all professions and nationalities had to be unique; it was boutique manufacturing, not production-line stuff.

Nurses and teachers required extra doses of patience and tolerance, politicians needed extra-thick skins and two faces, television personalities needed permanent smiles and the ability to fake sincerity, and authors and editors required extra doses of endurance and intelligence.

God had managed to create most types and professions when an angel working on quality control noticed that the creation process had slowed significantly. The angel, whose name from memory was Steve, was just starting out in his new job as apprentice archangel; I believe the Catholics later made him patron saint of spanners and wing-nuts and you can pray to him instead of swearing when you skin your knuckles under any vehicle.

'You're slowing down, Boss,' said Saint Steve. 'You seem to be taking a lot of time on this one. What's the problem?'

And the Lord answered, 'Thou shouldst see the specs on this order, it's near impossible even for me!'

'Maybe you're just getting tired,' said Saint Steve gently. 'Have another go after smoko. What is it you're trying to create, anyway?'

'It's a thing called the "Aussie truck driver" apparently,' said the Lord, checking the front of the manual.

'Sounds relatively straightforward,' remarked Steve. 'What's the problem?'

'Well,' answered the Lord, 'this one has to be able to drive ten to twelve or more hours per day, through any type of weather, on any type of road. They also have to know the highway traffic laws of six states and two territories plus the federal laws and be ready and able to unload 40 tonnes of freight after driving all night and have the ability to sleep when they can in places that the police refuse to patrol.'

'Gee, Boss,' said Saint Steve, checking out the front of the manual as he stood beside his leader, 'that means extra doses of concentration and endurance, amazing memory and superhuman strength plus extra vigilance and the ability to work on minimal rest!'

'Just as thou sayest,' replied the Boss, 'and this model also has to be able to live in a truck 24 hours a day, seven days a weeks, for months on end, offer first aid and roadside assistance to his fellow travellers, meet tight schedules and still maintain an even and controlled composure through it all. These people also have to keep their heads in a crisis and act to very detailed specifications with a high level of motor-skill accuracy in an accident.'

'I also see here,' said Saint Steve as he examined the specifications, 'they have to be in top physical condition at all times and be able to operate on black coffee and half-eaten meals and have six pairs of hands.'

'Yea, verily,' said the Lord, tapping the page Saint Steve was reading, 'but it's not the hands that are causing me problems, it's the three pairs of eyes a driver needs to have.'

'So I see,' gasped Saint Steve, 'and that's on the standard model!'

'Yes, just as thou sayest,' the Lord replied. 'One pair that sees the herd of cattle in the scrub 3 miles away, another pair here in the side of his head for the blind spots that motorists love to hide in, and another pair in front that can look reassuringly into a spouse's face and say, "It'll be all right, I'm fine, I'll get some rest when I get home."'

'Speaking of rest,' said Saint Steve, closing the manual, 'you're looking tired. Why not have a spell and tackle this one later, after a nice cup of tea and some smoko?'

'I can't,' said the Lord, 'much as I wouldst liketh to. I've already managed to get this model to the point where it can drive 1000 kilometres a day without incident, raise a family of five without ever seeing them and survive on one dollar a kilometre.'

Saint Steve rubbed his chin and looked reflective. 'What model brain are you installing?'

'The best,' said the Lord. 'When operating properly this model brain can tell you the elements of every chemical load invented, recite Australian road rules and regulations for each state while asleep, offer timely advice to strangers, search for missing children and help make good parenting decisions that help raise a family of decent citizens without ever going home . . . and still keep its sense of humour.

'This Aussie truck driver also has to have phenomenal personal control. He has to deal with delivery and pick-up areas designed by our main rival in Hell, coax a loader to actually work for his money, comfort an accident victim's family, pay all taxes and fines and put up with endless misguided criticism.'

With that, Saint Steve leaned over his Boss's shoulder to take a look at the unfinished model lying on the construction table. 'It looks almost finished,' he said with surprise. 'How have you managed to put all that's required in there?'

'It hasn't been easy,' said the Lord, 'but it has to be done. This model needs all those specifications and features to operate successfully.'

'Are you sure it will all fit?' asked the angel as he bent over the seemingly sleeping figure.

'I think I've almost managed it, but it's taken everything I had,' said the Creator with a sigh.

'Hang on, what's this?' asked the angel, bending lower and touching the cheek of the sleeping model. 'There's a leak, look. I told you that you were trying to put too much into this model. No living thing can handle all that, surely.'

'That's not a leak,' said the Lord, bending low to examine the droplet of water. 'It's a tear.'

'Well, that's amazing; along with everything else you added a tear. What's the tear for: bottled-up emotions, fallen comrades, or for the mate's family without its father? You're a genius, Boss,' said Saint Steve reverently.

The Lord straightened up and looked gravely towards the angel.

'I didn't put that there,' He said.

RENT-A-WRECK

KINGSLEY FOREMAN

I worked in the transport industry for 25 years from the 1970s into the 1990s; fifteen of those were with Richmond Heavy Towing, a company based in the city of Adelaide.

South Australia is a vast state, stretching from a mostly isolated coastline to the hot and dry deserts of the outback. Richmond Towing do a lot of long-range heavy truck and rental-car salvage, involving hundreds of kilometres of outback driving. Sometime in the late 1970s I did three rental-car salvage trips to Woomera in three days.

Now, Woomera is a vast area of government land in the middle of South Australia; controlled by the federal government, it consists of hundreds of square miles of flat, dry and very barren land which has been used since World War II for test-firing rockets and all sorts of explosive weapons. A group of NASA people from the US had gone up there to do some rocket tests. The problem was that the NASA mob didn't quite realise how big kangaroos were, until they hit a few of them with a rented car or two . . . or three!

The kangaroos up there didn't know much about cars either. Roads on the Woomera range are on government land and there are so few cars that the wildlife just run wherever they feel like running, and that can be straight in front of your car, so you have to slow down and watch out for them . . . or play chicken with them and take the consequences.

Woomera is about 600 miles from the Richmond Towing depot in Adelaide, and that's only one way. It's a 1200-mile trip each time, and I did three of them in three days; it was good for the wallet but not so good for my sleep pattern.

After doing work for a number of rental-car companies over many years, I now know why they like their customers to pay by credit card. You would be amazed at how roughly people treat rental cars!

I once had to go and get a little Volkswagen Golf from Coober Pedy, an opal-mining town in the outback desert of South Australia, some 550 miles from Adelaide. Normally, if you want to drive a long way in Australia, you rent a four-wheel drive or a bigger sedan like a Ford Falcon or a Holden Commodore. The bloke who rented the Golf was a German tourist who apparently told the rental company he was 'only driving around Sydney'.

Not only was he 1700 miles from Sydney, he had been up to Darwin and was on his way back. That's a round trip of 5000 miles. He had hit a kangaroo and the little car was a write-off; he must have been really moving when he hit that roo.

One of the funniest jobs I ever did for a rental-car company started one quiet evening about 7 p.m. I was sitting in the phone room at the Richmond Towing depot talking to PJ, the radio operator at the time, when he took a phone call from a rental company. It seemed they'd had a call from a Japanese tourist whose car had broken down. He called from the roadhouse at Meningie, which is about 150 miles south-east of Adelaide.

When PJ asked me if I would like to do the job, I said, 'Sure, I could do with a bit of a drive tonight.'

'Good,' said PJ. 'You'll be back just after midnight, so don't bother returning to the depot. Just take the truck home to save time and get some sleep. Give me a call in the morning about 8. Instead of coming into the depot to start work, you can start work from home tomorrow.'

I drove across South Road to the London Road fuel depot to fill up the truck, then drove into the city to the rental company to pick up the replacement car for the customer. I loaded the replacement car onto the Ford Louisville sliding tilt-tray tow truck and headed off to Meningie.

When I arrived at the roadhouse at Meningie I soon found the tourist. He didn't speak much English, but I told him to hop into the truck and show me where the car was. Off we went, heading east out of Meningie.

We had gone about 5 miles when I asked him how much further it was to the car. He just pointed straight ahead and said, 'More . . . more,' so I drove on.

Ten miles later I asked again, 'How far now?'

Again he just pointed ahead and said, 'More . . . more,' so I just kept driving.

This time I drove about 60 miles in silence before I said to him, 'Look, tell me what's going on, where's the car? You told the rental company it was just out of town!'

He replied in broken English, 'Yes, it just out of next big town.'

Well, the next town was Kingston and that was about 140 miles from where we were.

'Why didn't you get a lift into Kingston and not back at Meningie?' I asked, exasperated.

He said, 'I just took ride from first car that stop, but it going the wrong way.'

I drove on to Kingston and, when I slowed down for the town, I asked, 'So, it's just out of town now?'

He answered rather sheepishly, 'Not this town . . . next big one.'

I looked at him dumbfounded and said, 'You don't mean Mount Gambier!?'

'Yes,' he said. 'Yes, that right . . . Mount Gambier.'

I shook my head and said, 'That's another 180 miles away!' Mount Gambier is actually closer to Melbourne than it is to Adelaide.

Anyway, I drove to Mount Gambier and finally picked up the car and headed back to Adelaide.

It was 8.30 a.m. before I was back in two-way radio range at Tailem Bend, 50 miles from Adelaide. I could hear PJ calling me, so I stopped on top of a hill and told him the whole story.

'I'm not quite ready to start work today, PJ,' I said. 'I haven't been home yet!'

DOING TIME FOR TRUCKING

IRWIN RICHTER WITH JIM HAYNES

My association with trucking began in 1950.

We came from off the land, down near Lockhart, New South Wales, and of course we had a truck on the property that we used for delivering cereal hay around the district. Dad also used to supply fodder to the police stations in the area, which all had horses back then.

We decided that the trucks would provide a more reliable income and be a back-up to the farm, so my father and my brother and myself set up in the freight business together, originally using rigid Bedfords. When Dad passed away we were hit by death duties and had to reorganise the business so that our mother would be financially secure.

We were always involved in produce and always generated our own freight. We ended up with five vehicles on the road, mainly servicing the produce markets and building-materials industries.

Road transport had really only begun in the late 1940s and there were many restrictions in the form of road taxes. They had a Road Transport Restriction Act in the 1940s—in reality it was a Railways Protection Act—which imposed a heavy tax on all road transport.

Freight crossing state borders was subject to a confusing variety of laws up to the early 1950s. As the Commonwealth Constitution did not specify federal control over road transport, it effectively meant that jurisdiction was controlled by the states and territories.

In 1952, truck drivers became frustrated by the levies on interstate road transport, which were designed to protect the state-owned railways. At Wodonga in New South Wales, vehicles had to line up to buy permits to go into Victoria; it was the same on every border. The idea was to force the trade onto the railways.

The drivers got together and placed a copy of the Constitution in a wheelbarrow and pushed it from Melbourne to Sydney. The trip took eleven days, which was two days faster than a parcel mailed at the same time and carried by rail.

They then launched a legal challenge against the validity of the New South Wales Transport Act, on the basis that section 92 of the Constitution provided that trade and commerce between the states should be 'absolutely free'. This legal challenge became known as the *Hughes and Vale* case, and eventually led, in November 1954, to a successful constitutional challenge in the High Court which opened up the development of interstate road transport around Australia. The Privy Council ruled that the New South Wales Transport Act indeed violated section 92 of the Australian Constitution.

Hughes and Vale was the catalyst for the growth of interstate road transport. The growth of this business soon highlighted the limitations of the different road transport regulations between states. Following the case, taxes could only be levied for road maintenance purposes. The end result was that the tax burden on interstate trucks was somewhat reduced, making trucking more profitable.

The states then got together in an attempt to get revenue from road transport, as they did from the railways. New South Wales introduced the Roads Maintenance Contribution Act. Each state then followed suit and a new tax was introduced whereby each driver had to file returns for each vehicle for each month. The tax was so much per cent per mile on your gross vehicle weight.

Drivers who took the option of using federal 'interstate plates' soon found that state laws prevented the use of those plates unless a load crossed a state border.

A record of all journeys had to be sent to the state Department of Transport, which had hundreds of inspectors sitting at strategic points along the roads and highways. They wouldn't pull you up, they'd just jot down your vehicle number as you passed and then check their records against your monthly returns. If they didn't coincide, you got a 'bluey'—or summons—and a hefty fine.

There were massive protests in every state against this new tax, which applied to all vehicles over 4 tonnes. This meant farmers were also caught up in the tax and the Farmers' Associations soon joined the trucking industry in the protests.

In New South Wales we formed a Road Transport and Commercial Vehicle Owners group to organise opposition to the new taxes. There were thirteen members on the committee and I was the representative of the freight industry. The farmers, apiarists, coach companies and others were all represented, and 1800 people attended a conference held at the Trocadero in Sydney in 1958. At the meeting we decided to appeal to the High Court to test the validity of the new taxes.

In the meantime, our barristers suggested that we continue to file our returns but not to pay the charges, pending the outcome of the High Court appeal. In spite of the fact that stiff penalties applied to failure to pay, as well as failure to send in returns, hundreds of us continued to send in our monthly returns without paying the tax. My brother and I had four vehicles running at that time and we set up a special account for the funds in the event that the case was lost.

The High Court ruled that the new taxes were valid, and an appeal to the Privy Council in London was denied. The new taxes therefore became legal and binding in 1961.

While this went on we'd had to dig into the savings we'd put aside and the fines had added a considerable amount to what we owed in taxes. Consequently, we didn't have on hand the £4000 we owed. We had a pile of warrants for non-payment and had to come up with a plan to pay the back taxes and the fines in instalments. There were hundreds of other truckers in the same position.

Some of the bigger companies went straight to the Department of Motor Transport and came to an arrangement to pay a proportion of what they owed. In some cases the New South Wales parliament accepted a third or half of the outstanding amount plus a written guarantee to comply in future. Many of these arrangements were brokered through the hard work of legendary rural MP Wal Fyfe.

In my case the powers-that-be were not so sympathetic, as I'd been involved in organising the protests and authorising the legal actions against the tax. Wal Fyfe attempted to help us out and we made immediate representation to the state government, but we were hit with a further £6000 worth of fines and penalties for failure to remit the money, although we had sent in all returns and accepted that we had to pay the back taxes.

Wal Fyfe put in a representation on our behalf, but the summonses had already been issued and had fallen due at court in Sydney. Our representation was not accepted and I was told that unless I paid up immediately I would be sent to prison.

Specially commissioned police turned up at my office door one day early in 1963 and demanded the money or me. They even turned up at my mother's home and threatened her, as she was a part-owner of our business.

When they turned up at my door at work I told them I had chosen to serve out the time. They allowed me to go home and say goodbye to my wife and four young kids, then they escorted me to the railway station. Another fellow from Wagga and myself were taken by train to Goulburn. The escorting officers had a pile of warrants about a foot thick which they dumped on the desk at Goulburn Police Station.

The desk sergeant, who had migrated to Australia from the north of England, looked at the mountain of warrants and exclaimed, 'Fook me dead!' and called for everyone in the station to come and have a look at the pile. He'd never seen so many warrants issued against one business or individual. They chose the warrant that had the largest amount owing, about £300 it was, and I had to serve out the time for that warrant, which amounted to 123 days.

So, I spent 123 days in Goulburn Gaol as a fine defaulter. My first cellmate was a convicted murderer. I shared the prison facilities with many violent criminals and murderers, one of whom was the man who had been convicted in the infamous Thorne case some years earlier, when the young son of a lottery-winning family was kidnapped and murdered and the family blackmailed.

After the classification process, I was assessed as low-risk. (My brother-in-law was actually a policeman in Wagga—maybe he put in a good word for me.) I was appointed to be 'house-maid' to the deputy governor and perform household duties for him and his family. As the deputy governor was a strict Methodist and I was a practising Lutheran, we had many chats over a glass of cold ginger beer. By then I was in low-security accommodation at what they called 'the farm' and he'd often sign me out in the evenings for a chat.

Our business went bankrupt while I was in prison, but that at least protected my mother from financial ruin to a degree.

It took two more decades before the Razorback blockades and the huge protests and strikes of 1979 finally saw the end of the iniquitous road taxes that had strangled the freight industry for so long.

Luckily our company started up again and I continued to be involved in the freight business until quite recently. I'm now in my 80s and can look back on a lifetime in the business; it's been an interesting ride.

THE NULLARBOR CROSSING

RAY GILLELAND (THE NULLARBOR KID)

I was one of the first truck drivers silly enough to do regular crossings of the continent from Sydney to Perth, across the Nullarbor Plain, back in the early 1950s. The trucks we drove were basic, plain, slow and reliable. British trucks like Leyland AEC, Albion, Thornycroft, Foden and Atkinson were the backbone of Australia's road transport in those days, mostly due to the minimal sales tax they incurred compared to European and American trucks. The British trucks were always available immediately from the dealer's floor. Anything else had to be ordered, and delivery from overseas took up to six months. Although there were a few Macks, Federals, Diamond Ts and Mercedes-Benz to be seen on the road, they were few and far between. The 1954 AEC Matador and Albion HD models were good reliable trucks. Both were fitted with straight six-cylinder engines and a five-speed gearbox. The trailers were single or dual axles, mostly McGrath or Freighter.

Those British diesel trucks, which were the backbone of long-distance transport in the 1950s, had forward control cabins. The motor wasn't out the front of the cabin under a bonnet; the cabin was built around the motor. Between the driver's seat and the small passenger seat, the cabin was divided completely in half by the metal engine cover. The noise was indescribably loud; you had to shout to be heard above the roar of the motor. We placed all sorts of covers over the metal engine casing: the best was a canvas refrigerator cover, but even that only deadened the noise a little.

When it was time for a sleep, the driver had a choice. He could sleep out on the ground or build up the driver's seat and passenger seat level with the top of the engine cover with suitcases or boxes and try to sleep across the top with a couple of blankets.

Sometime in the late 1950s, after a few trips across the continent, we invented the original Aussie 'sleeper cabin'. The Albion HD had plenty of room between the front of the trailer and the rear of the cabin. The cab wasn't a tilt cab, it was bolted to the chassis, and so you had to be able to get to the motor from the rear. We extended only the top half of the cabin, leaving space to put extra tanks underneath the bunk on top of the chassis. The back of the cabin was cut out down to the top of the engine bay and the cabin was extended back on both sides to a width of just over a metre. The floor was cut to fit and the sides tapered in towards the base of the original cabin. Small glass windows with rubber edging were cut into both ends and some foam rubber was cut to fit for a mattress. It was primitive but worked unless you were really tall.

We always allowed three weeks for the trip in case of problems. And there were always problems out there in the 'Never Never' land: copper fuel lines could crack and break and there were many punctures. You might find yourself fitting and joining a new pipe or stripping wheels apart to repair them. Things like that were all a normal part of the trip . . . and I mean every trip. Broken springs might need to be wired together till a place could be found to park and fit a new leaf, or a broken centre bolt, or a wheel bearing that had given up the ghost. As there was nothing out there but you and your ability to get out of any trouble, all the extra parts that you might just need were carried in an extensive toolbox underneath the trailer. It was great fun.

There was no air conditioning or refrigerators in trucks back then, so in the heat and dust nothing fresh lasted longer than a couple of days. Any fresh food items were best bought at the last outpost of civilisation. The main food supply was tinned stuff and fruit in season, like apples and oranges. We survived on tomato soup, baked beans, Irish stew, peaches, pears . . . anything in a tin. I always carried a second tin opener, just in case. I bet very few readers have ever tried to open a tin of baked beans with a hammer and chisel. It can be messy . . . the sauce spurts up into your face and half the beans are lost on the ground.

There were a few water tanks scattered across the desert but they were usually dry, so it was in your best interest to be as self-sufficient as possible. I always carried around 200 gallons of diesel, a 44-gallon drum of water and a Primus stove, and that was it.

Perth to Sydney was a distance of 3000 miles, and over a thousand miles of that was only a goat track. Through New South Wales, Victoria and part of South Australia the 'highway' was a narrow sealed road that still had long gravel stretches. After leaving Port Augusta, at the top of Spencer Gulf in South Australia, the road became a sandy dirt track for the next thousand miles, crossing uninhabited desert to the little town of Norseman in Western Australia. The last 500 miles into Perth had only a few gravel stretches.

The Nullarbor was quite a trek back in the 1950s, real pioneering stuff. There were a few scattered properties off the main track but people only knew you were passing if you took mail in to them. That was always a bonus as they could use their wireless to notify those further on that you were around. If you had no mail to deliver no one knew you were out there. So, in any emergency, you had to rely on yourself . . . alone.

The wilderness was the home of kangaroos, rabbits, wombats, camels, wild scrub turkeys and not much else. Things like scorpions and snakes worried me most. If a death adder bit you, you were a goner. You would be dead long before the next traveller who ventured over the east–west track found you.

Out of the truck I always wore boots called Leather Necks. They were like sixteenth-century pirate boots that came up nearly to the knees and had a folded top. The death adder was well camouflaged and had a habit of lying still and striking quickly at the ankles. I felt fairly safe in my boots but I constantly surveyed the ground around me when out of the truck, and I always carried an old 1911 model Colt .45 pistol. If you had come across me out there back then you would have seen a tall, slim young man, brown from the sun and wearing a battered old Stetson hat and a pair of swimming trunks, with a pistol hanging from his waist, walking around in pirate boots. It was quite a sight!

Back in those days there were not many drivers who took on the challenge of the Nullarbor Plain. Maybe you had to be odd to do it! To get to the Nullarbor stretch from Sydney you could cut across the lower part of New South Wales and use the gravel road across the Hay Plain, or stick to the bitumen and go through Victoria. That Hay Plain road was fine in the dry, but when it rained the plains turned into a black-soil bog that clogged up the wheels till they were jammed to a stop. When that happened you had to wait till everything dried out and then chip off the dried mud before you could start again. So, when it was doubtful, it was best to take the longer route down through Victoria to join the sealed road to Adelaide.

I usually went over the Hay Plain because there was a conflict of interest between the state of Victoria and myself that made life dangerous when I was in their territory. If they picked me up I was in trouble for unpaid taxes and fines; I refused to pay road tax for using roads that were goat tracks most of the time. Taking the Hay Plain route meant that I only needed to drive a couple of hours across the edge of Victoria to get me into South Australia . . . and back to safety. It was then an easy run to the top of Spencer Gulf and Port Augusta, the last big town and the jump-off point to the wild west. Back then it took a couple of days to fuel up, check everything, buy provisions and then double check everything again. It was not the time or place to be in a hurry or to be forgetful.

I usually took off about sundown and travelled the thin sealed road to the Iron Knob turn-off, which was where the road to the 'Golden West' became a dirt track. I'd stop on the edge of the bitumen to have a last check around the truck with my torch, kick the tyres and tighten the ropes. At that point I always mentally ticked everything off for the last time . . . did I have everything? I always had that feeling that I'd forgotten something.

Penong, about 40 miles west of Ceduna, was the very last bit of civilisation—a shop, a couple of houses and a pub. On most trips I tried to get there in the afternoon. Getting towards sundown was a bad time to drive west looking through the windscreen for the smoothest parts of the track ahead, so it was good to stop here till the sun went down. From Penong it was about 145 miles to the sheep and cattle property called Nullarbor Station. Sometimes the post office in Ceduna would ask me to deliver mail to the station.

The enormous properties out there are measured in hundreds of square miles and, every now and then, gates had to be opened and closed on the way across. The area around the gate was often a sandy bog from vehicles constantly stopping there. I would usually stop a truck-length back and walk up to the gate, swing it open, make sure it wouldn't swing closed, and then trudge back to the truck. I'd roar through the sand in low gear and stop a trailer-length past the gate, then walk back to shut the gate. I always felt, as I walked back through the deep sand to the truck, that someone was going to get bogged there sooner or later. I didn't want it to be me.

If it was dark it was often a good idea to get through the gate and then call it a night about a hundred yards further on. I'd check the tyres and ropes and the fuel tanks before settling down for a sleep.

There are unaccountable happenings out there on the Nullarbor, strange lights that move around in the heavens and on the horizon and a wind that blows suddenly and then stops just as quickly, then starts blowing again, hot then cold then hot again—very strange. Back then the Australian government was letting the Poms use the area just a few hundred miles to the north to let off atomic bombs. I often wondered if a strange cloud was overhead in the night sky and what it might do to me out there all alone. You always stirred just before dawn, and then you realised it was bloody freezing! How can it be so hot in the day and so cold at night?

There were bores put down in a few places along the track; the water wasn't drinkable but you could have a shower and wash off some of the grime after days of rattling along the corrugated desert road. There was one I remember where a pipe stood out of the ground quite high, and then there was a horizontal pipe at a right angle and another that pointed down. A large wooden handle on the upright part could be vigorously moved back and forth and a large volume of cold artesian water would come pouring out as long as it was pumped. The only problem was that, if you were alone, it became difficult to pump and then jump the few feet or so to get under the water before it stopped. An inner tube cut in half with a small length of rope fixed the problem. You could stand and pump and hold the rope tight, forcing the water across to the lone pumper. You could feel it doing you good!

There was no official government sign to tell you when you entered the state of Western Australia, only a post in the ground with a tyre hanging off it and a few messages left by travellers. Out there no one cared what state they were in.

Often when I crossed the border I hadn't seen anyone on the track for days.

The next stop for human company was Roy Gurney's place at Eucla, which was down on the lower plain near the sea, surrounded by sand hills. It was just an old-fashioned wooden house built many years before for staff at the original Eucla telegraph relay station, which was a repeater station for messages between the east coast and the west coast. Telegraph systems back then were not very powerful. The old sandstone building could be seen occasionally when the constant wind blew the sand away; then it would be lost for months, sometimes years, hidden beneath a sand hill or two.

To get from the high plain down to the coast the road had been dug into the cliff face with no guardrail or fence and, wonder of wonders, that mile or so of road was a sealed bitumen surface. I always stopped at the top and gazed out to Roy's place in the far distant sand hills, marvelling at the scenery and thinking what a bloody big country this is. We didn't know back then that the Nullarbor Plain was riddled with underground caverns, a catacomb of unexplored water caves waiting to be invaded by scuba divers in years to come.

It was a good time to stop and check everything and look down the cliff face at that beautiful black bit of road and think, 'If only it was all like that across here.' But that dream was many years away in the future. Back then we had to settle for this bit of bitumen at Eucla and another section up the cliff face at Madura Pass, about 200 miles away.

Eucla Pass and Madura Pass were sealed because they were the two sections that could actually close the only road across Australia through lack of maintenance. Erosion from the wind and occasional rain left nowhere to detour. It was impossible to climb down from the high plain to the basin and back again if those two sections fell away. I'd roll down in third gear to the bottom and all too soon I'd be back rattling and clanking on the corrugated track across the basin to Roy's small wooden house and the old telegraph station. He had put in a couple of hand-pump petrol bowsers and always had some spare fuel available in 44-gallon drums if needed.

It was only a short distance over the sand hills to the Southern Ocean. I was always going to go for a swim but could never be bothered walking in the heat of the day over the sand to the sea. I went swimming on one trip at Ceduna, and after swimming well out in the bay I was told that a 20-foot great white shark had been seen where I was swimming only a few minutes earlier. I sort of lost my urge for swimming in the Southern Ocean after that. Bore water was not as dangerous.

Roy was ahead of his time as a tourist entrepreneur and had some metal badges designed with two holes at the edge that could be screwed onto a metal surface. They had a map of Australia in colour with the words 'Trans Australian' at the top and below, in a boomerang, the word 'Overlanders'. He sold them to the few travellers who came along; the cost was 75 pence.

I used to take Roy's shopping list to the shop in Norseman, nearly 500 miles away. The goods would be sent by the first truck coming back east. It would probably take a week or two; it might even be me that brought it.

The couple of hundred miles of road from Eucla to Madura Pass was fairly easy as it was all soft and sandy, not hard corrugations like the sections to the east. The biggest worry were wombat holes that the sand had covered over. There'd be a jolting lurch as the wheel dropped down and up again, the truck squeaking and groaning and me hoping it all hung together without a blowout—at the same time hoping the steering wheel didn't break my wrist as it whipped back and forth.

The Madura motel turn-off would eventually come into view on the left. It was a strange place, just a couple of buildings some distance off the road. One building was made of fibro and divided into a couple of rooms with iron frame beds. On the verandah there were a few well-worn old lounge chairs with springs poking out of them in all directions. The other building had a tiny, sparsely furnished dining room with a couple of tables. A traveller could get a meal there—but only in the dining room and only at specifically stated hours. The motel was hundreds of miles out in the wilderness but if it was five minutes past the time advertised on the noticeboard at the door there was no meal, nothing.

There were a couple of fuel pumps, one diesel and one petrol, but you were never sure if there was fuel available or even if the proprietors could be bothered serving customers.

This was the only place I knew at the time that used the American name 'motel'. This was a new word in the Australian vocabulary back then; we only knew about it from the movies. The 'motel' part was a sideline. The place was a large property and the motel had been added because they didn't really like visitors at the station. I wondered why they bothered with a dining room at all; they certainly were not friendly folk.

I had a run-in with them once, after I'd taken their mail east from Norseman, along with some supplies, and arrived about mid-morning. I didn't get a 'thank you' or even the offer of a cold drink. They seemed to consider that it was my job to do those things for them, when I was actually doing them a favour. That was the last time I ever went in there; I decided I'd rather cook my own meals and sleep in the truck.

After Madura the road cut through low scrubby bushes—some could almost be called small trees. It was about a day's drive from there to that section of road that was 90 miles long and straight as a gun barrel. The surface there was usually reasonable, unless it rained. When it was dry, as it was most of the time, the light 'bull dust' covered everything, as fine as cosmetic powder.

On one memorable trip, part of that stretch of road was covered in a sheet of water after rain. The main problem was that there could be wombat holes in the water. The best way to invite trouble was to drive into it without checking it out.

Luckily, I knew what to do. I stopped at the edge of the water and left the motor ticking over. I had a pair of sandshoes and a piece of old broom handle, about as long as a walking stick, which I kept for just such an occasion. Walking along through the muddy water, roughly in line with where the driver's side wheels would come through, I'd poke the broom handle around looking for deep holes, all the way to the other end of the wet section. Then I'd come back doing the same in a line about where the passenger-side wheels would be splashing through. If I found a deep hole, I'd rip a small branch off a bush and poke it into the muddy bottom enough to hold so I'd have a green leafy marker poking out of the water. Then I'd crawl through in low gear, avoiding the markers. Sometimes you couldn't drive through in a straight line and you had to zigzag.

Towards the end of the 90 miles I often called in to Balladonia Station to see the Jackson family and camp for the night.

The next hundred-odd miles was very slow and was often the worst of the whole trip. The road was rock hard and it had corrugations about three feet wide the width of the road. The only way to drive it was to put the driver's wheel in the very edge of the road, which had a sort of gutter of soft sand, and rattle along till it was time to swap and put the passenger-side wheel in the gutter of sand on the other side. While you did this the cabin and steering wheel would be vibrating so badly that it was hard to hold on to the wheel. This went on for hours and I always felt sick inside on this bit of road, knowing what it was doing to the truck. It was a real nightmare. I could imagine nuts slowly unwinding and spring leaves flexing up and down, getting ever nearer to breaking point. The only thing to do was to grit your teeth and keep going.

Eventually the little town of Norseman would slowly emerge from the setting sun and you could breathe a sigh of relief and finally relax as you hit the sealed road on the edge of town. The worst was over. A few sections of dirt between the sealed sections north up to Coolgardie and then it was just 400 miles of black bitumen to Perth.

These days it's a bitumen highway and takes three days' driving. Back then it was three weeks and 3000 miles of goat track—but we knew we were alive!

LONG ROAD TO THE TOP

JOHN ELLIOTT

In a career that spanned more than 50 years, Slim Dusty touched the hearts of Australians all around the country . . . and along the way the man with the crooked hat became a national icon.

It may be a long way to the top if you want to rock and roll, but try climbing into Slim Dusty's well-worn R.M. Williams boots.

Despite a gruelling touring schedule that began in the early 1950s, Slim remained a prolific singer, songwriter and musician. It was a commitment that continued throughout his career, and his celebration of 50 years in the entertainment industry was the perfect opportunity to release his 99th album . . . appropriately called *Slim Dusty '99*.

From the beginning, Slim took his music on the road, putting together an annual show that toured extensively. For many of those miles Slim was behind the wheel driving the trucks from show to show. While Slim didn't travel by truck over the last two decades of his career, his association with the trucking industry lasted a lifetime. It was the inspiration for many of his songs and his happy memories of life on the road never faded with time.

'My first tour was in '54,' Slim recalled when we were chatting one day. 'From Sydney to Toowoomba and back. We had a '38 Ford and a caravan with a great big tow bar on it. The caravan took four of us to pick up and we'd put it on the back of that poor old Ford and she'd just about lift off the ground.'

The first tour hit the road with wife Joy, daughter Anne, rope-spinner Malcolm Mason and guitarist Barry Thornton. In those early days the accommodation was usually just camping outside the halls where they performed, with some of the crew bunking down in the dressing rooms.

'I remember on that trip it was quite wet,' Slim went on. 'We had to cross the river below Taree and the water was up over the low bridge. Even today when we're travelling we look at those old bridges . . . most people wouldn't even know where they were.'

Over the years the Slim Dusty touring show grew and eventually needed a couple of trucks to put the show on the road. Slim had two Internationals; the big one was affectionately called Old Thunder and the small one was called Lightning.

'Boy, oh boy! They were good trucks,' Slim fondly recalled of those old petrol-powered machines. 'During one of our trips we put a hole through the side of the motor and all we had was self-tapping screws and Bostik. Those self-tappers were still in the side of the block when we sold the trucks.'

With a couple of trucks to haul his show to town, Slim could now attempt larger and longer tours and in the late 1960s the bush troubadour took the tour across the Nullarbor to Western Australia.

The Eyre Highway across the Nullarbor was still 90 per cent corrugations and 100 per cent bull dust. At that time the touring party included the two trucks plus four caravans to slow down the proceedings.

'It would take three to four days to get across,' Slim recalled. 'I remember one trip—there were big signs up that said, "BEWARE OF BULLDUST HOLES"—it was like talcum powder. If you went into them too fast it would spray up over the car and you would have to put your windscreen wipers on to clean it . . . and there was about 750 miles of dirt.'

Back in those days, Slim and his family would have a break at Metung in Victoria over the Christmas period before heading off on the road again.

'We had a mate who went over the old trucks with a fine tooth comb and fixed up anything that he could for us,' Slim said.

Barry Thornton and Slim were the truck drivers most of the time. They carried their own spares, and on the road they kept the trucks well serviced, oiled and greased. The vehicles were hosed down once a week and the cabs kept tidy.

'We felt if we kept them clean and tidy we would be more particular about the mechanical side as well,' Slim remembered. 'It seemed to work. We never had many breakdowns or hold-ups because we were prepared. We were only ever held up twice on the track; once at Rowena, a little town south of Walgett with no pub . . . fancy being stuck for four days in a town with no pub.

'There was another time we got stuck on a stretch up the top of Western Australia at a place called the Pardoo Sands. There was a big boggy flat below Roebourne; there were trucks, tourists and caravans stuck with us and luckily for them we always carried supplies of fruit juices, tinned meats and things under the bunks in the caravans. We ended up supplying a lot of people with a bit of tucker.'

Slim and wife Joy always felt close to truckies. 'We had a lot in common with the truck drivers in those early days. Just like the truckies, we had to really watch ourselves. Some of those roads were pretty isolated in the mid- to late 1960s, the truck stops were at the old-time stations. They were pretty wild and woolly places.'

Slim remembered one of the trips across the Nullarbor that tested their ingenuity. 'We took our show across on the train and drove back in my Ford Ranchwagon pulling a big 25-foot caravan with bogey wheels. The bloody Ranchwagon snapped its chassis. We made it through to the old Cocklebiddy Station, which the McDonald family owned. They'd stopped there years ago when they were going across the Nullarbor on the show run. People stopped to get cups of tea off them and they eventually set up a building and it became one of the first roadhouses in that part of the world. They couldn't do much with the Ranchwagon so we got saplings and wired the chassis together until we got across to the eastern side of the Nullarbor.'

The constant travelling may have seemed tedious to some people but Slim claimed those times held a fond place in his memory.

'We travelled 40,000 to 60,000 miles over eight months around Australia every year . . . year after year. We had our own advance agent ahead of us. He'd ring us once a week and we'd go to a post office and wait for his call.

'We were our own bosses and we treasured Sunday nights when we'd pull our vans way off the road and park them in a circle. That was our night to howl.

'One of these camps I remember well,' Slim recalled. 'We were about 80 or 90 miles out of Norseman and we'd pulled off the road to have our night off. We had a good time, a barbecue and a few beers. The next afternoon in Norseman one of the blokes on our tour said, "I can't find my wallet, it must have fallen out when I was lounging around the fire last night." We couldn't go back because we had a two-and-a-half-month tour ahead of us.

'Well, we did our tour and on the way back we camped at the same spot. We drove to the spot and the coals from our campfire were still there and right next to them was the wallet. The money was a bit dirty but it was still there.'

Eventually progress caught up with the Slim Dusty touring show. Slim's growing popularity meant that the day had come when people wanted Slim in all parts of Australia at the same time. The days of travelling by truck and caravan were over.

'While we swallowed a lot of dust, we were free, we breathed fresh air,' Slim said with a hint of nostalgia. 'Our vehicles weren't air conditioned and then all of a sudden we were in air-conditioned cars, planes and motels. I still reckon our old rough life was healthier than what we do today.'

The Slim Dusty Show was growing. With the advent of television people expected a bigger production with lights and sound systems, so Slim had to employ a production crew with a truck. From just a few people on the road Slim eventually travelled with a crew of about eighteen. 'We ended up with a regular sound crew from Canberra. They were just as important as the band. It doesn't matter how good the band is, you still need good sound equipment and operators,' explained Slim.

'I liked being on the road. It's similar to the trucking scene. You really have to balance every day, nothing is done haphazardly, and everything has got to be planned. Wheels are what got us there and kept us moving, just like the trucking scene.'

John McFarlane was the production manager on the Slim Dusty touring show when I did the interview; he ran a Hino FD 22-foot Pantech.

'We're pretty compact,' John explained. 'All up we'd carry 9 or 10 tonne on the road. We used to carry tons and tons of gear and we still carry a heap but it's now more efficient in how it's utilised.'

Like most delivery jobs, access could be a problem. John reckoned now and then they'd get to a venue that was difficult to get the gear into.

'If they can stick a theatre on the top floor they will. We've backed up to a loading dock, loaded into a lift, and then had a 60- or 70-metre push and then had to lift it up onto a stage. It was a bonus when we'd get to a venue that was easy to load into.

'A day off, or even a day with only 150 kilometres to travel, was a real luxury, but when you had 300 or 400 kilometres of winding and hilly roads with an average speed of 80 kilometres per hour . . . that took its toll on the truck and crew.'

By necessity they needed a truck that was absolutely reliable, as the consequences of not getting to a gig with the lighting and stage equipment could be catastrophic, especially when there were over 1000 Slim fans at the front door waiting for the show to start.

'In twelve years I never had a problem getting to a gig,' John said while touching wood.

Just to make sure any problem could be taken care of on the spot, John had tickets in rigging, electrical safety, first aid and a truck driving licence. If problems crop up the show must go on . . . in the great entertainment industry tradition.

'It's a pressure job,' he said of his work. 'There's no room for error, and it has to be perfect first time.

'In the studio you can spend all week getting the right sound but when you have 1000 screaming fans expecting CD-quality sound at the concert you have basically about 30 seconds to get it perfect. It can be demanding and you learn to fly by the seat of your pants very quickly. Once you got it right things normally stayed pretty stable.'

Slim had the final word on the touring life. 'The young ones who tour today often complain about their room because it mightn't have enough light in it or the carpet doesn't look right,' he told me. 'They don't know they're alive.'

It's a long road to the top . . .

MRS WARD

FRANK DANIEL

The Hay shire in western New South Wales has the distinction of being one of the flattest sections of land in the world, with a difference in elevation of only 55 feet between the highest and lowest points on the famous Hay Plain.

It is no wonder then that the general feeling of most truck drivers was that the Hay Plain is 'uphill both ways'. This was especially so in the days when we had less power! We always seemed to have a headwind whichever direction we were going.

Big Jack Rice and I used to cart wool from Pinnegars' wool stores in Parkes, New South Wales, to the Elizabeth wool stores in South Australia. It was a seasonal job and we usually backloaded with South Australian plonk or fruit juice for Sydney.

On one occasion during the wet season we were en route to Adelaide and had just passed through Rankin's Springs when we saw a Holden 1-tonner towing a small caravan parked in a clearing to the side of the road. There was a lady driving and it appeared she was waiting for us to pass before entering the highway.

'It's a good job we got in front of her, mate,' Jack called to me over his radio, 'I'd hate to be following that thing all the way to Hay!'

The CB radio was all the go with truckies in those days and some fellows never laid off. You could hear them for miles in some cases and other times you'd be flat out hearing them if you were virtually side by side. They weren't much chop but nearly every truck had one.

I was driving an old Mercedes-Benz 1418 at the time, and Jack had a Kenworth. He was always happy to follow me along and keep me entertained. The 1418 was only capable of 55 miles an hour in good going and I can remember many a time I crossed the Hay Plain at 45 miles per hour when the wind was against me and I had wool stacked four bales high. (Yes, I know three tiers was the legal limit . . . but that's another story.)

We'd passed through Goolgowi and got out onto the Hay Plain without any worries. It had been raining and the table drains were awash and more rain was imminent. The highway was built up about a metre above the surrounding countryside, so we were able to maintain a good speed.

About 15 miles short of Hay, Jack announced that the Holden 1-tonner had caught up to him. Then, almost immediately, he gave a startled cry. 'Look out!' he called. 'She's coming round!'

In my rear-view mirror I could see the action quite clearly. The Holden was taking a fairly hairy sort of a course weaving on and off the bitumen as it overtook the Kenworth.

The next minute I heard him call, 'Look out, Frank! She's coming again!'

She sure was: she was right on my hammer and trying to pass me. I was soon using all my concentration as I tried to keep to the left as much as possible and give the old lady room to pass. Between looking where I was going and keeping an eye on the overtaking vehicle I had my work cut out. One second she was there, the next second she was gone.

Suddenly she reappeared, out in the mud on the off-side, with the caravan up on one wheel and gracefully executing the first of two rolls, as the ute got a new grip on the bitumen and ploughed into my front wheel. The big nuts on the wheel of the Benz screwed the bonnet clean off the Holden as it straightened up and came to a halt on the roadway.

The force of the impact on my steering altered my course, and within no time at all my truck left the highway and I was smack bang into the table drain. All I could see was a shower of red mud at least 20 feet high as I flattened the old girl, hoping to drive out of the mess. Eventually, of course, I came to a stop with the wheels spinning wildly and no traction.

I didn't know whether I was upside down or not. I had a sore head from where I hit the panel above the door, and the world had turned into red mud. I managed to jump down from the cabin and get across the water in the table drain. Then, suddenly, I felt a bit dizzy and sat down on the edge of the road with my head spinning.

It's amazing where people come from when you think you are out in the middle of the desert with no one around. Before I knew it a bloke was checking me out for any damage. Not only that, he said he was an ambulance man.

Another truckie who was going in the opposite direction reckoned it was the funniest thing he had seen in years. 'You shoulda seen the caravan!' he laughed. 'There was bits going everywhere!'

Eventually the old lady who was driving the Holden came over to talk to me. She was rather nervous and flustered as she asked, 'Are you all right, son . . . are you all right?'

I just sat there dazed; my head hadn't finished spinning yet.

'Oh my God,' she said. 'I'm so sorry! I was just learning to drive . . . I was only in second gear!'

After I recovered enough to nod my head, she seemed a bit more relaxed. She told me her name was Mrs Ward and she and her husband came from somewhere up the Central Coast.

When I finally recovered my wits enough to look around I saw the most amazing scene. All that was left of the caravan was the chassis and wheels, and the fridge and stove, which were bolted to the chassis.

In no time at all another half a dozen trucks had come upon the scene. After each driver had told his version of the incident to each new arrival they all got together and helped load the contents of the caravan back onto its frame or onto the tray of the 1-tonner.

The shell of the caravan was tossed out onto the roadside, where it remained for several weeks as a reminder of the incident.

It was agreed that it was too far to drag the cops out from town, so we arranged to meet at the police station after we'd towed my Mercedes back onto the road.

My load was now leaning precariously to the left and didn't look like it would make it into Hay, so I drove into Hay on the wrong side of the road where the camber would be of some benefit in keeping the load on the truck.

I stopped at the first servo that I came to on the edge of town. Luckily for me a bloke was there with a front-end loader and he offered to push my dangerously leaning load back into position. After he'd done just that and Jack and I had resecured the load, we continued on our journey.

By the time all this was done, we had completely forgotten about our promised rendezvous with Mrs Ward at the police station. She may be out there somewhere creating havoc still, but we never saw her again.

THE FRIENDLY TRUCKIE

STEVE THEOBALD WITH JIM HAYNES

I have one eternal, but very sketchy, memory of the lengths to which a truck driver went in helping us many years ago. It happened in the late 1960s, when I was fairly young.

My mum and dad had emigrated from England in 1959, when Dad got a job with AIS in Port Kembla. They paid for him to come over in return for two years' service. Needless to say, we never went back to the UK. Maybe it was meeting people like the friendly truckie that kept us all here in Australia.

I was born in 1961 at Wollongong, but my older twin brothers were born in 1958 in the UK and they came over on the *Orontes* as babies with Mum and Dad. My younger brother was born two years after me, in 1963, and Mum and Dad adopted my younger sister Alison a few years later. Mum really wanted a girl and, with five kids in the family, we were quite a big and happy mob.

Mum and Dad first lived in a migrant hostel in Berkeley and then a flat in Wollongong. Then they bought a house in Kiama and that was where we all grew up.

Dad did shiftwork a lot and it wasn't until we were quite a bit older that Mum began working to earn a bit of money, too. In hindsight, things must have been pretty tight. We all had hand-me-down clothes and I can remember the home haircuts, but we never felt poor. We had chooks, like most people did back then, but we also had a couple of cows and a goat, all of which were milked.

I can remember a bloke coming around and selling rabbits. Everything was cooked on an old Everhot stove. Dad was always fed first, then Mum, and then us kids.

With five kids in the family and not a lot of money to go around we needed to be patient and remember our manners. We had to ask permission to leave the table. Mum handled most of the discipline but if we were really naughty it was: 'Wait until your father gets home.'

All in all we were a happy family with a hard-working dad and a caring mum. As we got a few pennies together we managed to obtain a few luxuries, and one of the big events was when Dad bought an EH Holden. Now the family could go holidaying and visiting.

Mum's mother lived at Miles in Queensland—she was 'Nan in Miles' to us—and Mum's sister lived in Brisbane. So, every couple of years we went on a trip to Queensland to see them.

It's funny talking to Dad about it now. As a kid I never picked up on the fact that he absolutely hated going up to Miles. Apparently Nan up and left England before Mum and Dad and she left them to sell all her belongings and dispose of quite a few animals. You can see why mother-in-law jokes were always a big hit! I have been to Miles quite a bit since I was a kid and like the town, but Dad still hates it.

Usually we headed inland towards Mudgee from Kiama and then went straight up, but coming home we must have come down the coast way. We have photos of all us kids at the Big Banana at Coffs Harbour, which would have been taken on that trip home.

Anyway, we were coming home from that holiday in Queensland when the car came off the road at 2 a.m. on a range just south of Bulahdelah.

Here's my dad's memory of the event:

The road in those days was very windy with a narrow verge and where it happened there was a small ditch a little way in, not deep, only about 30 centimetres, but enough for the front wheel to drop into. I accidentally got into the ditch, which wouldn't have mattered much except I'd already collected a couple of guide posts which disabled the car.

For the first hour or so that we sat there only three vehicles stopped: a car full of young blokes, a tourist bus and a truckie. The young blokes couldn't do much to help and the tourist bus offered us a lift if we paid all the fares for the family!

The truck was carrying cars and the driver was about the nicest bloke you could meet. He offered to drop us back to Bulahdelah so that we could report the accident. He said he needed a break and it would be no trouble. We accepted the offer as it was not far back into Bulahdelah.

When we got there, the police station was closed but there was a phone connected to the policeman on call. We rang and the cop told us very curtly that we would have to wait until 9 a.m.

The good Samaritan truckie insisted on waiting, and when we finally got it sorted at about 10 a.m. he offered to take us to Sydney, even though there wasn't room in the cab for us all. Your mother, Alison and I travelled in the cab and the rest of the family, all the boys, travelled inside one of the cars on the back.

Further down the highway we picked up a couple of hitch-hikers who were put into another car. The truckie said, 'If you see any police cars, duck down!'

We were a bit worried when we had to go into an RTA inspection stop because it was rather cold weather and the windows of the two cars containing 'passengers' were all steamed up. Luckily no one seemed to notice.

I forget where the hitchhikers departed but the driver took us all the way to his home at Narrabeen, where we were given a meal. This amazingly friendly truck driver then suggested it would be no trouble if he took us to Central Station. However, it appeared that his wife thought that was going a bit too far, so he compromised and took us to where we could get a taxi.

I remember our car vaguely—it was a grey EH Holden—but I really remember bugger-all about the accident, except that it was near dawn and the car was in against a cliff face. I can remember it being dark when the bus pulled up but I think it was lightish when the truck stopped. The only impression I have of our saviour the truckie is that he was a big and really smiley sort of bloke.

My only recollection of the trip home is stopping beside the road opposite a Shell service station so that Dad could organise a tow or something. That must have been when we went back into Bulahdelah to report the accident and they had to wake up the copper.

My younger brother Jim says he remembers that the truck was white and he reckons it could have been a Bedford. He says that the driver fed us bananas, and told everyone to stop breathing and keep down when he went through the weighbridges so that the car windows didn't fog up because it was raining. Evidently he also told us to duck down if he honked the horn.

I can definitely remember that it had Citroën cars on the back; they were comfortable to ride in, too!

Mum and Dad moved to Cootamundra to retire in 1985. The family are scattered around the coast and the Illawarra, Canberra and Cootamundra districts. One brother still lives in Kiama, and he drives trucks for a living. Oddly enough he mostly drives car-carriers at the moment. I'm not sure that he ever has any passengers in the cars he carries, though—I suppose not.

Times have changed but telling this story is like saying a big and very belated 'thank you' to the unknown truck driver who went way beyond the call of duty to help an Aussie family in a spot of bother—we never knew his name, but he isn't forgotten in our family.

THE GOOD SAMARITAN

RAY GILLELAND (THE NULLARBOR KID)

My truck at the time was called 'the bus'. She was a long-tray truck on an AEC long-wheelbase bus chassis, painted a dark green with yellow signwriting. She was used mainly for quick deliveries to the various capital cities.

Back in the 1950s the Sunday newspapers were not printed in Melbourne. It became standard practice for the Sydney Sunday papers to be loaded early Saturday night and dispatched by fast truck to reach Melbourne by midday on Sunday. The truck that made the run was the only commercial truck allowed on the road in Victoria on a Sunday except for live stock transport.

The red 'paper truck', as it was called, was also an AEC bus chassis, a sister truck to mine, although it only had half a cabin for the driver and low wooden sides just high enough to hold the bundles of papers. It had a slightly higher speed than mine but because it had to stop briefly at the highway towns through Victoria and throw bundles of papers off, I was able to beat its time from Sydney to Melbourne, point to point.

My time from Liverpool in Sydney to Coburg in Melbourne was usually about twelve and a half hours. This included quick fuel stops in Yass and Albury. The paper truck only went once a week and always on Sunday. On the other hand, I was in and out at all different times of the week, night and day, sometimes twice a week. My truck was also referred to at times as the 'green ghost' by the authorities, as she used to slip in and out of Victoria at speed.

On one trip I had to take an urgent load to Adelaide. Now, one way to Adelaide was over the Hay Plain in New South Wales to Mildura and then down into Gawler to Adelaide. The only problem with the road over the Hay Plain was that it was all black soil, and with a few spots of rain, trucks just bogged in it till it dried out. It was not the road to take for an urgent delivery.

The surefire way was down to Benalla in Victoria and then to zigzag across Victoria via Bendigo, Donald and Warracknabeal and hit the Melbourne–Adelaide highway at Dimboola. That way was all sealed and the only gravel road was through the Little Desert around Tintinara and Coonalpyn, in South Australia. But that was a hard white gravel surface, passable even in the wet.

My last refuel stop was at Keith just past Bordertown in South Australia. Keith was a tiny hamlet of a few houses, a small garage, a butcher's shop and a few other shops, which were on a side road off the highway. My boss had arranged with the garage there to fuel me at any time through the night so that I could be in Adelaide the next day. The garage welcomed any business out there in the middle of nowhere. Any cash sale was welcome in that farming community. I usually arrived there between midnight and dawn and rang the night bell. The owner would come out in his pyjamas and dressing gown, pump the fuel, take the money and I'd be off, all done in about ten minutes.

On this trip I pulled up at about 2 a.m. and rang the bell. Out he came and started to pump the fuel into the tank. On the opposite side of the road was the little butcher's shop and parked on the road outside was an early-model 1930s canvas-top open-sided Ford or Dodge car with an ex-army jeep-type trailer hooked on behind with wire-mesh sides. In the trailer four sheep were shuffling around and 'baa-ing' away quietly.

As I leaned against the cabin, stretching my legs, I looked across and, even in the darkness, I could see there were people sitting in the old car. Looked like Mum and Dad in the front and a couple of kids maybe in the back.

The garage man was holding onto the petrol hose and noticed me looking across the street at the sheep.

'That's the butcher's brother-in-law,' he said, nodding at the car. 'They came down to sell him some sheep but he went away for a couple of days, and no one knows when he's back. The poor bastard's broken down now as well,' the garage man added. 'Can't even get back home, lives a couple of hundred mile up north in the bush. We can't help him here. The nearest bet for him is Adelaide.'

At that moment fuel gurgled up the spout and she was full. I handed him some money and while he went inside I walked around the truck checking tyres and ropes. Everything seemed OK. I went back to the cabin to climb in, and there was the car driver waiting for me.

I sized him up as I reached for the door handle. He was in his late 30s or early 40s, tall, thin, a typical farmer type—he had that weatherbeaten look about him. He looked directly at me and asked hesitantly and quietly, 'You wouldn't be going Murray Bridge way, would you?'

'Yep,' I replied. 'I have to be in Adelaide in the morning.' I nodded towards the car over the road. 'You having trouble?'

'Yeah . . .' He explained to me how he'd brought down the sheep to sell, only to find his brother-in-law away. 'On top of that I've cracked my distributor cap and can't get home. I told him last week I was coming, got the missus and kids with me as well.

'It hasn't been a good year for us,' he added. 'Trust the bastard not to be here when he's needed.' He pulled out a packet of cigarettes and offered me one. 'Any chance of giving us all a lift to Murray Bridge?' he asked as I leaned over for a light. 'The missus has some more relatives there.'

'Sorry, mate, the cabin's full of boxes of spare parts, there's no way I could fit you all in there.' I nodded towards the cabin.

'Bloody hell,' he said. 'I don't know what to do now. The missus and kids are freezing to death, the car won't go and I've got four sheep I don't know what to do with in the trailer.'

I stretched my hand out for the door handle to climb in. I felt sorry for him, but there was nothing I could do. I had to get going. I was thinking of the next few hours when I knew I would be feeling tired and wishing I was nearer to Adelaide so I could have a couple of hours' sleep.

Then, on an impulse, he burst out, 'Listen, mate, I'll give you the sheep if you will tow us into Murray Bridge. How about it? They're worth good money.'

I let out a chuckle. 'What the hell am I going to do with four sheep? If I can't get you in the cabin, how can I get four sheep in there? Even if I could . . . what the hell am I going to do with four sheep?' I couldn't help laughing thinking about it. I'd seen a few trucks with dogs poking their heads out the windows, but sheep!

'Yeah . . . I know,' he said, sadly. 'It's . . . . it's just that I'm desperate. What am I going to do?'

I looked at him and thought, Murray Bridge is one hell of a long way away, about 150 miles from Keith, and most of it was white gravel and not the best road at any time. I dropped my hand down from the door handle and looked at him and then across to the figures in the car over the road. It was a freezing night with that biting cold wind from the South Pole that seems to go right through you.

The sheep were restless and an occasional thud came from the metal floor of the trailer as they shuffled around and a low 'baaa' could be heard every now and then.

Then one of the kids, who must have been very young, murmured something to the mother and I could see her leaning over the back of the seat trying to rearrange a rug or blanket over the kids.

I suddenly felt very sorry for them. I let out a deep sigh and looked at the farmer. 'OK, I'll tell you what, I'll hook you on the back with as long a rope as I can find and see if we can make it to Tintinara. At least that's on the way and we'll see how we go from there . . . no promises. What do you say?'

'Hey, that's great, mate,' he said. 'Thanks, it's better than sitting here.'

'Wait there till I turn around,' I said. I drove down the road a little and turned around, then drove past his car and reversed back.

In the meantime he had told his wife and she'd agreed to give it a go.

I took some spare ropes from the toolbox and tied one end to his bumper bar and the other to my rear tie-rail. I told him to wave the torch when I had taken up all the slack in the rope, then everything would be tight and ready to roll.

'Now, it won't be any good blowing the horn to attract my attention,' I told him. 'The motor's beside me, so I won't hear it.'

He looked at me a bit blankly, so I continued, 'If, for any reason, you want me to stop, then move out a little to the right and blink your lights, but don't use the brakes till you see me answer by blinking my lights. OK? When I blink my lights I will very slowly lose speed and you try and keep the rope tight till we have stopped. Got it?'

Everything was agreed on and we slowly moved off down the street and turned left onto the highway.

The road from Bordertown to Keith was gravel, with just a small length sealed through Keith and then it was gravel again to Tintinara. This gravel was unusual as it was a white type of granite. It must have been quarried somewhere locally. All the gravel roads I had used around the country were a brown colour and very heavy, leaving only a low cloud behind which quickly settled to the ground after a vehicle had passed. This bloody stuff was different. It billowed up like a white fog.

When we had gone only a tiny distance, after blinking my lights I pulled up at the end of the sealed road just where the gravel began. I left the motor running and ran back to the car.

'Well, how's it going?' I asked. 'Will you be OK?'

'I think so.'

'OK,' I said. 'Don't forget to blink if you want me to stop.'

With that I ran back and slowly took off, bumping down onto the white gravel road where I kept a very slow speed to see how he was handling it.

After about half an hour I blinked my lights and slowly came to a halt.

I ran back to the car. 'Well?' I asked.

He smiled a little. 'It's a bit hard to keep focused on the back of your truck,' he said. 'It's the only thing I can see, like a big green wall in front of me. The white dust blows everywhere so we pulled all the window curtains down but I'll leave mine up so I can look out if I have to. But no, mate, it's great, just keep going. We're OK. The kids are asleep.'

'I'll stop and check you now and then, and stop at Tintinara,' I said. 'OK?'

So far everything was going like clockwork, but I had been a long time without sleep. I was feeling very tired and as time went on the motor noise started to lull me into a dream-like state. I wasn't going to sleep, I was aware I was driving, but it was a bit like being hypnotised—the white road, the motor, the warmth after being out in the cold.

I had checked the lights behind me a couple of times in the first hour and everything seemed OK.

Time crawled on.

Slowly but surely and without really thinking I must have gradually pressed my foot down harder on the accelerator. With a diesel truck, a driver presses the pedal to the floor and lets the motor find its own way faster. A petrol truck's accelerator needs to be feathered like a car's, but it was natural for me to press the pedal all the way and evidently I did so without thinking and somehow completely forgot I had a car with

Mum, Dad and the kids, plus a trailer full of sheep, dangling behind me . . .

Thinking back now it seems impossible that I simply forgot this, but I did. Time slipped by in this dream-like state. I wasn't going at top speed because the road was too rough, but I was definitely going too fast for a bloke with an early-model car full of people and a trailer full of sheep hanging on to his tail.

Suddenly, I hit two bumps in quick succession and then it hit me. 'Caesar's ghost, what have I done?' I thought in a panic. 'Are they there?'

Thoughts spun through my head at express train speed, faster than a computer! 'Are they still there? Are they OK? Stop quick . . . NO . . . not quick, he might run into the back of the truck if he's still there. Have they lost control? ARE THEY STILL THERE, DAMN IT?' I leaned out of the window with my foot hovering over the brake pedal. The adrenalin was pumping and I was in quite a state of panic.

'YES . . . it's still there . . . pull up gently, Ray . . . steady, steady. OK, now run back and hope like hell everything is OK.'

As I reached the driver's door of the car I started to shout, 'Sorry, mate. Are you OK? I started to go to sleep and forgot you were there. I haven't had much sleep for the last couple of nights. Are you OK? . . . Are you? How's everyone in there?'

The poor farmer didn't move.

He didn't even turn his head.

He just stared straight ahead with his eyes bulging from trying to see through the white gritty dust for the last hour or so. It was caked all over him, his wife and the blankets over the kids, who were still asleep. Even the sheep were covered in white dust.

The knuckles on his hands were white from gripping the steering wheel. As I stood there I could see he was still gripping the wheel so tightly I thought he was going to crush it.

Still staring at the back of my truck and without turning his head he said quietly, 'Everything is OK.' He wouldn't look at me and I'm sure he was in a state of shock.

I suggested he should get out and have a walk around. At first he shook his head, but his wife piped up and said, 'Hop out, darling, you will feel better after a little walk.'

He slowly relaxed his hands and turned his face towards me. That poor man's face was just a white mask. Only the grooves etched around his eyes and nose showed through. His eyelashes were heavy with what appeared to be white mascara and his brown hair was snow white.

'Have we stopped, have we?' he said weakly.

His wife got out and went around to his side. She opened the door, leaned in and grasped his arm, helping him to alight onto the road. 'Yes, dear,' she said gently. 'Come walk around a little.'

I didn't know what to do. I just stood there looking at that fit, brown-haired, lean, well-spoken farmer whom I had turned into something out of an MGM horror movie.

He shuffled across the road, then turned and shambled back. As he came closer he asked very softly in a hesitant voice, 'How far to Tailem Bend?'

With a sense of great relief I smiled and said, as jovially as I could, 'Not far at all from here.'

He climbed back in behind the wheel, 'I'm OK, no,' he murmured. 'Let's get there. At least that's back on a sealed road. We've come this far, let's finish it.'

I checked the rope and it was still tight, so I jumped in the cabin and slowly took off.

•

We arrived in Tailem Bend after a very careful drive by me and I went back and checked that everything was all right.

'Murray Bridge is just down the road now,' he said. 'Come on, let's get there.'

'I'm game if you are,' I replied.

The dawn was just breaking as we pulled into Murray Bridge and parked outside the relatives' house. I unhitched the car and rolled the ropes up and put them in the toolbox.

The farmer was now almost back to normal and said to me, 'Well, the sheep are yours. That was the agreement.'

'No mate,' I said. 'It's OK. What the hell would I do with them? I don't want your sheep.'

He looked at me and then said, 'Do you think you could squeeze just me into the cabin to Adelaide? We'll be there before anything's open and I can have the part and be on the bus back here and away home by tonight.'

He had to lie on the boxes with his head out of the window, like a puppy with his face in the wind, but we got there OK and I dropped him off.

He shook my hand and thanked me for all I had done for him.

That was the only chance I ever had to become a primary producer . . . and I turned it down.

REPOSSESS *THAT!*

KINGSLEY FOREMAN

An important part of the work of a truck driver employed by a large towing firm in a big city is vehicle repossession. It's often unpleasant work, but you get used to it.

Although Adelaide is a major city, it's not so big that you don't occasionally have a conflict of interest in your job when someone you know is on the receiving end of repossession. One day in the 1980s I went to do a repossession at a transport yard where one of the owner-drivers I often worked with was based. It turned out that the ute I was sent to repossess was actually his.

As I was winching it onto the back of the tilt-tray tow truck, this bloke I knew quite well was standing there calling me every four-letter word he could think of and threatening that next time he came to the depot he was going to blow my head off.

When you do repossession work you get used to that sort of thing. People are often surprised and upset when the repossession occurs, but they usually calm down and, at the end of the day, it's all just talk. Men threaten and abuse you, but often women are worse as they have a bad habit of throwing things at you as well as screaming abuse. In the heat of the moment they are not too fussy what it is they throw, either. I have had hammers, knives, screwdrivers and various items of food thrown at me. Once I even had a woman throw a baby's stroller at me; luckily the baby was not in it at the time.

Some repo jobs require cunning and ingenuity, and many take quite a long time to complete. I once spent hours trying to recover a Rolls-Royce for a repossession agent who was desperate to get it back. There had not been one payment made on the Roller. Apparently the bloke who had it was a good con man who had used the name of a real company director to get hold of it. Naturally the finance company wanted it back rather badly. The problem was that it was parked in the yard of a friend of this con artist and the friend had his own car parked behind it so we could not get to the Rolls-Royce.

The police were called in to help and did what they could. The police can get you onto the property, although they can't get you inside the front door under South Australian law. So, we could get to the vehicle, but we could not legally move the friend's car to get the Roller out. It was a stalemate.

After I thought about it for a while, I told the agent I could get it out without moving the other car, but it might do some damage to the Rolls-Royce.

He looked at me a bit puzzled and said, 'We have to get it at all costs.'

I think he thought I was a bit mad when I said I'd get it out but, when I asked him to sign my worksheet to the effect that any damage was not my responsibility, he did as I asked.

Then I called PJ on the radio and told him to send down the 'Big Wrecker' that our company used for crane-style salvage jobs. I put bars through the windows of the Rolls-Royce, fitted chains to the crane and then we lifted it over the other car and straight down onto the tilt-tray I was driving. I was worried that putting the bars through the windows of the Rolls might damage the car, but they build those things pretty well and we managed the job without any real damage.

It's amazing what some people will do out of spite when they know their vehicle is to be repossessed for failure to keep up the payments. I remember one job in the Adelaide suburb of Pennington where this bloke who had not met his payments came up with a novel revenge on the finance company.

When I met the repossession agent out the front of the house he said, 'Mate, the car's in the backyard. I think you'd better have a look first.'

I went with him into the backyard and couldn't see a car anywhere, so I asked him where on earth it was.

He had a grin on his face when he replied, 'Look behind the chicken hutch.'

I thought he was being silly and said, 'The chicken hutch isn't that big, and there can't be a car behind that.'

The agent just kept smiling and said, 'Go and have a look.'

I went behind the hutch to have a look and, sure enough, the car was there. It had been cut into three pieces, which were stacked one on top of the other. It was just as well I had a tilt-tray truck that day!

You might think that's a hard story to top, but life is full of coincidences. As fate would have it, within days of the three-piece car incident I had another job that was almost the same.

When I rolled up to the house the agent was waiting and he said, 'Prepare yourself, you'll love this one!'

We went around the back of the house and, without a word of a lie, the whole yard was covered in pieces of the car we were there to repossess. The bloke we were repossessing from was there too, smiling his head off at the back door.

'Does this make life hard for you?' he asked, like a real smart arse.

'No, mate,' I said. 'We charge by the hour, so the more time it takes, the more money I make.'

'That's good,' the bloke said. 'The finance company will have to pay, that's why I took it all apart . . . it took me hours.'

I said, 'Do you want the bad news?'

'What do you mean?' he said, with the smile starting to fade.

'The way this works is that you are charged for the tow,' I told him, 'and because you have done this to the car and it will take forever to recover it, you'll get nothing much from the auction after costs are deducted.'

'That's all right,' he said. 'I've handed the car back to them, so that's it.'

'No it isn't,' I told him. 'You still have to pay out the loan.'

That took the smile right off his face.

One of the oddest repo jobs I ever did was one I did 'on the move'. A certain repossession agent had been after this particular car for a long time; the driver was a petty criminal and well known as a druggie and a dealer. He was hard to track down, as he didn't stay in one spot long enough for the finance company to locate the car and get it back.

I was on my way back from a routine job when PJ called me on the two-way radio to tell me that the agent had spotted the car and was following it through the suburbs. As I was not far away with the tow truck, he wanted me to catch up to him as he followed the car, so I did a U-turn and sped up and I was soon behind the two cars.

The agent relayed a message through PJ on our two-way radio system to ask me to get in front of the car he was following, so I passed both cars and got in front of the wanted vehicle.

Then all I had to do was to gradually slow down to a stop while the agent stayed up close behind the car we needed to repossess. The bloke in the car had no idea we were even on to him at this stage.

I slowed to a stop, jumped out of the truck, lowered the lifting gear and had the front of the car off the ground before the bloke knew what was happening.

When I looked back I could see the driver's face and he was terrified! Maybe he had some enemies in the criminal fraternity because he looked as if he thought this was a hit and his time was up. Or maybe he thought we were the drug squad and he was finally busted.

THE AEC GOVERNMENT ROADTRAIN

LIZ MARTIN

The 1930s were very turbulent times for Australia.

The country was still reeling from the devastating loss of men in World War I, the economy was depressed, and a second world war was imminent. Men were forced to earn a living as best they could. The rail was stretching further inland with The Ghan having started its service from Adelaide to Alice Springs in 1929.

Road transport had just started to establish itself as an effective mode of land transport and, in the more populated areas of Australia, had already taken over from routes previously serviced by various forms of animal transport.

It was certainly an era of transition for the way things were done in the transport industry. The rail had been long established in most areas of Australia and trucks were reaching into places that only ten or twenty years before had not even been settled. The horse-drawn buggy was still in use in many areas, and camel teams and bullockies were still servicing the more remote regions of Australia.

At the time, operators of the railways, the camel strings, horse teams and bullockies believed that the road transport industry had finally reached its peak and would not create any further competition for the beast-driven freight market.

That was until, on 19 May 1934, a very unusual piece of machinery arrived in Alice Springs and changed the face of outback transport forever. Certainly no one realised it at the time, but it was a seed from which a great Australian adventure would grow.

The Government Roadtrain, as it became known throughout the outback, is reputed to be the first real motorised roadtrain in Australia in today's sense of the word. And, as unlikely as it may seem, until this vehicle started to operate in the Northern Territory the camel had all but cornered the market in moving freight to outlying stations and communities not serviced by rail or road.

This roadtrain, with its Dyson self-tracking trailers, is directly credited with the eventual downfall of the Afghan camel trains which had served the transport needs of outback Australia so well. The Afghans and their camels had served the freight needs of the red centre for so long that they were considered to be an intrinsic and irreplaceable part of the outback landscape.

When the roadtrain began to travel the unmade roads and bush tracks of the Northern Territory, no one believed that it would really have much of an impact. It was described by sun-hardened ringers and cattlemen, who watched in amazement as the unit snaked its way through the scrub, as a passing 'typical Pommy phase' that would never handle the Australian bush.

The roadtrain was one of three manufactured by the Associated Equipment Company of England (AEC) for the British Overseas Mechanical Transport Committee, under instructions from the British Army.

AEC was a British company which began production in 1912 and made over 10,000 trucks during World War I and produced the famous Matador gun trucks in World War II. The company later merged with Leyland.

The British Overseas Mechanical Transport Committee designed the 'Overseas Tractor' units for the specific purpose of opening up the underdeveloped countries of the British Empire. The British FWD Tractor Lorry Co. and Hardy Motors, originally a rail company, assisted in the design and production.

As early as 1927 the British government was convinced a second world war was imminent and commissioned the construction of a heavy transport vehicle that could carry large quantities of supplies and cope with the rigours of desert warfare. The result was this unusual six-cylinder indirect-injection diesel giant, reminiscent of the earlier clumsy steam-powered roadtrains but far more practical in the bush. It had high ground clearance, a high-mounted radiator located at the rear of the cab to prevent clogging by grass seeds, and two Dyson self-tracking trailers designed to follow in the tracks of the prime mover.

The roadtrain project was initially funded by the British and South African governments, but Australia and New Zealand and another 23 countries of the British Empire were later to contribute financially to its development and construction.

The three huge 'Overseas Tractor' units were prototypes that never actually went into commercial production. The more advanced unit was sent to Australia for trials in desert conditions and the other two went to South Africa and the USSR.

Of the 27 countries involved in the 'Overseas Tractor' project, Australia was the only one to take up the concept of the roadtrain after World War II.

At the time the units were constructed, the British Empire was still reeling from the Great Depression. So, the Overseas Tractor units were largely built from scrap metal; one unique feature was the turntables, which were made from old World War I gun turrets.

It was a peculiar vehicle even by the standards of the day. In modern terms, the truck was an 8x8. All wheels drove through single tyres but only two of the axles steered—from opposite ends of the truck. Axle one and axle four pivoted on the centre tandem.

Traction was applied to all eight wheels through four differentials. Odd though the configuration sounds, the vehicle soon proved itself capable of handling the various terrains and hardships of the outback, thanks in no small part to the men who operated it.

The roadtrain's 24 axles were articulated and independently sprung, enabling it to negotiate uneven terrain, sharp bends and snaking bush tracks without fear of overturning.

Its unusual braking system acted on the rear trailer and moved, with decreasing power, through each of the trailers to the prime mover. Each tandem axle had the unusual configuration of having only one brake drum fitted; each was placed opposite the other.

Although the unit was fitted with an electric starter, it also had provision for a crank-handle start, which required the full efforts of two men. Initially, some problems were experienced with the cooling system and the aluminium cylinder heads, but bush mechanical skills soon overcame most of them.

The roadtrain originally hauled two imported, purpose-built Dyson four-axle self-tracking trailers. Soon after its arrival two locally built trailers were added to the train, giving it a carrying capacity of 30 tonnes, although it mostly carried loads weighing far in excess of that.

The Dyson trailers were eight-wheelers set up in a bogie-bogie configuration. Each bogie was fitted with a turntable connected to the other by a spring-loaded linkage. This massive roadtrain was what would be called a rigid-plus four in today's modern trucking terminology.

It was the life-blood of the remote and isolated communities it serviced in Central Australia. During the years of Japanese hostilities in the Top End, following the bombing of Darwin in 1942, many residents in the bush received unchanged quality and quantity of haulage services, at the same rates, as they received prior to the onset of war—thanks to the Government Roadtrain. Without that service many would have had to walk away from their properties.

The AEC Roadtrain was self-tracking, which meant that the trailers would follow exactly in the wheel tracks of the prime mover. This was essential as the roadtrain trailblazed its own roads in most instances, often towing and winching the trailers, one at a time, over hundreds of kilometres of inhospitable terrain.

So perfect was the self-tracking mechanism that the unit could perform an L-turn in a tight area and run a near-perfect circle on its own tracks. Unfortunately, this precision also meant that if you were unlucky enough to stake a front tyre, it was highly likely that you would stake several other tyres on that side of the roadtrain.

Following a few months of trials in the South Australian desert, the AEC Roadtrain arrived in Alice Springs under the supervision of Captain (later Brigadier) Dollery of the Australian Army's Motor Transport Division. He was accompanied by a British officer of the same rank, two soldiers who had accompanied the truck on its long sea journey from London, and a 'bush cook'.

The trip from Adelaide to Alice Springs, a distance of 1770 kilometres, took nineteen days. Captain Dollery travelled by car ahead of the truck to survey for the best route. Planks and matting were used to get across the shifting sand dunes and trailers were unhooked to be winched across the twisting and winding beds of the Finke and Hugh rivers some eleven times in about 30 kilometres.

After further testing, the Commonwealth of Australia purchased the vehicle from the British Overseas Mechanical Transport Committee and the army handed it over to the Northern Territory government. It then became the responsibility of Douglas David (D.D.) Smith, resident engineer of the Commonwealth Department of the Interior in Alice Springs. A new chapter opened in road transport history.

In spite of the amazement (and amusement) the roadtrain initially created, it soon became a welcome sight to the pioneers who lived and worked in what was then considered the trackless deserts and scrub wastelands of the Northern Territory.

The roadtrain was to travel an amazing 1.28 million miles (2 million kilometres) before it was sold off to a timber dealer in Pine Creek in 1946. Its top speed was 28 miles per hour (45 kilometres per hour), and since it averaged around half of that most of the time they were 1.28 million slow miles.

The roadtrain's first real job was to take supplies and building materials from Alice Springs to Tennant Creek for the construction of a new hotel. There was no road to speak of in those days, only a rough two-wheeled track that followed the Overland Telegraph Line. As the AEC Roadtrain was a full 45 centimetres wider than the standard vehicle of the time, having a gauge of almost 2.4 metres, thousands of steeple-shaped anthills, some 1.5 to 1.8 metres high, had to be hand-cleared off the winding track that the narrower trucks of the day had carved out.

Another early job was hauling two trailers of stud bulls from Katherine to Wave Hill Station, a distance of 480 kilometres. It took a whole three weeks to complete. Carting cattle meant copious rolls of fencing wire, pickets and fodder had to be taken so the cattle could be unloaded and spelled. Water had to be brought too, as wells and other sources were often weeks away.

The roadtrain went on to haul many unusual loads during its years of service and never ceased to surprise, not only the public, but also its drivers, with its ability to cope with the rigours of the rugged Northern Territory bush.

In 1942 it hauled two prefabricated railway carriages, weighing 45 tonnes each, over the 1000 kilometres of dirt track between Alice Springs and the Birdum railhead south of Darwin. The railway carriages were for the Red Cross, following the Japanese bombing of Darwin. There was no railway line between the Alice Springs railhead and Birdum in those days and road was the only hope of getting the carriages north in this time of crisis. The load was three times what the roadtrain was designed to carry and authorities were amazed and delighted at the result.

The roadtrain's last major job was to haul 126 bales of wool from McDonald Downs Station to the Alice Springs railhead, a distance of about 400 kilometres. This was freight that was previously carted by 60 or more camels taking up to five times longer.

During its twelve years of operation for the Department of the Interior, many drivers operated the roadtrain. As was customary practice within the department at the time, a co-driver was also assigned to the vehicle. The second driver, or offsider as he was called, not only did his share of driving, but roadside repairs such as changing axles, springs and replacing tyres—just a part of the normal day's operation. The roadtrain had to be loaded and reloaded in areas where no assistance was available from machine or man. It was tedious and backbreaking work for two men, but an impossible task for one.

Territory truck driver Ewen Clough started on the roadtrain at the beginning, helping the army test the machine. When it was handed over to the Department of the Interior, Ewen stayed with it, and drove it from 1934 to late 1936. His bush skills and mechanical expertise were partly responsible for the roadtrain's eventual success.

During the dry season (May to October) the roadtrain worked out of Katherine supplying remote communities and isolated cattle stations in the Victoria River, Wave Hill and Borroloola regions.

With few roads to follow, it was simply a matter of getting the map out, drawing a line from origin to destination and heading off in the general direction. Ewen carted cattle, windmills, boring equipment and supplies to remote cattle stations, and building material and goods to outlying communities and the goldfields.

The wet season played havoc with the waterways of the north. Tracks that had been blazed just the year before were totally washed out and often the drivers and offsiders would have to walk for kilometres up and down the creeks looking for a suitable place to cross, up to six times a day.

They had to dig with shovels, sometimes for days, to cut away the riverbanks to allow the prime mover to get through. After this the truck was driven back and forth many times in order to compact the riverbed. When it was a bit wet, scores of barrowloads of dry soil or small rocks were tipped into the holes. The trailers were then winched through one at a time.

When there were four trailers the road often had to be repaired several times during the process as the weight of the trailers caused them to bog. Sometimes, massive tree trunks and other river debris had to be sawn up and moved out of the way of the path of the best crossing. Drivers always carried a supply of dynamite in case an obstacle had to be cleared or the road had to be blasted through. Some drivers said they felt like blowing up the truck instead of the obstacle.

Of course, there were no facilities along the lonely tracks the roadtrain followed. Drivers slept in swags under the stars, or under the truck if it was raining, and they had to live off the land; good bushmanship was essential.

The roadtrain had no windscreen and, in the sweltering heat of summer, 40-degree winds swept through the cab, burning the drivers' faces.

The radiator was mounted at the back of the driver's cab for protection and a large slow-speed fan mounted in front of it was driven by an auxiliary shaft on the engine, which also operated the compressor supplying air for the brakes. Although the position of the radiator, at the back of the cab, was conducive to the comfort of the driver and his offsider, on freezing winter nights the huge fan located behind the cab would suck below-freezing air through the cab and chill them both. Ewen said driving the roadtrain was like standing in front of a movie-set wind machine.

'It was murder sitting up there with the cold wind of the Centre whistling over you,' he said. 'I used to wear a leather coat to keep me warm.'

The engine didn't like the cold weather and the water in the radiator turned to ice at night during winter. Each night Ewen recalled he would have to empty the water out of the radiator, all 80 litres of it; after his evening meal he would spread his campfire coals under the engine.

In the morning his breakfast campfire would melt the ice and warm the water for the radiator, and the coals were then spread under the sump, slowly warming it enough to encourage the engine to start. If possible the truck was always parked on a downgrade or slope so that it could be rolled and clutch-started if the batteries refused to fire.

It took Ewen Clough around six months to complete his rounds. The roads and tracks he blazed made it a little easier for those who followed in his footsteps. His pay was £7 per week.

The AEC Government Roadtrain was not the first multi-trailer combination to operate in Australia. A variety of other steam, traction and electric models were used in the late 1800s and early 1900s throughout Australia, none of which proved particularly successful. Additionally, many early road transport drivers, keen to improve service and profit margins, built or adapted a wide variety of trailers to pull behind their small transports.

The AEC was unique not only in its construction and configuration but in the service it provided to the people of the Northern Territory. Before it began operating, the Afghan and Pakistani cameleers charged a rate of two shillings and sixpence per ton per mile to move freight. The efficiency and carrying capacity of the AEC and its two (or sometimes four) trailers meant the Department of the Interior could drop the rate to just six and a half pence per ton per mile. This rate was also less than half the rate the railways charged at the time.

The roadtrain was also an essential part of a scheme known as the Road/Rail Service. This was a joint initiative of the Australian government's Department of Transport and Works and the Commonwealth Railways Department. The Service was administered by D.D. Smith and the Department of the Interior.

The idea was that an efficient and effective land transport service, using road and rail, would encourage settlement in the remote areas of the Territory. It started in 1938 just after the coastal shipping service from Darwin down the Victoria River ceased operations.

At the time, the only other reliable service in the area was Bert Drew and his donkey teams. Bert was renowned for his reliability and dedication to the job, as well as his willingness to cross crocodile-infested waters, but the service was still slow and in an increasingly competitive environment road transport was the obvious choice.

The idea was that freight would come into the Alice Springs or Birdum railheads by train, and then be transported by road to outlying stations. The Department offered a discounted rate for goods that were for new developments. Naturally World War II made the service even more essential.

Initially the AEC Roadtrain took most of the freight between Alice Springs and Katherine or hauled down from Darwin to Katherine, and two smaller trucks—an AEC Monarch and an AEC Matador—operated out of Katherine hauling to cattle stations and remote communities.

The Katherine service ceased in 1940 and the main Northern Territory service ran out of the Alice for the remainder of the war years.

In 1946 the government decided to sell the AEC Government Roadtrain. Bought at auction by a company called Territory Timber, it was used primarily to haul timber in the Edith River area. It is believed that it also did some work for a gold-mining operation in Pine Creek until, finally, it suffered a major engine failure.

It was then sold as scrap metal and eventually ended up in the hands of Stan Kennon, who owned and operated a scrapyard in Winnellie (near Darwin) where it sat deteriorating for many years.

Stan knew its historical significance and, although he lacked the wherewithal to do anything about it, at least he had the foresight not to cut the vehicle up for scrap or otherwise dispose of it.

Renowned Central Australian camel breeder, racer and tour operator Noel Fullarton recognised the vehicle in 1973 and later purchased it, taking it back to Alice Springs. It was in a sad and sorry state. The bodywork was decaying and the wheels were missing, but the mechanical equipment and the chassis and frame were all still in position and in a repairable condition.

'It was barely recognisable,' Noel said. 'I just knew I had to do what I could to save it. I didn't have too much cash, but Jim Cooper helped me out with various things.'

When Noel bought the 'old girl' for $1500 it was surrounded by jungle with a gum tree growing up through the trailer on the back.

Noel believed at the time it was the only one of its kind in the world, and research to date indicates he was right, although there were similar prototypes in the USSR and South Africa, of which no trace can be found.

It is largely thanks to Noel's foresight and vision that the old AEC Government Roadtrain still exists today. He tinkered with it for a while and, after extensive lobbying, was able to convince the Northern Territory government of its historical significance, not only to the road transport industry, but also to the development of the Northern Territory and Australia.

In 1980 Noel sold the truck back to the government and it was returned to Darwin to the old Department of Transport and

Works plant workshop where staff took on the restoration project on behalf of NT Museum and Art Galleries. Tom Bertenshaw was the government's foreman in the Plant Section of the workshops at the time and took the project under his wing.

The restoration took about two years to complete, with many of the apprentices and mechanics using their own time to help with repairs and restoration. Tom played a major role in ensuring the job was completed.

One of the conditions under which Noel Fullarton sold the roadtrain back to the government was that it be displayed in Alice Springs. On its return to Alice Springs, it eventually ended up in the Central Australia Aviation Museum, displayed with the Stuart Auto Collection. That museum needed the space for aircraft, and when the steering committee of the National Road Transport Hall of Fame applied for funding to build a truck museum, one of the things the Northern Territory government stipulated was that the new building should house the AEC Roadtrain and the car collection.

The vehicles were initially placed in the Hall of Fame on a five-year loan agreement and, in 2000, at the fifth anniversary celebrations for the Hall of Fame, the Northern Territory Minister for Transport, Peter Adamson, presented ownership of the AEC Roadtrain and the Stuart Auto Car Collection to a very excited Hall of Fame committee.

EXTRACTS FROM THE DIARY OF GEORGE NICHOLS

George drove the roadtrain from 1939 to 1944. His diaries are part of the collection of the Road Transport Hall of Fame, Alice Springs.

Thursday 2 May 1940

Left Alice Springs for Katherine at 12 noon.

Blown tyre—out 8904945, replaced with 967396.

Camped at Hanson Creek. 150 miles.

Friday 3 May 1940

Hanson to Tennant. Arrived 8.30pm. 170 miles.

Saturday 4 May 1940

Offloaded and dismantled fire plough and reloaded. Left Tennant Creek at 5pm. Travelled 47 miles to Attack Creek.

Sunday 5 May 1940

Bogged near Renner Springs. Something broken in transmission. New tyre 937969—Old D967404.

Monday 6 May 1940

All day in bog replacing a broken axle. Got out and all ready to pack up by dark.

Tuesday 7 May 1940

Four miles south of Renner Springs after packing up. We move on to Newcastle Waters, very rough and heavy going with several minor bogs.

Wednesday 8 May 1940

Offloaded approximately ½ ton and reloaded it again and proceeded through Daly Waters to Rodericks Bore.

Thursday 9 May 1940
Rodericks Bore to the Warlock Crossing. 80 mile. Hopelessly bogged in the middle. New 963531, Old 937969, blown out.

Friday 10 May 1940
Got out of Warlock at 2pm and proceeded to Mataranka.

Saturday 11 May 1940
Proceeded to Katherine. Bogged near Maranboy.

Sunday 12 May 1940
Arrived in Katherine.

Monday 13 May 1940
Getting the truck ready to load, greasing up. Commenced loading. Changed tyres old 7995541, replaced with 938076.

Tuesday 14 May 1940
Completed loading. Started out for Victoria River Downs. 20 miles. Camped King River Crossing.

Wednesday 15 May 1940
King River to 3 miles from Delamere St. 120 miles from Katherine. King River very steep pull.

Thursday 16 May 1940
Delamere to Victoria River Downs. Arrived 8pm. Making creek crossings all day, road in bad condition. Tyre blown out, old 938016, new 963502.

Friday 17 May 1940

Offloaded and started back for Katherine. Camped at Delamere.

THE AEC GOVERNMENT ROADTRAIN: SPECIFICATIONS

Width: 7 ft 6 in (2.3 m)

Bogie wheelbase: 5 ft (1.5 m)

Bogie centres: 9 ft (2.7 m)

Wheelbase 1st axle to 4th: 14 ft (4.3 m)

Track

    1st and 4th axles: 6 ft 4½ in (1.94 m)

    2nd and 3rd axles: 6 ft 1⅜ in (1.86 m)

Body space: 11 ft 2½ in (3.4 m)

Min. ground clearance: 11 in (28 cm)

Height to top of frame: 5 ft 2⅝ in (1.59 m)

Platform height: 4 ft 6 in (1.37 m)

Turning circle: 58 ft (17.67 m)

Chassis weight (including fuel, oil and water): 7 tons 19 cwt (8 tonnes)

Capacity: 3 tons 16 cwt (3.9 tonnes)

Laden bogie weight

    Front: 5 tons 17 cwt 2 qr (6 tonnes)

    Rear: 5 tons 17 cwt (5.9 tonnes)

Total laden weight: 11 tons 15 cwt (11.9 tonnes)

Tractive effort with 10½ x 20 inch tyres: 15,000 lb (6800 kg)

Fuel tank capacity: 50 gal (227 litres)

TRUCKING CHICK

JAYNE DENHAM WITH JIM HAYNES

I was nineteen when I met my husband, Paul. He drove trucks for his family's business and also played guitar in a band.

We met when I auditioned for his band. I was attracted to this guy, who was a great guitarist and very creative, and we started dating. In fact, we spent many of our early dates in his truck delivering pipes and dreaming of being a singer (me) and a cameraman (him).

Now I sing and he films my video clips.

It's a dream come true!

So, I have always had an admiration for truckies. They keep this country moving and I'm astounded by the amazingly complicated work the big trucking companies manage to do across this huge nation. The logistics are terrifying!

I was speaking to a friend some time ago, while I was writing songs for a country album, and she said, 'You should meet my cousin Jude in Tamworth—she is a truckie. You won't believe it,' she went on, 'she has beautiful long dark hair, always wears makeup, and looks like Sandra Bullock!'

Well, I was in songwriting mode at the time for my first album, *Sudden Change in Weather*, and I immediately thought, 'What a top idea for a song.' I picked my friend's brains and asked her more about this unusual and apparently very cool 'trucker chick' from Tamworth.

John Kane and Mark Walmsley, who were producing the album, helped me write the song 'She's the Queen of the Road', and Paul did quality control on the lyrics.

As far as my career was concerned, the rest is history. Suddenly there were stories about me and the song in every truck magazine and newspaper in the country and I was invited to perform at truck shows all over Australia.

I had not met Jude when I wrote the song so I didn't really know if what I had written was a little exaggerated or took any liberties. I finally met her at Tamworth in 2008 and was greatly relieved to discover that she was all that I had said she was in the song . . . and more. It was obvious she took her job very seriously. She was also one of the funniest people I have ever met, a true 'larger than life' character.

Each album an artist does usually has three 'radio singles', and we decided to release 'Queen of the Road' to radio and have Jude star in the video clip. When she suggested we use her everyday truck in the clip I thought, 'Oh dear, I hope it isn't a little truck with chickens painted on it, or something that doesn't match up to the lyric from the song: "Her truck's no toy, she's the Queen of the Road".'

When we met on the highway on the way to Sydney through the Blue Mountains it was quite a shock for me to realise my song was not even close to the real story. Jude's truck was much more amazing and powerful than I had imagined, the most beautiful Kenny with a cream interior and three sticks of different-coloured lip gloss on the dash to match the interior!

She really was the 'Queen of the Road'. We were allowed to use the truck in the video clip and it was a huge success.

•

I had obviously struck a chord with the trucking industry so, for my next album, *Shake this Town*, I knew I needed to have a few more trucking songs for the fans I had been lucky to find in the trucking world.

With Colin Buchanan and producer Garth Porter, I wrote 'Trucker Chicks', and Colin also wrote a song called 'Road Train Fever' especially for me.

'Trucker Chicks' was an obvious single, and we needed a bigger budget this time for a really great video clip. We also needed quite a few trucks for the clip we had planned.

As a result of the success of 'Queen of the Road', I had performed two years running at the Wickham Freightlines Christmas party. Wickham Freightlines is one of Queensland's leading freight companies. They specialise in refrigerated, general and express transport companies and run a fleet of 51 Kenworth trucks.

In spite of their size, Wickham's are basically a family-owned and -operated company. I remember a conversation with Graham, the managing director, when we first met, telling him that I had seen heaps of their trucks during the year in Sydney. His first question was, 'Were they clean?' I really came to admire the work ethic and spirit of excellence they always attempted to achieve as a company and the fact that they manage to still be a great friendly family.

After meeting them, and discussing the idea with my management team, we asked if they would like to sponsor me for the year 2010. The idea was that we would use their trucks to make two video clips of my songs, which would also be a great promotion for them. It turned out to be an amazing union.

Wickham's were excited to be a part of what I was doing and naturally the sponsorship created publicity in both the trucking and country music industries. Stories appeared in both truck and music magazines, and radio stations took up the idea as a great talking point too.

People involved in road transport are always happy to have positive publicity. The connection between the trucking industry and country music has always been strong. Slim Dusty was a champion of the truckies and recorded many albums of truck songs, and I was helped along the way by another country singer, Travis Sinclair, who has continued the tradition. Coming from a Victorian trucking family, Travis has four generations of big rigs in his blood and drives a big gold Kenworth when he isn't performing his travelling country music show.

Two Wickham Freightlines B-doubles turned up for a day of filming with real working truckies at the wheel. The clip looked great and had a real spirit of fun and action. The song became a hit on Australian country radio, reaching number three in the charts, and the video clip was a hit on the country music channel CMC.

The relationship with Wickham's was working for both of us and they decided to put a picture of me on the side of one of their refrigeration vans as part of the sponsorship. The truck is on the road all the time so it is seen a lot—suddenly there was my face rolling along the highways of eastern Australia.

When I had a show somewhere, Wickham's would make an effort to arrange schedules so that the truck would be parked out the front as advertising for us all. It really created a stir: fans would be out there, lining up and getting photos of themselves and the 'Jayne Denham' truck, or the 'JD' as it became known.

It was an amazing feeling for me to see that truck parked out the front of the Golden Guitar at the Tamworth Festival in 2011. It was truly a dream come true and it was certainly hard to miss the fact that 'JD was in town'!

For me the connection with the trucking industry has been a wonderful thing; it is such a thrill to be able to cheer on the trucking industry and the incredible people in it.

I just know that this is something I am meant to do. I am spending time reading and learning more about the industry and its history, and plan to write plenty more truckin' songs!

Born in Brisbane, Jayne Denham grew up in the Blue Mountains near Sydney listening to her father's collection of country music. She had formal vocal training from an early age and formed an all-girl band at school when she was fourteen.

Jayne developed a career as a backing singer for artists like Tina Arena and toured Europe, the USA and New Zealand singing for various Australian artists before recording an album as a solo artist and having success with her debut single 'Chick Ute'. She has now developed a successful career in country music.

CONFESSIONS OF A WHEAT DUMPER

FRANK DANIEL

In 1985 I purchased a new Ford LTL prime mover and a new Alcan aluminium tipping trailer.

It was no trouble to buy a new truck in those days; all you had to do was walk into Stillwell Ford in Milperra, in Sydney, and they would just about throw the keys at you.

Borrowing money was not a problem either if you were prepared to make the loan repayments and pay the interest being asked. Interest was set at a mere 23 per cent! At least we were guaranteed that it wouldn't rise during the term of the contract or lease.

Interest rates were indeed shocking, but in the trucking industry we were used to putting up with such hardships. We just went along for the ride, knowing that after five years of monthly repayments the trucks would be paid for.

Of course, what we tended to forget was that the truck was usually buggered by then and we'd have to trade it in and buy another one. Still, cartage rates at that time were good enough to cover our costs and give us a fair to comfortable living.

Farmers, however, were in a different boat. They were paying around 12 per cent on money borrowed, and their returns were fairly static—not too high, but not too low either. It wasn't until they were hit with 4 and 5 per cent increases, and the rate very quickly jumped to 24 per cent, that things really went wrong.

Budgeting on farm income included costs set against returns from sales, and when the increase was forced on them they were not in a position to pay. No farmers had budgeted for more than a 1 or 2 per cent rise in their cost of borrowings.

Bob Hawke was the prime minister then and 45,000 farmers rallied outside Parliament House, Canberra, in July 1985 to protest about the impact of taxes and charges and the lack of government concern over their welfare. There were promises of some relief, but the relief never eventuated and the protestors vowed they would return.

Farmers faced another harvest that year with no expectations of relief, knowing that the government would not come to the rescue. Incomes were being sucked up by the banks. The big banks didn't care, as they felt assured of getting their money back. Many farmers went to the wall, suicide was not uncommon in the rural sector, and families were left destitute.

Farm machinery bought with bank loans was often sold at a loss in an attempt to relieve interest charges. The loss of capital was added to the farm overdraft, which was still attracting high rates of interest.

In the midst of all this, meetings were held and the Australian Farmers' Fighting Fund, or AFFF, was officially launched.

And that's where I came into the picture!

One night a few days before Christmas I was dragging a pretty heavy load of grain up Mount Victoria, New South Wales, bound for Allied Mills at Rhodes on the Parramatta River, when the bloke reading the news on my truck radio announced that the AFFF was planning an assault on Canberra.

My ears pricked up straight away, and when he said that the farmers were threatening to dump a load of wheat on the steps of Parliament House in Canberra if no action was taken by Bob Hawke I really took an interest.

I remember thinking to myself, 'I'd be in that!' But I never realised, as I chuckled to myself at the thought of such an opportunity for a bit of devilment, that it was just around the corner.

I didn't hear the rest of the news as I was too engrossed in my plan of attack and escape, should I get the job. My mind was also busy with a strategy for getting into Sydney without being caught for overloading.

It was a chance in a thousand but you wouldn't believe it, back in my hometown of Canowindra a few days later I was approached by a couple of cockies, who laid their plan before me. These blokes represented a group of farmers known locally as the 'Magnificent Seven' and they had a plan to make the politicians and the media sit up and notice the farmers.

A sizable load of grain had been collected at the local silos, which wasn't hard as it was harvest time. The plan was that I would dump the load in Canberra early on New Year's morning. They assured me 'that there was nothing to worry about'. 'We'll be right behind you, Frank.' How many times did I hear that? I'd been hearing blokes tell me that since I was a kid in the playground.

Anyway, I listened and I probably believed them as well. The plan seemed simple enough and they had it all worked out pretty well . . . for farmers.

Came the big day: New Year's Eve and the truck was loaded. My wife Kerry came along for the 'drive'. She wasn't going to miss out on such an adventure. Two young farmers followed me; I think they were supposed to be there for moral support.

We made the trip to Canberra via Cowra, Boorowa and Yass, and it was quite uneventful—we didn't have any worries with scalies (weight inspectors) that day.

At Yass I gained a passenger by prearrangement. The Magnificent Seven had arranged for a journalist from the *Australian* newspaper to join me for the rest of the trip. It turned out that he had already written a story about my journey and his paper would be the first with the news on New Year's Day. I wasn't too sure why he had to be there with me, other than the fact that he wanted to be sure that his article in the paper came true.

I remember thinking at the time that the newspaper trucks would be well on their way out of Sydney delivering the morning news statewide as we headed down the last leg of the journey to the nation's capital. Those trucks would be making many of their deliveries with the early editions of the paper to rural towns and cities before I had even completed my part of the deal.

I'd planned my part of the job pretty well . . . so I thought.

I'd go straight through Canberra city, over the Commonwealth Avenue Bridge, take the first left after Lake Burley Griffin then wriggle around a couple of streets to the front of Parliament House. (It was still the old Parliament House in those days; the new one hadn't been completed.) I'd tip the load on the front steps and then race out along Kings Avenue, over the lake again, hang a right into Morsehead Drive and make a bolt for freedom on Majura Lane near the airport. I'd driven Majura Lane in the past and I remember it used to be a very dusty road. Maybe it was dusty that day, too, but, as it turned out, I never had a chance to find out.

When I approached the national seat of democracy there was no sign of any security anywhere, just a small dark blue sedan parked in the side street before the 'target area'. I didn't know then that Canberra cops drove small blue sedans. I was only on the lookout for the white Ford Falcons that were standard cop cars in those days, and I hadn't seen one since entering the Australian Capital Territory.

Two of my mates had found the plan so exciting when it was divulged to them that they had motored down to Canberra to be part of the action. When I pulled up outside the building, right at the entrance to the old place, they jumped to attention and opened the tailgate on my trailer as I sent the hoist up as fast as I could. They had brought a couple of protest signs to put up as well.

In seconds the load was dumped and the signs were almost erected. Things were going well.

Then, all of a sudden, the aforementioned blue sedan came screaming around the corner, did a wheelie and spun itself crossways in front of my truck. It was real cops and robbers stuff, just like in the movies.

Of course, it was driven by a policeman! He turned out to be a pretty good bloke and only new at the game. He didn't seem to know what to do.

He was soon knocking on my truck door and yelling at me, but I couldn't hear him over the revving of my engine. When I finally decided I'd dropped most of the load I rolled down the window and asked him what his trouble was. He asked me why I was dumping a load of sand on the driveway entrance to our national parliament.

I was taken aback by his question at first; then I realised that he wouldn't have known shit from sugar, let alone the difference between sand and wheat.

Eventually, after a short and confused conversation, I got down from the truck and he placed me under arrest. I wasn't too concerned at this point, however, as the Magnificent Seven were surely 'right behind me' . . . somewhere . . . or so I thought . . .

But they weren't!

However, large numbers of Canberra police *were* quickly on the scene, even though it was only 4 a.m.

Pretty soon at least twelve of those white Ford Falcons, the ones I hadn't seen so far that day, had joined the blue sedan and my truck was surrounded. It was like a scene from the last reel of a bad American action movie.

Not only that: word seemed to travel fast in the nation's capital and no less than 25 journalists and reporters representing the world at large appeared from nowhere, some still in pyjamas, all clicking cameras and asking questions. I wasn't interested in what they wanted; in fact I wasn't overly sure or too concerned as to why I was dumping the wheat or what was to become of it, or me. I was in it more for the fun than the politics.

The police took me to the Federal Police station in Civic and placed me in a charge room while they decided on their course of action. I could hear most of their conversations until I eventually fell asleep across a small table.

My wife and two mates felt a bit left out of it all and went off looking for some breakfast. I think they found an all-night pancake parlour and coffee shop in Civic.

Meanwhile the load of wheat was labelled 'poison' by the police for some reason best known only to them. Maybe they thought it was a clumsy plot to poison the food in the members' dining room.

The police took me back to my truck about four hours later and I found out that the Department of the Interior had been summoned to supply half a dozen employees, a front-end loader and a large mechanical broom to clean up the 'mess' and load it back onto my truck. I bet they all got good money for working on New Year's Day.

With the truck reloaded I was given an escort to the Australian Capital Territory/New South Wales border by a couple of white Ford Falcon chase cars driven by attractive blonde female police officers. They pulled over at the border and with sirens blaring and lights flashing they gave me a big wave and a final 'good riddance'.

Back home, the Magnificent Seven declared me a local hero and, as a gesture of good faith, they presented me with the load of grain. I sold it to a local agent, who consigned it to a chook farm in Sydney's west. On top of that he paid me to deliver the load. So if you remember having some blue metal in your frozen chooks around 1986, I can tell you where it came from.

Twelve thousand farmers rallied at the Canberra Court House on Valentine's Day 1986 where, unsure of my destiny, I faced the wrath of the law and the criminal justice system.

Once the prosecutor started to read the charges against me he didn't look like he was ever going to stop.

The judge was a decent sort of a bloke. He stopped the prosecutor in his tracks as he reached charge number ten. His honour then came down from his bench and told the prosecutor to forget the charges. He said that I was only representing the mood of many and he gave quite a nice speech on my behalf and wished the room packed with farmers all the best in their endeavours.

And the Magnificent Seven paid all the bills. They were right behind me after all!

TRUCKING WITH SLIM

JOHN ELLIOTT

Not only did Slim Dusty record many trucking songs, he also had a long association with the Australian Truck Drivers' Memorial at Tarcutta and regularly performed fundraising concerts for it.

When Slim decided to do another album in 1998, he spread the word among his team of songwriters and, naturally, the songs began to come in.

Evidently Slim decided that he needed to be in the right mood before he began the album, so he decided to make a roadtrain trip across the Nullarbor from Adelaide to Perth. Luckily, he decided that I might be useful and he called me up and invited me to come along. There would be plenty of photo opportunities and some good stories, which would help promote the album. Of course, there was lots of fun to be had and Slim always enjoyed having mates along when there were good times ahead.

Slim had always said that truck drivers were just like show people. 'We've spent a lot of time on the showgrounds over the years,' said Slim, 'and we seem to have something in common between the showies and the truck drivers. If you're not in the game, you're an outsider. There is a great bond, a great brotherhood—they all stick together.'

Now, it isn't all that easy to arrange travel by roadtrain. It isn't the kind of travel request that you can take to your local travel agent. When you travel with Slim Dusty, however, there are ways of making things happen. A phone call to an old mate, Noel Brown, national sales manager of Re-Car, soon had the trip becoming a reality.

Slim and his wife Joy McKean were patrons of the truck drivers' memorial at Tarcutta, which is sponsored by Re-Car, and Noel was soon in touch with Keith Thompson of Thompson's Transport in Victoria. Keith agreed to provide the trucks and the trip was on. He even managed to procure four genuine trailer loads, two from Colgate Palmolive and two from Bridgestone Tyres.

Every truck driver in Australia would have loved to have made that trip with Slim, but executive privilege was called into play, with Keith Thompson driving one of the Kenworths and Noel Brown, after years in retirement, making his driving comeback to pilot the other one. The wives decided they were not going to be left out either, with Bev Brown and Carol Thompson driving the back-up vehicle.

The itinerary for the trip was quite leisurely. Six days would be spent on the road, with stops at Port Augusta, Ceduna, Eucla, Balladonia and Kalgoorlie, before arriving in Perth.

The planning done, we all met up in Adelaide and set off on the short first leg to Port Augusta. Within no time at all Slim was reminiscing. 'This is just like the old days,' he said. 'It reminds me of back in the 1960s when we would head off across to Perth early in the year with our big road show. The roads were dusty back then and as rough as guts; the trip would just about destroy our old Internationals. It's a bloody lot more comfortable riding high in a Kenworth.'

Slim and Joy enjoyed travelling in the Kenworths every day, experiencing life on the road in the rigs. 'The trip has given me a whole new insight into how it is from a truck driver's perspective,' Joy said. 'I'm sure I'll get some good songs from it. When I'm writing I want to know how things work and I love travelling, so this trip is giving me the best of both worlds.'

At Ceduna there was time for a quick visit to one of the thriving oyster farms, which was followed, naturally, by a delicious dinner of local seafood. Everyone agreed that truck-driving tours like this one could really catch on!

The trip had been deliberately kept very low key, with no advance publicity. This gave Slim a chance to be just one of the boys, and things became more relaxed the further west we travelled. The truck drivers we met along the way welcomed Slim as one of their own and swapped yarns with him about their work and lives. Many of them commented on how well Slim looked after some recent health problems.

'I hope I'm going as well as you when I'm your age,' said one driver.

We stopped for quite a while at the Western Australian border and I took many photographs of Slim with the quarantine inspectors. Then it was on to Eucla, where the local police had arranged a late afternoon tour of the scenic delights of the area.

Constable Phil Kuhne was given the job of driving Slim across the now sand dune–covered site of old Eucla. He then took Slim for a drive along the amazingly beautiful 20-kilometre section of beach. In spite of Constable Kuhne bogging the four-wheel-drive vehicle on the return trip, a good time was had by all.

That evening we took a light drive around Eucla's new golf course. The highlight of that adventure was chasing a bunch of kangaroos along the eighteenth fairway. Then the whole crew headed back for dinner at the Eucla Motor Inn.

Slim was in a great mood that night and said to me, 'I think I'll have a quiet one tonight, so when I've finished dinner it's out the back door and back to my room.' As it happened, Slim changed his mind and ended up, unsurprisingly, in the bar.

Slim loved a beer or two and, during his busy touring schedule, there was rarely time to party with his mates. Normally he would finish a concert, meet the fans, pack up his gear and then head back to the motel for maybe one or two stubbies with the band before getting to bed, ready for an early start the next day with several hours of driving to the next concert. That routine could go on day after day for up to six weeks at a time.

But then at Ceduna there was no concert the following night and Slim was able to take advantage of being with a couple of good mates and a bunch of party-loving locals in a bar in the outback.

It was a night to remember, a night for yarn spinning, research for future Slim Dusty songs and reminiscing. In fact, there was so much of a good time that night that the bar ran out of Bundaberg Rum at 11 p.m.

Because there was often someone who would take the chance to bail up the famous entertainer, Slim usually had someone designated to be his 'minder'. On this particular evening I was the one who had the job.

The locals had taken the liberty of warning us earlier about one particular local woman who was especially argumentative. There is always one in every town and this woman was the 'one local stirrer'. If she turned up at the bar they told us she would definitely start an argument of some kind and the only way to deal with her was to tell her, in no uncertain terms, to 'bugger off'.

I had been keeping an eye on Slim in the crowded bar, making sure he didn't get into any trouble. As the evening wore on I looked up and spotted Slim and, sure enough, a woman had him cornered; even from across the room I could see that they were having more than just a chat. I edged my way over so that I could hear the conversation.

'You are always sucking up to the black fellas,' I heard the woman say.

'Half my mates are Aboriginal,' Slim replied, 'so I have no need to suck up to them. I probably wouldn't have had a career without all my Aboriginal fans.'

In spite of Slim's attempts to reason with her, the woman was in no mood to listen. She continued her belligerent badgering. I was about to intervene and save Slim from any further aggravation when he looked her straight in the eye and said, 'Why don't you bugger off?'

I realised then that Slim was well aware that this was the 'one local stirrer' that he had been warned about.

It was quite late in the evening, or rather early in the morning, when the crowd dwindled and the locals departed. With just myself, Slim, Noel, Keith and the barman left standing, it was the barman who said he'd had enough.

'Bugger you blokes,' he said. 'I'm off to bed.'

It was only then that the trio decided to call it quits.

Now, it seemed like a simple process: all I had to do was get the three of them back to their motel rooms and, after all, the motel was right next door. Surely it couldn't be all that difficult.

How wrong can you be?

All three of them had had quite a bellyful of booze, and the gravel driveway to the motel seemed to be proving just a little difficult for them to negotiate; maintaining any dignity while trying to walk along that drive was seriously beyond them.

The motel was in darkness, all other guests were sleeping soundly, and my mates were getting progressively louder and louder. It crossed my mind that if the manager of the motel chucked us out we probably wouldn't get another bed in Eucla at that time of the morning. To top things off, Slim couldn't remember what room he was in.

Thankfully, Joy had guessed that her husband might have some difficulty in that department and she had conveniently left their motel door ajar, so I gently pointed Slim in the right direction, through the door, and said goodnight to Noel and Keith.

Back in my own room I was very grateful to be able to kick off my shoes and rest my weary bones on the nice soft bed. It had been a long day. Just as I dozed off the whole motel was rocked by what I thought must be an earth tremor. Once I had recovered from the shock, I dozed off to sleep wondering just how common earth tremors were on the Nullarbor.

At breakfast the next morning I discovered the truth about that tremor. Keith Thompson has an artificial leg, and after he had staggered into his room, doing his best not to wake his sleeping wife, he had undressed, kicked off his artificial leg, and attempted to hop. As he hopped, however, Keith gained momentum and the further he hopped the faster he went. Having made it to the door of the toilet at an ever-increasing speed, he tripped and went head-first into the gyprock wall behind the toilet.

At first Keith's wife, Carol, thought he was dead but, apart from a hangover, Keith survived the night unscathed.

As a result of the 'night out' in Eucla, Slim gave the Kenworth's sleeper cabin a thorough road test for most of the next day.

Slim was always up for new experiences and it wasn't just the sleeper cabin that he road-tested on that trip. He had been spending much of his time travelling with Keith Thompson, who gave the legendary performer lots of personal tuition on the gentle art of driving a roadtrain.

Slim was a quick learner and was soon behind the wheel of the big Kenworth. He was full of enthusiasm at the first truck stop after his test drive.

'It's the biggest vehicle I've ever driven,' he said, beaming. 'It's an amazing feeling up there. It's hard to explain until you've done it and have felt the power under your control.'

Keith's assessment of the legendary entertainer's driving skills was very positive. 'He took to it like a natural,' said Keith. 'He changed gears so well I reckon he's been outback somewhere near Longreach practising in one of those cattle roadtrains; he wasn't tense at all.'

Slim's driving ability was certainly tested the next day when he asked for another go at driving the roadtrain. This time it was at the bottom of the Fraser Range. Slim was in the driver's seat of the Kenworth for the winding, gear-jamming section of the narrowest piece of road between Adelaide and Perth but, once again, he passed the test with flying colours.

'That's it for me,' Slim said with a laugh. 'I've driven a road-train and I don't need to do it again. I'm retiring, undefeated.'

Keith and Noel had turned it on for Slim with their never-ending supply of truck stories, but on day four of the trip it was Slim's turn to return the favour.

The place he chose was the side of the bitumen, halfway across the Nullarbor. The two Kenworths pulled over and Slim climbed down with his guitar in hand.

'"Lights on the Hill" was meant to be sung in front of a big Kenworth out here,' he said, 'so here we go . . .'

Windscreen wipers are beating in time,
The song they sing is a part of my mind . . .

This was one impromptu concert that would never be forgotten by the crew, and the two surprised tourists who just happened to be lucky enough to be passing by and pulled up, amazed, to join the audience for the free concert.

Two roadtrains roared past mid-performance, their CB radios crackling instantly to life.

'I can't bloody turn around,' yelled one driver into the CB. 'Maybe I could drop the trailers and go back and see what's going on. I'm sure it was Slim Dusty!'

Almost everyone we ran into had their own Slim Dusty story. During the overnight break at the Balladonia truck stop, one member of a team of Nullarbor road workers recalled the days of the Roy Bell Boxing Troupe. Aged fifteen at the time, he had seen the Slim Dusty Show back in 1964. Now, he and Slim traded yarns about life on the road.

Slim was forever meeting people who'd seen his concerts years before. Slim's explanation of this never-ending phenomenon was simple.

'After being on the road for 43 years I have come into contact with a lot of people,' he said, 'so it's natural that I run into many of them on my travels.'

The following day we had lunch at the Norseman BP truck stop. The Akubra-wearing manager, Karen Harris, already had Slim Dusty playing on the in-house music system when we arrived. By an amazing coincidence, the staff had decided to have a country music day. They couldn't believe it when the man in the familiar hat walked in.

'No one told us Slim was coming,' Karen Harris said. 'We got a big surprise, we didn't even know he was on the road.'

We drove on to Kalgoorlie and arrived about 5 p.m. We had been on the road for quite a few long days and long nights, so I was tired and looking forward to a good hot shower and a lie-down before we would all meet for dinner.

I had just finished my shower and was about to lie down when there was a knock on the door. It was Slim with guitar in hand.

'Joy wants to have a sleep and I feel like singing. Do you mind if I come in?'

It would take a braver man than me to refuse Slim, so in he came.

He sat on the end of my bed while I made a cup of tea and listened. He knocked out song after song, picking and strumming his trusty Maton guitar. He was singing for the pure pleasure of it, because that was what he did.

Slim never needed the excitement of a crowd or the charged atmosphere of the recording studio. Watching and listening to Slim in my motel room, I realised he didn't even need me there to listen. He was going to sing anyway. Singing was something that came to Slim as naturally as breathing. It was something he had to do every day.

I just happened to be lucky enough that day to be selected as the very exclusive audience for this one-on-one performance. He took great delight in singing his own songs. Some of the songs he had been singing for over 50 years, but to hear him in my motel room I realised he was singing them with so much passion and heart you would swear he was singing them for the first time.

There was never an ordinary show from Slim.

A phone call interrupted this special performance but only long enough for me to say, 'Could you please call back later? I have Slim Dusty in my room singing requests.'

Next day it was on to Perth to unhook the roadtrain and deliver the semis to Thompson's Transport depot at Welshpool.

Joy was being serious when she climbed down from the Kenworth cab for the last time and said, 'I'm just getting warmed up—I could keep going forever.'

The final dinner for all the crew in Perth was a time to swap memories and yarns and even make plans for future trips. Slim had been particularly impressed by the friendly folk at Eucla, so Keith Thompson, Noel Brown and Slim were already looking at putting on the show to end all shows right in the middle of the Nullarbor.

'It would be a good opportunity to get all the truck drivers, the country music people and the locals together,' said Noel.

'We can use one of my tautliners for a stage,' Keith Thompson chipped in, 'and we can truck in toilets and generators.'

'Let's do it,' Slim said. 'I'll get some of my country music mates over to perform.'

Look out, Eucla!

Everyone voted the trip a huge success and Joy said, 'I have enough raw material to keep writing songs for years. I have three definite song ideas that I hope will make Slim's truck album.'

'Just write another "Lights on the Hill",' was Slim's answer. It was his constant challenge to his wife during the trip.

The trip had served its purpose. Joy McKean did write three songs for the album, and Slim was mentally prepared to hit the studio, feeling much more comfortable about recording an authentic Aussie truck album.

Makin' a Mile, Slim Dusty's 93rd album, is the result of that epic truck trip across the Nullarbor.

IT WAS A GREAT IDEA

GRANT LUHRS WITH JIM HAYNES

It was Simon Smith calling me. 'I've got this great idea!' he said.

I had a sense of foreboding right away; Simon is a very enthusiastic bloke and isn't easily diverted.

'What is it?' I asked, not without some trepidation.

'Well, Grant, you see, back when I was at Radio 2WG Wagga Wagga in the 1990s we ran this trucking show. It went out on 2WG and 2AY Albury and was a big hit with the truckies driving down Sesame Street.' (Sesame Street was the truckies' name for the Hume Highway.)

'You've got a recording studio,' Simon continued, 'so why don't we put a radio show onto CD and distribute it to truckies all over Australia? We'll sell advertising, give 'em great music and comedy, industry news etc . . . and make a fortune!'

'Hang on, Simon,' I replied. 'It's a great idea and I'm interested, but it isn't that simple. For a start, when you put music on a CD it becomes a compilation album and you have to pay royalties. That costs a lot and you have to negotiate a deal with every record company and every publisher for each song.

'Then there's the distribution nightmare—actually getting the CDs to the drivers on the road all over Australia—and it takes quite a while to put a show like that together. For this sort of thing to be successful, we need a constant flow of shows, just like you have on radio.'

And so the idea was put into the too-hard basket.

The irrepressible Simon called me again a few months later. 'Just been talking to the CBAA,' he said. 'Do you know them?'

'Sure I do,' I answered. The Community Broadcast Association of Australia coordinates the community FM stations.

'Well,' says Simon, 'they have this thing called NatRadSat.'

'They do,' I said slowly.

Of course I'd heard of NatRadSat. It's a subscription service provided by the CBAA to all member community FM associations around Australia. It provides a 24-hour program service that stations can switch to whenever they choose to—typically from midnight to 5 a.m., when it isn't feasible for them to provide their own programs.

'Well,' said Simon enthusiastically, 'they'll let us do a trucking show between midnight and 5 a.m. on a Sunday night and Monday morning. I also ran into this bloke called Barrie Smith. He's no relation, but you wouldn't believe it—he has the same idea as me and he is keen to work with us. And he owns an advertising agency in Melbourne called Framework Media that specialises in the trucking industry! It's perfect! Mate . . . this is all doable!'

So Rig Radio was born.

The first Rig Radio show, aimed squarely at the trucking industry, went to air on 29 April 2001. Its aim was to provide not only entertainment for drivers but also industry information.

Our research found that truck drivers are huge fans of radio; in fact, 90 per cent of truckies listen to more than four hours of radio a day. Although there is a plethora of trucking magazines, the drivers themselves are not big readers of them and prefer radio. The reason is pretty obvious: when you spend most of your waking hours driving a truck you can listen, but you can't read!

Our research also showed us that truck drivers mostly like rock music from the 1970s and 1980s and tend to like female announcers. They seem to prefer a girl's voice and a warm and friendly attitude. Contrary to misinformed popular opinion they do not want smut or overt sexuality—just a kind voice to listen to while they are doing the hard miles.

Truckies deliver 2 billion tonnes of freight each year and the industry employs 220,000 people. It seemed a good number to make for a successful radio show.

We also found that 70 per cent of all Australia's trucking transport goes up and down 'Sesame Street', the Hume Highway.

•

The show ran out of Wagga Wagga from the studios of 2AAA-FM, Wagga's community FM station. It was broadcast initially from midnight Sunday to 5 a.m. Monday morning.

We sent our broadcast signal from the 2AAA studios in Wagga via ISDN to the CBAA studios in Sydney. It was then beamed up to a satellite. (ISDN is a circuit-switched telephone network system designed to allow digital transmission of voice and data over ordinary telephone copper wires.)

The show was a great success from the start. We soon had 100 stations taking the show all around Australia.

We started with Simon and a female presenter named Phoebe. The drivers loved Phoebe! But she soon found it difficult to work the night shift. We tried other girls after she left, but with no success.

Although we were now missing the warm female voice, Rig Radio went on to success after success with Simon and myself as presenters.

In October 2002 the show went to a second night and we hired two other guys, Rod and Mick, to do the second night—which was Monday night into Tuesday morning.

Listener input was a big part of the show's success. We encouraged all drivers and other listeners to call in and tell us their stories. We ran many competitions to encourage this and got 70 to 100 calls each night. Now, they say in the radio industry that one call equates to 1000 listeners, so we were doing all right!

On-air advertising was the only way Rig Radio made money. We quickly attracted advertisers, who saw an opportunity to effectively deliver their message in a way that the print media could not. Companies like Kenworth, Caterpillar, Iveco, Freightliner, Shell, Sterling, *Owner Driver Magazine*, Castrol and Mobil were just a few of those who were keen to come on board and support the show.

Industry groups also used the show to spread their message. The National Road Transport Commission, Natroad, Vic Roads, the RTA and the Australian Trucking Association all used the show to spread their messages and information.

Truckies' welfare groups like the ATA Women's Association and the Concerned Families of Australian Truckies were good supporters. We even had our own religious adviser, Transport for Christ—the Highway Chaplain!

The National Road Transport Commission in particular had a strong involvement in the program. They became a sponsor and used their airtime to propagate information about the issues they wanted drivers to be aware of.

In no time at all we had a wide variety of listeners from all aspects of the trucking industry. Roadtrain drivers across the Kimberley and northern Queensland and the interstate truckies all along the Hume were a big part of the audience, but we also soon discovered that city truck drivers doing shift work and delivering papers, milk, groceries, petrol and so on were interested listeners. We also started to hear from tow-truck drivers, furniture removalists, coal-truck drivers and blokes involved in waste management.

Some groups became dedicated listeners and used the show to stay in touch with each other. The Woolworths' drivers were a great bunch, as were the Australian Air Express drivers and the 'Barters Chook' drivers based in Griffith.

We had some odd and unexpected groups who became avid listeners and regular correspondents, like the street sweepers in the Victorian town of Shepparton.

What we hadn't counted on was the fact that the show also attracted listeners involved in night-shift occupations like taxi driving. For some reason we had a strong contingent of drivers from Townsville. They would keep us posted on how their night was progressing. One Townsville cabbie went overseas for a trip and rang us from England to speak to us on air!

Many of our most loyal listeners were not involved in transport at all. We had nurses and train- and bus-station employees and others who worked at night. The guys and gals working in the bakeries in Texas, Queensland and Portland, Victoria were regular listeners. One bloke would give us a blow-by-blow description of how his pies, sausage rolls and pasties were going. It is amazing what you find interesting on radio in the early hours of the morning!

Rig Radio certainly attracted its fair share of characters. A group of wood-chip drivers from Tasmania were all great characters who listened every Sunday night. They were known as Boofer, Jacko, Batch and Woody, and were also great contributors to the program. They were all great mates but never missed a chance to take the piss out of each other. How much of what they told us was true, we never really knew!

Boofer, apparently, was notorious for getting lost—that is how he got his nickname. Come to think of it, he always seemed lost when he called us! He drove a 'Fruit Box' (Freightliner) and had a jovial personality and a big laugh. Boofer was such a character that we had him do promotional stings for us—things like: 'Hi, this is Boofer from Tasmania—one of the wood chippers—and I love listening to Rig Radio!'

The boys and girls who drove for Murray Goulburn Milk, based in Shepparton and Warrnambool, would all listen to the show, those manning the depot and all the drivers out on the road. There was lots of interplay between the depot and the drivers on the road through Rig Radio. We had fun relaying messages, jibes, jokes and insults between them. We even arranged and effected a marriage proposal one night. Can't remember if it was for real or not, but it was good radio!

Then there was Squeak. Squeak worked for Moll Transport in Queensland. He was also known as Goog. He learned to drive trucks when he was eight years old, and he fell in love with our female presenter, Phoebe. We all met Squeak when he visited us on one of our outside broadcasts in Albury. He was a lovely bloke, but his fascination with Phoebe was pure old-fashioned unrequited love. Phoebe was already involved with someone else and Squeak accepted his fate with equanimity. He was still happy to listen to Simon and me after Phoebe departed the airwaves, but I don't think he listened with quite the same enthusiasm!

Rod Hannifey, the truck-driving crusader from Dubbo, was a regular on the show. Rod was and still is at the coalface of all issues associated with truck drivers. We would talk to Rod at around 2.30 a.m. from wherever he and his truck were at the time. He managed to eventually get himself onto the board of the Australian Trucking Association and has become a powerful voice for drivers.

Rod is an irrepressible advocate for the improvement of driver conditions across Australia. He has taken many politicians for a ride in his truck to give them first-hand experience of what it's like to be a truck driver.

One of my personal favourites from our audience was Cuddles. Cuddles came from the Gippsland area, had her own truck, and had been driving for over 30 years. Her husband Kevin was also a truck driver and when we were doing the show they both worked for the same company. Cuddles had been married four times before, so Kevin was number five!

THE BEST AUSTRALIAN TRUCKING STORIES

She was a regular on the program, a real character. She scared the 'proverbial' out of most men she came into contact with and she certainly scared Simon and me—and we never met her face to face!

Quite a contrast to Cuddles were Cheryl and Elaine. They were two lovely not-so-old ladies from Penrith, Sydney, who had no connection at all with trucks or trucking but for some unknown reason just loved the show! Cheryl and Elaine would ring up every week after their regular night out at the local club. They were usually more than slightly under the influence by the time they rang us and the chats were always interesting.

We tried hard to find a husband for Cheryl. For some reason, she was very keen to get herself a truck driver. (Maybe she fancied a husband who was never around.) We interviewed many candidates for the position of Cheryl's spouse, to no avail. As far as I know she is husbandless still and enjoying her weekly outing to the club with Elaine.

The Caterpillar team V8 Super Car drivers were regulars on the show. The team had a few different drivers over the years that Rig Radio was on air. Inky Tulloch, Simon Wills, John Briggs and John Bowe were among them. We also spoke to the team's engineers, mechanics, PR blokes and corporate managers from time to time. One of the prestige prizes that we offered in our competitions was the 'Cat Jacket'. This chunky, warm piece of clothing with its logos was incredibly desirable and seemed to be a thing that everyone wanted. We couldn't get enough of them!

Politicians from all sides of the fence appeared on the show, among them Labor's Martin Ferguson, who was Opposition spokesman for transport at the time, and John Anderson, the deputy prime minister and leader of the Nationals.

Ken Dennis, known as the 'Truck Whisperer', was another interesting personality who became part of the show. Ken has a secret method of dramatically improving the handling of trucks and we had many testimonials from drivers all over Australia attesting to his genius.

He had a plan to take his magic to the truck-driving world and launched a major franchise business opportunity through Rig Radio. Ken also tinkered with and had major success with trucks that raced, and became a major sponsor of the program, buying into our company.

Unfortunately we all got involved with a guy who ripped off Ken and Rig Radio in a big way, but that's another story!

Among the many positive and rewarding things we did as part of the show were the 'OBs' we ran. OBs—or outside broadcasts—were held at Albury, the Mildura Country Music Festival in 2001 and at Tarcutta, where we featured the memorial ceremony that is held each year to honour the truckies who have lost their lives in road accidents and feature on the walls at the truckies' memorial. We also gave lots of exposure to the Victorian Convoy for Kids, held in Melbourne each year.

Rig Radio also had a presence at the huge Warrigal Truck Show in 2002. We hired a caravan in Melbourne, towed it to Warrigal and recorded industry interviews for the show. We also were successful in attracting a lot of interest from potential advertisers. At these outside broadcasts, drivers would often drop in and have a chat and show us their trucks. It was all a lot of fun and we like to think the show provided some terrific services and entertainment for truck drivers and late-night listeners.

Like all successful projects, we had hurdles to overcome and we did have some problems to deal with. One of the significant limitations of the CBAA network was the actual power of each particular community station. It varied dramatically. Most stations only had a range of 60 to 80 kilometres—so drivers had to change stations constantly as they travelled.

ONE-FM in Shepparton was an exception to this situation. It had a very powerful transmitter and covered most of regional Victoria. As a result we had a lot of Victorian listeners. ONE-FM was therefore important for us, but they realised this and were the only station to ever charge us for putting the show to air!

Another limitation was the fact that the Community Broadcast Charter only allows five minutes of advertising per hour. This situation seriously restricted our income and the potential to grow the show and improve the quality and range of what we could offer.

We also had to deal with CBAA and local community FM station politics. The CBAA were always concerned about the quality of the show and had their own ideas about how it should be run. Naturally they had a charter and government requirements to worry about—while our response was always: Hey, the show works, leave us alone!

If local stations chose not to connect to the CBAA's subscription service, NatRadSat, for any reason we were up the creek. Many did this and their reasons ranged from 'it's too expensive' and 'we can just run canned music from our computer' to 'we couldn't be bothered'. Much of our time was spent constantly lobbying stations to take the show.

Like many great ideas that have been popular, Rig Radio came to an end just when it could have become something bigger and better.

The ultimate demise of the show in 2003 was due mainly to a lack of liquidity. We had to pay the CBAA a significant amount for the use of the satellite, 2AAA for the hire of their facilities, and Telstra for the ISDN service and 1300 number. We also had to pay our biggest broadcast partner, ONE-FM, to take the show!

In the end, five minutes of advertising per hour was just not enough to keep us going. But what fun we had and what wonderful memories we have of those few years of specialised trucking radio!

We still have so many friends from those days and many people lament the loss of something that was very special and valuable to a whole bunch of wonderful characters in a great industry.

Ah, well . . .

It was a great idea.

ODD JOBS

KINGSLEY FOREMAN

Among some interesting memories of jobs in the outback is one which concerns the night in around 1988 I spent in a boat, a mere 400 miles from Adelaide and at least 60 miles from any water you could use a boat in. It was near the town of Orroroo, east of Port Augusta.

Kenworth had just brought out their range of trucks with long rounded noses; truck drivers called them 'anteaters'. I felt sorry for the driver in this case. Apparently his boss had given him the new truck, with the instruction: 'DON'T SCRATCH IT.'

The truck's maiden trip was from Sydney to Perth and the driver was on his way back the short way, through the middle of South Australia, when he fell asleep and his wheels struck a hole just off the road. He survived but he rolled the new truck over on its side in the bush. He had a flat-bed trailer with a load of general freight. The load included a large number of car parts, air-cleaner elements mostly, and a boat. The boat was a nice neat 20-footer with a little cabin. It certainly looked a bit out of place, I can tell you, sitting there in the middle of the bush.

By the time my co-driver Ron and I had the truck and the trailer back on their wheels and hooked up to our tow truck ready to tow back to Adelaide, it was dark. But we had another problem. The truck that was coming up to get the load and take it on to Sydney had not arrived.

We were on our own, 400 miles away from the depot, with no mobile phones in those days to find out what was going on. We couldn't just leave the load and head back, so we flipped a coin to see who would stay and wait with the load. I lost. So Ron headed back to Adelaide with the wreck and I stayed all alone in the bush with the load.

Luckily for me the local station owner came down with some food his wife had made for me, so I lit a fire and waited for the other truck to arrive. About 11 p.m., with no truck in sight, I settled down for the night. I had no sleeping bag or swag, just two blankets that Ron had given me out of the truck. Sure enough, at about 2 a.m. it started to rain.

What was I going to do now? I was getting wet and I had no choice but to get into the boat. It was on a slight lean but I clambered aboard and spent the rest of the night in a boat in the middle of the bush in a rainstorm. I've done a few strange things but not many stranger than sleeping in a boat in the middle of outback Australia.

Just after sunrise the truck rolled up and I hailed the driver from the deck of my little boat. He said that a farm tractor with a jib was coming to lift the boat onto his truck and we started to load everything else by hand. We got clever and put a lot of the heavier stuff in the boat so it would all be loaded together when the tractor arrived.

It took most of that day to reload the truck-trailer; it was 4 p.m. when the truck driver said goodbye and headed off to Sydney. I watched my little boat disappear down the dusty road and sat and waited for the boss to come up from Adelaide to pick me up.

•

One thing I liked about working for Richmond Heavy Towing was the crazy and lovable characters that seemed to end up working there. One of my favourites was John Nash—we all called him Nashy—who would do some part-time work with us from time to time when he was short of a dollar. I'll never forget one long-haul job we did together many years ago on the Nullarbor Plain.

Nullarbor comes from Latin and means 'no trees'—and they weren't joking when they came up with the name. It's hot and dry and flat as a pancake. An old double-decker London bus that had been converted into a mobile home had broken down and blown a motor at the border between South and Western Australia. Nashy and I had to get it back to Adelaide.

Because of the height of the bus we had to do a straight bar tow all the way back to Adelaide, over 1000 miles one way. Out we went in the Richmond Heavy Towing W model Kenworth with Garwood 9000 lifting gear. We took turns driving and found the old bus at a place called Border Village. We then got it ready to tow. It was so low to the ground I took out the rear inner axle shaft rather than the drive shaft. Meanwhile,

Nashy attached the front axle clamp, a half-inch steel U-bar a foot long which went around the front axle.

After we hooked it all up it was quite late in the day, but it was still really hot, about 110 degrees Fahrenheit, so we cleaned up, had a meal at the roadhouse and tossed a coin to decide who would steer the old bus, which had no motor and no power steering.

I won, so I drove the tow truck.

We were both keen to get the first stage done in one go, while the sun was out and we had better vision for driving at speed. The first stage was from Border Village to Ceduna, which is 485 miles of long straight road with no towns, no farms, nothing to slow down for, and no police speed traps either, so it was 'foot down and hang on'.

Not long after the first hour I saw Nashy open the little driver's door on the old double-decker bus, quite a dangerous manoeuvre at the speed we were going. I gave him a blast on the air-horns to check if he was OK and he gave me the thumbs-up.

Then, about half an hour later, he opened the driver's door again, so I gave him another blast on the horns. Again he gave me the thumbs-up—all OK.

This went on for six hours or so and when we stopped at Ceduna I was keen to ask what all the opening of the door was about.

'Well,' said Nashy, 'it was hot as hell in there. I was nearly dying in the heat and I couldn't open the window.'

'Why couldn't you open the window?' I asked him, rather puzzled.

'It's odd,' he replied. 'There must be a switch somewhere for it, because I couldn't find the window winder anywhere.'

I started to laugh—poor Nashy had spent six hours in that hot box. 'It's a British bus, Nashy,' I told him. 'There's no winder because the windows just slide up and down.'

I noticed that for the rest of the trip the driver's door stayed closed.

•

Among many memorable heavy salvage jobs, I remember one just out from the town of Truro, 70 miles north-east of Adelaide, on the highway to the Riverland.

When we arrived we saw it was a Mitsubishi FM model with a 30-foot pan body. It was lying on its side about 15 feet off the road in the dirt, and I noticed a team of firemen from the Adelaide Fire Service were already there, dressed in those plastic splash suits. The local volunteer fire service was there as well.

It seemed there was something unusual about this wreck, so I went up to one of the local firemen and asked, 'What's with all the splash suits?'

He told me they were the first on the scene and thought they had it all under control when the Adelaide Fire Service rolled up and one of their officers said the accident was actually still in their area, and that he would take charge.

There were some drums among the load with no names on them, just numbers, and they were leaking. While the local guys believed it was just industrial cleaner, the over-efficient Adelaide officer had called in the chemical control unit.

I looked at the numbers on the drums, CT-18, and chuckled to myself. 'Was the fluid green in colour?' I asked the local fireman.

Ray Gilleland in the
'Perth Express'.

Trucks in
Tarcutta's
main street
in 1956.

Truckers' camp
during the Tarcutta
road closure.

Above: Richmond Towing's Ford Louisville.
Right: Wheat dumper and farmers' friend,
Frank Daniel.

Above left: Wheat delivery
to Parliament House on
New Year's Day 1986, and
(*left*) Frank's arrest.

Above: The AEC Government Roadtrain at work in the late 1930s, and (*left*) on delivery in 1934. *Below*: The AEC Government Roadtrain restored, in 2005.

Top: 'Jackie' and 'Julie': the Vestey's Rotinoffs in their working days, circa 1960. *Above*: 'Julie' Rotinoff in 2002, before restoration. *Left*: 'Julie' restored, 2010.

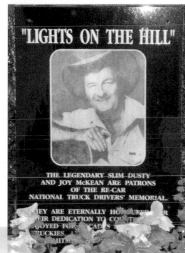

Above: Slim Dusty and two friends.
(Photo courtesy of John Elliott)
Right: Slim Dusty's memorial plaque
at Tarcutta. *Below*: The memorial.

"LIGHTS ON THE HILL"

THE LEGENDARY SLIM DUSTY
AND JOY McKEAN ARE PATRONS
OF THE RE-CAR
NATIONAL TRUCK DRIVERS' MEMORIAL

THEY ARE ETERNALLY HO
EIR DEDICATION TO CO
OYED FOR
UCKIES

Above and right: Jayne Denham, sponsored by Wickham Freightlines.

Grant Luhrs on air for Rig Radio.

Part of the U2 convoy, 2010.

The Claw being erected in Brisbane.

Rod Hannifey and the Roadsafe truck.

Cattle roadtrains at Helen Springs Station.

Left: Liz Martin, OAM, at the National Road Transport Hall of Fame Museum. *Below*: The museum.

'Yes,' he said, 'it was.'

I laughed and told him, 'That's truck wash, we use it by the gallon.'

The local fireman went up to the officer from the Adelaide Fire Service and they had a heated conversation. Then he came back to me after a couple of minutes and said, 'He reckons he's in charge and he knows what he's doing.'

'That's OK by me,' I told him. 'I get paid by the hour.'

Then I sat down and waited for the chemical control unit to unload the truck piece by piece, stopping every ten minutes to shower themselves down. They did my job for me by unloading the truck, and I got paid for the time they took to do it.

•

Another interesting truck rescue was one we did from the middle of the Murray River at the Swan Reach ferry crossing.

The Murray River is Australia's longest river, some 1476 miles long. It starts in the Snowy Mountains in New South Wales and cuts across the rear corner of Victoria, where all the waters of the inland rivers join it before it flows into our state of South Australia and runs down into Lake Alexandrina and then finally enters the sea near the town of Goolwa.

The little town of Swan Reach has no bridge across the Murray River; they have a ferry operated by cable from each side of the river and somehow a 5-ton Isuzu truck with a 15-foot pan body rolled off the ferry in the middle of the river.

The ferries they have at some local river crossings are quite surprising. You'd think they would only carry a few cars, but they can carry a loaded tractor-trailer. When they have a full-sized tractor-trailer on board they often can't close the gates at either end.

On that job we needed a bit of help. Although the river wasn't deep, it was quite muddy and too dangerous for us to go swimming in. We called in Rodney Fox, who runs a diving centre in Adelaide and is well known as a diver. Many years ago he was attacked by a great white shark while diving and had one of his legs bitten off at the knee, but that didn't stop him diving.

The truck was full of water, and it wouldn't be safe to attempt to lift it up using the ferry, so we had to winch it along the muddy riverbed and back to the road again. Rodney's team attached two chains to the front axle of the truck under the water. The other ends of the chains were attached to our pulling winch, which was on the back of our Mack 9000 Ultraliner.

We had no idea how it would go. We'd never towed a truck under water before. But it was surprisingly easy; the truck was floating under the water. It did get tough, however, when the truck got to the bank of the river, which was about 15 feet from the roadway, but we got it out OK.

Rodney did a number of underwater jobs for us while I worked for Richmond Heavy Towing. He helped us get a concrete mixer out of the manmade lake at West Lakes in Adelaide. He also helped retrieve several stolen cars dumped at the same place, as well as a few cars that ended up in the Torrens River, which runs through the heart of Adelaide City.

The truck that fell off the ferry is now back on the road doing the same work for the same driver. I bet he makes sure the park brake is on when he goes on the ferry.

AMERICAN BLUE DEVILS

FRANK DANIEL

Billy O'Connor, my mate of many years, is a real 'wheeler-dealer', trading in anything and everything, from rabbit traps to rhinestones, from shanghais to semi-trailers.

He's an avid reader of the rural newspaper *The Land*, which comes out weekly in New South Wales. Bill was never any great shakes as a reader, but when it came to reading *The Land* he was quite an expert. Always starting from the back page, he would read through the classified columns, studying up on all the clearing sales and 'For Sale' columns. He could tell you every property for sale in the country, the price of ewes and lambs from Cooma to Cobar and the price of store cattle from Tibooburra to Tumut. He never missed a thing.

If there was a two-bob watch for sale somewhere he would have seen it advertised and would more than likely be able to tell you from memory the phone number to ring. However, if he happened to say that something was going to take place on a Tuesday or a Thursday, it would be advisable to check the paper yourself and make sure, because they both started with a 'T' and he wasn't one for details like that, just phone numbers.

In around 1975 the famed American stunt rider Evel Knievel was touring Australia and my mate John and I took our kids to Orange to see this spectacular show. (I might add that the real hero of the show was our own Aussie boy, the late, great Dale Buggins, who performed all the motorcycle stunts.)

Anyhow, a week later Billy and I were travelling through the Upper Hunter region of New South Wales, near Muswellbrook. We were some miles out of town en route to Merriwa when a large pantechnicon passed us, going in the opposite direction.

'There he goes!' said Billy.

'Who?'

'Your mate, Evel Knievel! That's his truck, ain't it?' he said. 'It was red, white and blue and had the stars and stripes and "American Blue Devils" painted along the side.'

I had a disbelieving look over my shoulder at the truck and said that it couldn't possibly be him because I knew for a fact that the stunt show was scheduled for Melbourne after Orange.

'It's him, I tell ya—red, white and blue, stars and stripes,' said Billy. 'American Blue Devils! It's written all over the truck.'

'No!' I said. 'You're mad.'

'Now look,' he insisted, 'I know I'm not much good at reading and all, but that was definitely Evel Knievel! It's written all over the truck! Stars and stripes! Red, white and blue! The whole works! It was him all right—American Blue Devils!'

'No bloody way, mate! You're wrong!'

'Well, I know I'm right this time. I'll prove it to you.'

And, with that, he spun the old Ford around and gave chase, back towards Muswellbrook. He was determined to get a winner this time and had the Fairlane fairly rocking along at about 80 miles an hour in a bid to establish his reading ability and prove his literacy skills.

We caught up with the truck as it turned into a service station at the edge of town. Billy pulled the car up alongside. Full of confidence and glowing with pride he said, 'Go on! Read that! What's it say, eh?'

Sure enough it was red, and it was white, and it was blue, and it did have some stars and stripes. Billy was right in that respect but, on the side of the big pan, for the world to see, in huge letters, was a sign that read 'AMCO BLUE DENIMS'.

'Well, stuff me!' Billy murmured in disgust as he swung the car around and took off again in the direction of Merriwa. 'I reckoned I was right that time!'

A few miles down the road, after a lengthy silence, he brightened up and looked at me and said, 'Ahh, well, red, white and blue and stars and stripes . . . at least I got two things right out of three!'

THE TARCUTTA MEMORIAL

RON PULLEN WITH JIM HAYNES

I spent a lot of time working for Re-Car, the truck repair company, running their 24-hour base operation. During that time I saw a lot of tragedy as I also often drove the Kenworth recovery vehicle for Re-Car and attended the accidents.

I also became involved in the Trans-Help organisation, helping the victims of fatal accidents involving trucks, and seeing the results and the effects on families. My wife suggested some memorial was needed to give solace and closure to the families of all the men who died driving trucks. We took the idea to Re-Car and they agreed to help financially.

Since the 1950s, Tarcutta, being halfway between Sydney and Melbourne on the Hume Highway, had been like a lighthouse in a sea of bitumen. There wouldn't be many truckies who hadn't stopped for a rest at Tarcutta at some time.

In 1956, when the Hume Highway was cut off for many days during what became known as the 'Tarcutta bog', many truckies were stranded in Tarcutta and the town fed them and looked after them. A real sense of community developed around the town and the trucking industry. Trailers were often left there for other drivers to pick up, and Melbourne- and Sydney-based drivers often 'changed over' there. Tarcutta seemed the obvious place for a memorial.

There was already a memorial of sorts in Yass, at Rocky's Service Station. It was a steel, brass and bronze structure with a steering wheel, which had been erected by the Long Distance Transport Association (LDTA). At that time they were building a bypass, which meant that Yass would no longer be on the Hume Highway. So I contacted the LDTA, and asked if I could move the memorial to Tarcutta.

They agreed and gave me a letter authorising me to move it. We arrived to claim it just as the bulldozer was about to knock it down, and Re-Car had it all cleaned up and erected at Tarcutta. We then decided to build a memorial wall at Tarcutta and I dug the foundations myself in 1993.

I went cap-in-hand to the trucking industry to get the materials. Irwin Richter donated bricks and a bloke working for Re-Car did the brickie work, and we had a special drive and a bucket donation along the highway. Bruce Baird, Minister for Transport, opened it in 1994.

As time went by we found there was a demand from families of truckies who had passed on from natural causes to be remembered also, so we built a separate wall of remembrance for them. There are a total of 1500 names on the walls now, about half of them being those who died in accidents on roads in Australia.

My wife then had another good idea, which was to build a 'road' around the walls; there are five walls now, with a path connecting them.

We asked Slim Dusty and Joy McKean to be patrons. They accepted, and Slim sat in my kitchen and began to sing the song Joy had just started to write about the memorial, 'Names Upon the Wall'.

From 1995 on we had a special night each year with a memorial service and dinner. Slim would bring his show to Wagga Wagga and do a fundraising concert, and then he and Joy would attend the service the next day.

Other singers were involved in the services and fundraising also. Artists like Ian Castles and Grant Luhrs and even the person who put this book together, Jim Haynes, were involved as part of the Slim Dusty touring show.

The money raised was always intended to go back to the memorial or to the families. In the early days, Re-Car paid for everything, even providing the dinner and drinks free to family members of those on the wall. Eventually Re-Car had to pull out, and I became ill and had to pass the baton to a committee, which held meetings to decide how the work should continue and who should run the memorial in the future. I was made a patron, along with Slim and Joy, but it was hard to have any effective involvement once the committee had been set up.

Apart from Re-Car's contribution and donations from within the industry, Wagga Wagga Council helped to pay for the memorial to be built, and Re-Car footed the bills for the service and the dinner and also part of the original set-up.

In recent times the dinner numbers have remained static, although 50 names go onto the wall each year and you might expect more and more to attend. It's a shame to see that it hasn't been as well attended as we would have liked in recent years. Since Slim passed away, the concert hasn't been as big as in those early years either.

The names are sent on a special application form in the form of a 'stat dec' that gives us all the driver's details, such as their name, age, date of birth and death, and nickname, so that all information recorded on the plaques is accurate. Now it's all on a computer database, of course.

As well as the walls, nowadays Tarcutta has a large safe trailer and driver exchange area, and there's a welfare organisation for trucking families. This foundation, called Trans-Help, is run by a wonderful woman named Dianne Carroll.

Dianne and I had begun to realise that a memorial was only the start. It became apparent to us that help was needed not only for the bereaved, but also for those still involved in the industry. Truckies were often killed in accidents and their wives had no idea about things like insurance and superannuation, so we set up Trans-Help.

Trans-Help Foundation provides practical and emotional support and assistance to operators, drivers and their families connected with the transport industry who are suffering any form of crisis. One truckie's wife was about to lose everything and was crying on the phone. When we investigated we found out her deceased husband had insurance and she ended up with over $200,000, thanks to Trans-Help.

There is also a need for help to be provided to those suffering from depression, poor lifestyle situations or financial hardship, and to raise awareness about these issues. Trans-Help also assists in providing for the educational needs of children who would otherwise be deprived of opportunities due to family hardship.

The foundation eventually purchased the old nursing home at Tarcutta, and health checks and healthy lifestyle awareness clinics are now provided for drivers, along with free heart checks and other medical services.

Trans-Help also negotiates with state and federal government departments to develop road safety awareness programs, which encourage all road users to adopt safe driving practices.

Now Tarcutta itself is about to be bypassed and the future of the memorial is uncertain, but the great work of Trans-Help and the ideas of remembrance, closure and awareness that the memorial provides will continue as long as there is a road transport industry in Australia.

THE TARCUTTA BOG

RAY GILLELAND (THE NULLARBOR KID)

It happened many years ago, in 1956. We called it the 'Tarcutta bog'.

For some time there had been exceptionally heavy rains, and the area between Tarcutta and Holbrook on the Hume Highway in New South Wales—a distance of about 40 miles—became waterlogged.

Rushing waters from the high country filled the low areas and suddenly the highway started to disappear under a sea of boiling water, which rose over the paddock fences, flowing mile after mile from east to west.

Northbound traffic was halted at the town of Holbrook, and southbound was stopped on the south side of Tarcutta. Vehicles of all descriptions started to bank up at both ends.

The worst affected part was 17 miles of highway that had disappeared under 6 foot of muddy brown water which flowed relentlessly westwards, with the occasional sheep or cow carried away by the fast current. Highway 31 had completely disappeared.

Nothing like this had ever happened before. It made headlines in newspapers all over Australia.

I was bound for Melbourne with a load of washing machines, which were urgently needed by Melbourne housewives, or at least by retailers keen to sell them to housewives.

My truck, a 190 International pantechnicon, was sitting forlornly about fifth or sixth in line waiting on the slope with about twenty others, all parked higgledy-piggledy down the main street in the town of Tarcutta, near the Tarcutta Creek Bridge.

The top of the creek bridge rail was just visible as the current of fast-flowing water formed whirlpools around the tops of the bridge uprights. Looking beyond to where the highway should be, I could see a vast billabong of swirling water, which stretched to the horizon, with debris washing past and the tops of trees here and there looking like large bushes, with their trunks lost in the deep and fast-running water.

Eventually, days later, the waters receded and, to our amazement, the Hume Highway ended at the creek bridge. Beyond that there was nothing: no fences, no road. Nothing but bush, as if that was the end of the line.

It was incredible and the burning question was, 'What the hell do we do now?'

The authorities, in their wisdom, had placed a 5-ton limit on the only road south that was open, through the town of Wagga Wagga, to bypass this section of road.

Now, the Wagga Wagga route was really a secondary highway. It was used all the time by trucks coming from further out on the Western Plains. There was really no valid reason to put a 5-ton limit on it. Some truckies even said that it was done out of malice, to hinder the trucking industry, which was in a battle with the state governments, which owned the railways.

Anyway, there we were, stranded, while more and more traffic built up at each end of this 17-mile washout.

The retailer in Melbourne was now completely out of stock and, on hearing of the situation, our Sydney office decided to load a 5-ton truck with extra washing machines and send it down to me with a relief driver. The idea was that I would take the 5-ton truck via Wagga Wagga and the rest of the load could follow when the Hume Highway was open.

The Main Road engineers had quickly responded to the crisis once the waters receded and started to lay dirt-fill and rocks along the original road base of the highway, which had disappeared in the flood. They were trying to connect Tarcutta with the hill at Kyeamba, 17 miles away, as quickly as possible.

There was one very dicey low spot just before Kyeamba Hill, around Little Billabong, that needed a huge amount of fill. This area was very swampy and low lying.

As it happened, the little 5-ton Bedford with the extra washing machines on board arrived in Tarcutta on the same day that the engineers were about to open the highway for cars and trucks up to 5-ton. It was the only 5-tonner there, as all of the others had been going through Wagga Wagga.

I spoke to the engineer in charge and he told me that they were sending a semi-trailer with a heavy load of steel through to Kyeamba, to test if that section would hold its weight.

The engineer agreed that, as I had the only 5-tonner there, I could take the Bedford through to the low spot just before Kyeamba and wait there for the semi-trailer. If it held, they would let a limited amount of traffic through while they continued to strengthen the whole 17 miles that had disappeared.

I trundled off in the little Bedford, a few minutes after the steel truck.

It was slow going as the road was no more than a muddy track, slippery and bumpy. The track still being slushy, the front wheels would drop into an unseen hole and thick yellow mud would whoosh up over the bonnet and all over the windscreen. I needed the wipers to push it aside somehow and leave me a little bit of glass to try to see through.

It was a low-gear job, but I managed to catch up with the steel truck, which was making much heavier weather of it than I was, and we arrived at the crisis spot together.

Both trucks were covered in thick yellow dripping mud. The Bedford looked as if someone had sprayed it with thick yellow goo. On top of the tarpaulin-covered load the splashes had dried hard, but from cab-roof level down it was just a wet running mess.

The engineer who was in charge walked across and asked what I was doing there. I told him the engineer at Tarcutta sent me through as the first 5-tonner and said to wait for the steel truck and try to negotiate the tricky part.

He was OK with that, and asked the driver of the steel truck what he thought about the situation. They chatted and the engineer said that he had a Caterpillar grader on the other side that could pull the semi out if it became bogged. It was agreed that the steel truck would attempt the tricky section and I would wait till he was through and then take off after him.

The section we faced was about six semi-trailer lengths long and only just above the surrounding watery bog that had formed in the hollow. The water wasn't running; it was just lying there.

The steel truck managed to slip and slide through, sinking down here and there. When he went down into a hole the surrounding water quickly rushed in, but he managed to keep going.

It was obvious that more fill was needed before opening the road. The engineer told me I would be in the way where I was so I had better go through and get out of their hair.

I agreed with him, wholeheartedly!

The Bedford slipped and slid through and I overtook the steel truck on the climb out, as he was in low gear. At the top of the hill I was met by a reception committee from the south, a large group of newspaper reporters, police and locals. I was the first vehicle from the north to get through the bog and reach the southern, undamaged part of the Hume Highway. I was famous . . . almost.

A bunch of reporters hurried across to me as I rolled to a halt. They fired questions and more questions at me, as if I was a celebrity.

'Is the road open?'

'How bad is it?'

'Are more trucks coming?'

'How long did it take you to get through?'

'Where's the big heavy truck we were told was coming?'

In the middle of all this, a police sergeant followed by a constable pushed through and was suddenly standing between the reporters and me. I was still in the driving seat of the Bedford.

'Where did you come from, driver?' asked the sergeant.

I looked out of the driver's door window at him. 'Tarcutta,' I replied.

'How did you get here?'

'Through the bog,' I answered.

'The highway from Tarcutta to Holbrook is closed.'

'I know.'

The sergeant stepped back a little and cast his eye over my mud-encrusted truck. There was mud dripping down from the top of the headlights onto the road. He walked back to my window. 'Your front numberplate is obscured.'

I laughed. 'You should see the back one, if you can find it.'

The sergeant turned to the young constable and said, *sotto voce* for all to hear, 'Ask him for his licence.'

The constable looked ill at ease but stepped forward and said, 'Can I see your licence, driver?'

'Yeah, OK . . . here it is,' I said, handing it over to him.

While all this was going on, the reporters were standing around in a half circle a little way back from the truck, listening and watching closely. I'd had enough by then and stepped out onto the road, protesting.

'What's going on?' I asked loudly. 'The Main Roads Department engineer at Tarcutta let me through, with the semi with the heavy load of steel, as a trial. If it's OK they'll open the road to 5-ton trucks. As far as I know, he's in charge of the road and what he says goes.

'Have you been down to the swamp back there?' I asked the cops. 'It's 17 miles of yellow mud! Look at the bloody truck, for crying out loud! And you're talking about a dirty numberplate?' I walked to the back of the truck, fuming at this stupidity.

It was a sight to behold. Halfway down the side of the load the mud had splashed up so thickly that the ropes tying the load were lost in drying mud. It was a wall of mud. The numberplate, the rear lights—everything was covered in yellow dripping goo.

I walked back to the cabin in time to hear the sergeant say to the constable, 'Book him for an obscured numberplate.'

I stood, open-mouthed. I couldn't believe it.

I must have been the first 'pinch' for this new constable. The sergeant must have been training him. He fiddled with his book and kept looking back and forth between my licence and what he was writing. You could tell he was uncomfortable, scribbling and scratching away, looking around and then back to his writing. Finally he turned the licence over and looked on the back for I don't know what and then handed it back to me as if it was a death adder.

The sergeant turned his back and marched off towards the police car with the constable in step behind. I was tempted to call out, 'Left, right, left, right . . .' but decided I had better shut up. Maybe nothing would eventuate after they realised that I was entitled to be where I was.

As the law retreated, the reporters came dashing over.

'What did he say?'

'Did he book you?'

'Yeah, they booked me,' I said.

'You're joking?'

'Wish I was.'

'What exactly did they book you for?'

'Obscured numberplate, would you believe?'

'You're having us on.'

'No, they booked me for an obscured numberplate.'

The reporters were writing it all down and chorused that it would be appearing in the Melbourne newspapers the next day.

The injustice of the whole episode was laughable. In the midst of what was the biggest disaster to hit the main highway in Australia ever, a driver was booked for an obscured numberplate.

As I was busy laughing at the stupidity of the whole business, the steel trailer chugged up the hill and the reporters deserted me and converged on it as it pulled to a halt behind me, shouting questions at the driver.

I took off to Melbourne in my mud-encrusted Bedford and delivered the urgently needed load of washing machines to the shop. I returned to Tarcutta a few days later, swapped trucks and took the 190 to Melbourne.

The road had been opened, but some sections covered with water with no road base underneath still required a tow through.

Sometime later, I duly received a summons to appear in court to answer the charge of operating a motor vehicle on the Hume Highway while having an obscured numberplate on the front of my vehicle.

Needless to say, by the time it came to court I was somewhere out in the Nullarbor Plain or up in the New England high country or somewhere and couldn't answer the charge. In my absence I was fined a nominal amount of money for the privilege of being the first driver through the famous 'Tarcutta bog'.

ROCK 'N' ROLL TRUCKING

ROD HANNIFEY

When I first read in a trucking paper that Australian Touring Services were looking for trucks for the upcoming U2 tour, I thought to myself, 'This might be worth a look . . . it might be a bit of a change from normal general freight.'

What an understatement that turned out to be!

When I rang and asked a few questions, I was told they were looking for nearly 60 semis.

I left the information about the tour with my boss, Rod Pilon of Rod Pilon Transport, in my hometown of Dubbo, so he could check out the route to be taken and timing of the tour and decide if it was worth being involved in.

It seems it was, because a couple of days later I arrived at work to hear the news from some of the other drivers.

'Hey, we're doing the U2 tour.'

Twenty-one trucks from our fleet had been put on the job. It was the start of a great experience, a real adventure.

In late 2010, U2 embarked on the Australian leg of their 360 Degree Tour, which started in 2009 and travelled for over two years to twenty countries. All stadiums had to have 360-degree viewing, hence the name of the tour.

The tour arrived in Melbourne from New Zealand in six jumbo jets. From there, Australian Touring Services took over as the transport provider. Fifty-eight trucks transported the production equipment within Australia—from Melbourne to Brisbane, then to Sydney and on to Perth, with at least two shows at each Australian venue.

The tour then continued on its way around the world; next stop, South Africa.

With another 48 semi-trailer loads for each of the three 'space stations' that formed the centrepiece and stage, all built in advance of each show, it was the largest ever show transport task undertaken in Australia.

I am sure if you asked any of the patrons who saw the show what role road transport played in the tour, they would probably just look at you mystified, but the task of moving the show across the Australian continent was mind-boggling.

As a logistics exercise, just consider coordinating 48 trailer-loads for the space-station staging area (or 'the Claw', as it became known) to be constructed and in place four days before the show and then the 58 trucks, carrying all the sound, lighting, electrical and stage gear, to be on site at the correct time and in the right order!

Simply organising somewhere to muster and hold these trucks while the concerts were underway, and to deal with all the drivers and companies involved was a logistics exercise of massive, almost military, proportions. I wouldn't want that job for quids.

One issue that arose early on was that ATS were told 'no tautliners, we want all pans'. This was understandable when it was explained that they could load a pan in ten minutes or less. Just load the gear in against the front wall, put a couple of straps in as you go and some at the back and shut the doors, done. Try to do that with tautliners, with the gates, the curtains being pulled back and forth and needing to feed straps through the load and then tighten them, and you can see the cost in time and crew and wages if you multiply all that across the entire course of the tour.

Some drivers were already on the way to Melbourne with tautliners, which are much more common than pans in Australia, when this demand became clear. So there was a bit of a scramble to access enough vans, and a few companies did pull out due to these issues, which left ATS trying to get enough replacements and have all in readiness to start the loading in Melbourne. Finally, though, enough vans were found and we assembled for the start of the marathon adventure.

At the drivers' briefing we were introduced to the world of rock 'n' roll touring. We were told, 'This will be different from anything you normally do. You will be stuffed about, you will find yourself thinking, "Why are they doing this?" You just have to trust that it is all being done for a reason, so just do your job and it will all happen.'

It didn't take long before we had a taste of the kind of being 'stuffed about' that was to become the norm for the tour. Show business runs differently from the normal world of trucking.

We had nearly all our trucks in Melbourne ready for the start of the tour and in time for the briefing. But the last couple were coming down 'bobtail' (without a trailer) and we rang to confirm the briefing time. We were told noon for the briefing. We were also told, initially, that we would not be required for loading till 9 p.m., so we decided to take two drivers per truck to the briefing and then go back to the depot and rest up, have a meal and return to the site.

When I'd asked if we needed anything like licences or loading equipment and clothing, I was told, 'No, just the drivers.'

After the drivers' briefing, however, we had to get our drivers' passes and this was to be done within the show venue, Etihad Stadium, which at the time was in construction mode, so vests and boots were required.

Some of the drivers had come in whatever they were wearing, as you do when waiting, plain clothes and good old Aussie safety boots—known more commonly as thongs. So we marshalled those needing gear and sent them back on the 30-minutes each way trip.

We were then told loading for some drivers could commence earlier, in some cases immediately! One truck was sent off right then and there to pick up a trailer in the venue. The fun had begun.

By default or design, or both, I was asked to be 'road foreman'. Maybe it was because I had made the initial inquiry about the tour and was in a way responsible for our involvement, but being road foreman mostly meant that if anything went wrong on the road, it would be my fault.

In retrospect I often wished that I had gone and taken that first trailer, but I was now responsible for marshalling the rest of the trucks and organising the passes, so another driver, Eddie, said he would go.

As it turned out, that trailer was the one carrying all the guitars and personal band gear and Eddie had quite a good time throughout the tour, detouring if the band decided to rehearse or practise somewhere else, and becoming mates with some of the band's minders.

As our drivers were travelling back to collect their gear, we had a call to say we all had to be in place by 6 p.m., not 9 p.m., so the phone ran hot for the first of many times over the next few weeks as I tried to coordinate all 21 of our drivers.

Although we had been told we would get a snack at the briefing all that was available was a cup of tea, and the change in time, plus the fact we were not all ready to stay on and start work after the briefing, meant little time to get a meal before 6 p.m.

This was the first of many lessons I learned about being prepared to be 'stuffed about'. To make matters worse, by the time the first batch of drivers returned to get their passes, the tour staff involved had been employed on other duties and the drivers were left waiting for over an hour and told, 'Sorry, it will have to be done later.'

I was learning fast.

During this time trailers were being allocated to the drivers, and all drivers' details, phone numbers and vehicle details were recorded and the trailer tags given out.

Each truck and trailer had ID tags to go on the windscreen of the truck, on the rear of the trailer and on the inside of the door of the trailer, so that the right gear went in the right trailer and everyone could see from front and rear exactly what was what.

Finally, at about 7 p.m., pizzas and drinks arrived for the drivers, kindly supplied by ATS. You might get 'stuffed about' on a tour like that one, but the other side of the coin is that someone thinks to do things like giving food and drink to 58 hungry truck drivers!

Some drivers were sent off to the 'dog yard', the area closest to the venue where some trucks could be parked ready to load and for access to additional gear if needed in a hurry.

Other trucks were marshalled and drivers told to be ready to load from 9 p.m. Others would be needed from about 11 p.m., as soon as the show finished, and the rest would follow.

I was to be in the last group to load, so I put my head down and tried for some sleep. Rest at last, or so I hoped. However, at some stage they must have opened the roof at Etihad Stadium and we could hear the show from the wharf were we were parked, about a kilometre away.

There was also another venue at the wharf, and a large and noisy Christmas party was going on there. On top of all this, the seagulls seemed to be enjoying the music, as they squawked along with it at full volume.

All this noise, along with some excitement and trepidation about what we were in for, made sleep hard for some. I was woken at about 2 a.m. and the last of us were pulled up in a queue ready to load.

The order was changed several times, as we had been told it would, and we had to get some trucks around others in the narrow street, but eventually I got to back in and load.

I was carrying parts of the hydraulics and rigging for the enormous expanding screen that hangs from the Claw. This consisted mostly of large heavy frames on four wheels, which were loaded by forklift and then manhandled into place and strapped and secured with some smaller pieces packed in between. Plywood was used to separate the various pieces of equipment and there were some aluminium frames at the rear.

It was not a heavy load in the scheme of things, but much of it was on wheels and it was all very valuable and critical to the show, as was every piece of gear that was carried by the trucks that took part in the tour.

I was the last of our trucks to load and the second last truck out of the venue at 5 a.m. We had plenty of time to get to Brisbane. We had been told we must go via Sydney, but many of our drivers were keen to go up the centre through Dubbo in New South Wales where Rod Pilon Transport is based. Naturally, many drivers wanted to visit family and change and wash clothes, as some had already been away for a week and were due to be away for the next two.

There were flood concerns about taking the route through Dubbo, but I conferred with Rod Pilon and we were confident we had time and alternatives available to cover any possible flood issues at the time.

During these discussions I learned that a truck involved in another tour had left Townsville to travel to Adelaide and the driver had rested near Emerald and woken up flooded in. The floods in eastern Australia were a big concern and we were told in no uncertain terms that we must be at destinations safe and on time.

A few of our drivers went via Sydney, while myself and the rest went via Dubbo. We did have two trucks slightly delayed for minor repairs, but we were all in Brisbane on the Monday and on time.

Our Brisbane parking area was the old wharf at Hamilton. I had memories of this being a badly organised site. I recalled being sent, as a young driver, to pick up a piece of machinery and being left waiting there for hours. Devoid now of any buildings, but right on the river, the area we had to use as a depot was really just vacant ground with some portaloos.

With the gang getting a bit restless, I decided to get all our drivers to line up their trucks and we took some company truck photos as well as some with each driver and his truck. The photos kept us occupied for a couple of hours.

Once we were unloaded on the Tuesday we were free until we'd be needed to load again on the Wednesday night. There's a shopping centre just down the road from the wharf, so some drivers stayed on site the whole time.

Others took the chance to go visiting friends and family and I was able to visit my father. Sadly, Dad died less than two weeks after the tour finished and that was the last time I saw him alive and well.

It was wonderful to watch the crew of well over 200 people set up the show. They seemed to put it all together like a big electrical jigsaw. Seeing the end result made me marvel at the magnificent effort of coordination, all that widely varied equipment coming into place with the help of so many casual local staff, plus of course the tour staff, loaders, forklift drivers and truck drivers.

Apart from the construction itself, many other people oper-ated away from the sight of the truckies. There were other staff coordinating all the different aspects of the tour, media, venue, catering and, of course, looking after the artists and music. A team of 145, with three additional specialist teams of twenty, travelled full-time with the show around the world, and hundreds of locals were hired at each site.

With such a large event and the number of drivers involved, there were many problems with marshalling and holding trucks in readiness, not to mention getting such numbers of vehicles in and out on time and in the required sequence.

To make things worse, plans and schedules changed, as we were warned they would. If one driver didn't show up on time, or failed to go along with the changes as they occurred, a big spanner was put in the works and it could hold up the whole construction or dismantling of the set for hours.

For many drivers it was their first time working on a show tour. Generally speaking, by the time we had been in and out of Brisbane most blokes were coping well and said they were enjoying it.

Because of the nature of the work and all the down time, many were able to visit long-lost mates and family during the time between unloading and reloading. A large number of drivers who generally only passed one another on the road or in a depot were able to spend time together in a way they normally never did.

As the largest group of drivers from one company, the blokes from Rod Pilon Transport in Dubbo had a unique opportunity to be together at close quarters and socialise and get to know one another. Other smaller groups and individuals were happy doing their own thing and, as I said before, some drivers were simply happy to head off on their own to see mates, or do their washing and shopping and relax.

We had been told at the briefing, 'No free passes', but the Aussie Truck Driver security passes we had been issued allowed us access to any part of the show. There were at least two shows in each venue and we were welcome to attend and watch the show on the first night. On the second night, however, we would be loading immediately after the end of the show and had to be rested and ready to load and go. We all thought that this arrangement was more than fair and many drivers saw the shows at different stops. One driver even ended up in the mosh pit at the Brisbane show and rang a disbelieving mate to tell him where he was 'working'.

I saw part of the Brisbane show and then left to watch over some of my 'flock' who had gone off to have an ale or two. Truckies get very little chance to have a beer now, what with the zero blood alcohol tolerance for truck drivers, and not being needed till the following night was like heaven for our blokes. A few beers while we were all together seemed only fair.

Some had more than a few and I had a couple of beers myself just to be sociable while keeping an eye on things. At the end of the night, which was actually the late early—or early late—morning, we had to drag a couple of our 'merry men' away to taxis and back to the wharf. Many did not surface till late that afternoon.

That was about as close as we came to the rock 'n' roll lifestyle. Some of our drivers danced with local girls that night, but the end results were far from the legendary wild and steamy late-night antics of superstars. Our blokes all behaved like true gentlemen and went home alone—though some might have wished it otherwise.

A few things about the rock 'n' roll lifestyle stuck in my head from the tour.

During the first of the two Brisbane shows, Bono said to the audience, 'Thank you for the life you have given us and for helping us to be able to have this magnificent space station.'

He also commented in an onstage chat with the drummer, 'Australians and the Irish are much alike, they are generous and stick by those who are down.'

The drummer replied, 'Yes, but Australians are still the only people who have made the use of expletives into an art form.'

Bono was said to be very approachable and genuine by all who met him and wrote a substantial article about the tour for the *West Australian* Sunday paper.

I had a great curiosity about how the whole operation worked and I got to speak with the Englishman who designed the Claw, and with many others during the tour.

All of the crew were friendly, professional and efficient. With very few exceptions—which were understandable given the stress and time constraints involved—they were happy to talk about and explain their work.

It was truly amazing to watch the show and see the end result after seeing the myriad parts we carried. I arranged a meeting with Jake Berry, the production manager, and asked him for some of the details about the logistics of the whole operation.

He explained to me that most venues have grass playing surfaces and these must be covered and protected using a 'field cover' of aluminium sheeting—fitting this over the turf takes one day. It then takes four days to erect the Claw—or 'space station', as Bono called it during the show. Then the trucks turn up and it's another day to fit all the production gear, and another to test and be ready for the show.

The sound gear was from the USA, the video equipment was from Belgium and the UK, and the crew came from all over the world. Just one example of the League of Nations character of the crew was Flory Turner from Costa Rica. He was the head carpenter and one of the happiest people I ever met.

With such a huge amount of gear, there were a lot of repairs along the way. The Claw weighed 546 tonnes. With all the lighting and sound gear fitted it weighed over 1000 tonnes. There were 412 speakers in operation and the custom-designed 360-degree video screen was the only one of its kind in the world. It had one and a half million pixels, just a bit bigger than your average TV, and the screen expanded and moved up and down during the show.

The tour provided its own power with two 1750-kW CAT 3216 V16 2304-hp generator sets with 100 per cent back-up, so if the one in use failed the other kicked in. The show carried enough cable to do 50 runs at 200 metres; the Sydney shows had them near full stretch at 190 metres.

From our point of view, the Brisbane venue was the easiest to get into as you could drive in, go round one corner and then drive into the stadium. We got most of the trucks inside and it made for some good photos.

While all the stadiums we visited had a ring road around them under the grandstands, the size, width and room available to manoeuvre varied widely. Why you would design a multi-million-dollar facility and then make the access road for trucks into it a zigzag is beyond me.

We had a couple of W900 Kenworths, which are long-bonneted trucks, mainly used on long-distance roadtrain work. These vehicles are not ideal for city work and were a real handful when it came to getting into and out of the stadiums. In Melbourne I was on the phone to one of the transport coordinators when he said, 'Hang on a minute while I watch one of these barges try to get around this corner!' At first I wondered what he was doing watching boats, then I realised he was talking about one of the Kenworths.

While things could be difficult inside the arenas, working around the streets of the major cities was also often a nightmare. Just finding the correct yard for parking was fun and generated hundreds of phone calls. When all this had been organised months before, the yards we were to use were usually empty and available.

The week prior to the Sydney concert, however, there was a huge motor race event and all the stands and gear were still stored in the yard we were to have used, so we were all put into a car park which had a tight entrance and a missing road sign which led to many drivers doing U-turns up the road to get in after missing the turn.

I did go and put up a temporary sign, but as the only means I could find of keeping it in place was to balance it on a chair, it didn't help much. Also, it wasn't big enough to be seen from any distance.

The following day, once we were all settled after unloading, we cleaned trucks and went visiting. Some of our drivers even headed home for a day, knowing they had to be back to load on the Wednesday night.

One enterprising driver went shopping and brought back a barbecue with meat and all the gear to cook on site. That barbie became quite popular and travelled to Perth and back.

Our first night in Sydney went well, until we found out that security locked the toilets at 8.30 p.m. On the second night we enjoyed another barbie and I made a number of phone calls to security and also took the precaution of sticking a big note on the toilet door. Thankfully, we managed to get the toilet block left unlocked during the night.

I had some fun on the Tuesday afternoon in Sydney. As I said before, once we had been given our tags the load in each trailer was to remain the same for the whole tour. The load I was carrying consisted of the heavy-wheeled frames that formed part of the screen operating gear. The trailer I was towing had an aluminium floor and the wheels had started to dent the floor, and one spot in the floor had split. We had used a forklift to load and unload in Melbourne, but we were now using a ramp and I was starting to imagine the wheels going through the floor during the trip and getting stuck.

I arranged to get the floor fixed at an old mate's place not too far away, delivered the trailer to them and was on the phone talking to one of the additional drivers we were flying over from Perth. As the next leg, Sydney to Perth, was very tight for time, we were required to do two-up—two drivers in the truck, one driving and one sleeping—to be able to get there legally and on time for the Perth concerts.

As I finished the call I was thrown into another of those 'you will be stuffed about' situations. And this one was a doozie!

I had an urgent call saying we had to shift from where we were parked as the area was needed to be part of the car parking for the show that night.

Ninety thousand tickets had been sold and they needed the extra parking, so we had till 5 p.m. to vacate the area or there would be a heavy fine for the tour transport operator. It was now just after 3 p.m.

We had to shift every truck and trailer into a much smaller yard. Some drivers were still away and had locked up their trucks, and we had all their trailers to shift as well.

It was a mad rush and this time some drivers were not as accepting of the situation as they might have been. 'Getting stuffed around' was starting to wear a bit thin and I had a few dissenters to settle down!

Anyway, it was finally done. I rushed back to pick up the trailer and found my 'old mate' still cutting and welding merrily, but he'd had enough time and, with a bit of a hurry-up, it was all finished and I was on my way.

We had some other driver issues later that night, and then on the second night the Perth drivers who were needed for the long haul across the Nullarbor were due in while we were still queued up to load.

Naturally I could not go to get them and they had to be dropped off at the venue to wait for the trucks they were to help take to Perth, which had all been pulled inside the perimeter road by that time.

They were told a few different stories and it was not the best start to their involvement in the tour, but finally we found them and they found us. This time I was the very last truck out. After we had the new drivers sorted out, the race to Perth was on.

Whereas we had been given three days to get from Melbourne to Brisbane and another three days to get from Brisbane to Sydney, we had two days to get to Perth.

It had been decided that we would run as roadtrains to Perth, with eleven trucks and 22 drivers, and so we set off to

Dubbo as single semis. Once there we were to hook up the dolly (the set of axles and drawbar with a turntable on top) to each of the eleven trucks, then hook up the second trailer and off we would go . . . as roadtrains.

There was another flood scare on at the time and it took a number of phone calls to confirm that the road was open and we could carry on as planned. I left Dubbo as the last roadtrain with just one last truck to leave after me and follow behind as a single, when his 'two-up' driver finally arrived.

At Port Augusta I handed the second trailer over to the last truck, which had caught up by taking a short cut that was available to him as a single semi.

My partner and I were to run as 'tail-end Charlie' in case of any trouble. Tyre trouble on one dolly at Ceduna was fixed before we even got there and we took off again. Later that night my co-driver Rod was driving and I was snoozing when I heard him call the truck in front to ask if everything was OK.

Rod thought he smelled rubber.

In the middle of the night, in the middle of the Nullarbor Plain, we both pulled up to find two dolly tyres on the truck in front destroyed . . . and we only had one spare left.

Luckily there was a truck from another firm coming behind us. They pulled up and had a suitable spare, so we got to work and changed the tyres and were back on the road before the spares truck caught us up.

The spares truck was a dedicated truck and 'A-trailer' following at the very rear of the entire tour convoy with spare tyres, fuel and bits and pieces, ready for such events as breakdowns and wrecked tyres. It was also able to pull a second or 'B-trailer' as a 'B-double' if there was a major truck breakdown.

We rolled on into Norseman and decided to give the second trailer of the roadtrain that had the tyre problem to the spares truck as both it and the B-double could then go straight into Perth.

All the roadtrains had to drop their second trailers at Northam and make two trips into Perth as single semis. Everyone was on track and we again followed in the rear. I took over the driving while Rod went to bed.

Suddenly, in the middle of nowhere, the truck simply shut down. I got out to check and I could smell radiator coolant, but could not find a leak anywhere.

Another truckie pulled up and chatted to me while I checked the radiator carefully and got the water bottle out of the toolbox. Then slowly, a litre at a time as the neck of the radiator was deep behind the grille, I filled the radiator. I always carry a bottle with a rubber hose neck in case this needs to be done, except now it was in my trailer in Dubbo and consequently not much help.

It took ages to refill the radiator, but the truckie who stopped chatted the whole time—boy, could he chat—and at least I had some company as I filled the radiator slowly! Rod, on the other hand, never stirred and was still sleeping when I got underway again.

Coming into Perth we were finally back into phone service range and there were a heap of messages from the early hours of the morning telling me to be at the venue by 7.30 a.m. or all hell would break loose.

Another phone marathon ensued. This time it was mostly regarding 'dog runners', drivers who come out and pick up or deliver your second roadtrain trailer for you.

Mixed in with all those calls were a few more dealing with upset drivers, the big boss asking how things were going, unprintable comments and suggestions from drivers losing their patience after weeks of 'being stuffed about' and calls telling some drivers who had pulled in and gone to bed that they were needed to bring in the second trailers.

It all made for an interesting morning's entertainment.

Just to top it off, as I was coming into Perth I could smell the radiator coolant again, so I put the Horton fan on manual. The radiator fan in a truck pulls nearly 30 hp (22 kW) and is thermostat controlled, so it only works when needed. It can be turned on manually, however, and that's what I had to do.

We pulled up at 7.45 a.m., just in time to prevent all hell from breaking loose. Exactly 30 seconds after I finished unloading the truck, it shut down again. I topped up the radiator to get it off the dock and, when I took the truck for repair that afternoon, we discovered there was a pinhole-sized leak in the radiator hose.

I had to organise my truck and another to be repaired that afternoon, as well as trying to coordinate return loading with our drivers. Luckily Eddie stepped in and sorted out the return loads while I got the trucks fixed.

All the trailers were now empty and all the gear from the show would go into containers for the sea trip to South Africa after the Perth shows. So, we were finished. However, as a parting gesture we were to be 'stuffed around' just once more. When we returned to the parking yard we were told all trucks had to be moved again, to another yard. That finished the evening off nicely.

Some of our drivers got away that afternoon, but some were not happy about the loading on the way home and we had to play 'mix-and-match trailers' to make sure that lead trailers with the coupling that the dolly connects to were in the right places to tow the second one.

Just when I thought we had it all sorted out and I was to be the last away, hopefully on Sunday, I found that I had my trailer reallocated twice—each time I'd already cleaned the skid plate.

The final twist was a request to do a return load to Melbourne, but it would not be able to be loaded till Monday. I was to be the last truck out and, to be fair, I was quite prepared to do the right thing and help out those who had helped us.

Rod and I then had the last two trailers to unload on Saturday morning. Rod's wife had flown over to do the trip back home with him and they left straight after unloading.

That left me and another of our drivers, named Mick, who had decided to stay for the show and leave for home on Sunday morning. Both Perth shows had sold out—50,000 tickets plus two . . . Mick and me.

We went and parked up inside and went to the first of the two Perth shows. It was terrific.

Over the nearly three weeks of the tour I took photos at the venues as we went along and also spoke to nearly all the drivers and took photos of most of them with their trucks. All except a couple were glad to have been involved and said they would happily do it again.

Adam Notley, a driver who operates a construction company in Sydney, said he had always wanted to do some long-haul trips, and applied for the tour because it ticked all the boxes on his wish list, with trips to Brisbane, Melbourne and Perth. He said the Nullarbor crossing was a bit boring except for the time he had a friendly reminder from a Western Australian copper, who called him up on the UHF radio to tell him to 'back it off a bit'.

Another driver did not get on so well with his partner during the crossing and they were not on speaking terms in Perth.

I managed to get my faulty truck fridge fixed on the Monday; I didn't want to cross the Nullarbor again without one. Then I cleaned the truck inside from top to bottom while I waited to load for the run home, via Melbourne. Wind and rain meant loading was further delayed till Tuesday morning, when the call came to be ready to load at 1.30 Perth time.

I'd already picked up the trailer at 12.45 and I got loaded as quickly as I could. By the time I'd finished loading, however, the canteen had closed, so I set out to cross the Nullarbor with a can of Coke and two bottles of water.

My first day of the homeward journey finished early in the morning in the middle of nowhere on the Nullarbor. At least it was overcast and cool when I went to bed at 6 a.m.

On the second day I was just near Iron Knob at 6.30 a.m. and it was getting warmer and harder to sleep.

The third day of my return journey was Christmas Eve and I made it into Melbourne to unload. I then had another dolly loaded into the trailer and another from one of the other roadtrains to tow home.

I left Melbourne and made it into Dubbo just after 7 a.m. on Christmas Day. I had driven for four days across the country and Santa had beaten me home, but at least I was with my kids on Christmas Day.

The U2 tour was a remarkable experience and I felt a real debt of gratitude to all the crew of the tour, especially the ATS staff and all the drivers who took part and got the show along the road. I certainly enjoyed it. I did a number of radio interviews during the tour and hope to keep in contact with some of those I met for many years to come.

When I was asked at the start of the tour if I was a U2 fan I replied that I enjoyed some of their music. Now? Well, I have been converted. I enjoyed the show and the spectacle as much as any of the other show patrons, but knowing what it took to make the whole thing happen made it even more enjoyable.

It was a truly unique and fascinating experience being a rock 'n' roll truckie.

THE VESTEYS' ROTINOFFS

LIZ MARTIN

This is the story of two rare and unusual trucks that changed the way cattle were transported, helped develop an industry and a nation, and hastened the demise of the iconic 'Aussie drover'.

•

At the end of World War II many individuals and companies around Australia took advantage of the huge supply of surplus military trucks in government disposal sales. Recently demobbed men with newly acquired mechanical and driving skills bought and modified these vehicles to suit civilian applications. In the Northern Territory, huge ex-US Army 980 Diamond T tank transporters and Federals were adapted to suit multi-trailer combinations.

As this second-hand fleet diminished over the next decade, British and American truck companies competed for market share in Australia. At a time when British vehicles were being replaced by the big US trucks, the R Internationals and B Model Macks, two amazing British-built vehicles made a name for themselves in the barren deserts of Central Australia, thanks to Lord Vestey's refusal to invest in an American product.

Vestey Brothers had earlier used an American Diamond T roadtrain and two self-tracking trailers and decided it was a concept worth following up but, initially, they were reluctant to spend too much money on it.

Stan Mason, a British engineer who had spent his life maintaining large vehicles both here and in Britain, had worked for Vestey since 1951, maintaining their vehicles and studying the use of road transport to haul cattle.

'Vesteys had been impressed with the success of Kurt Johannsen's Diamond T roadtrains and were hoping to develop a more efficient method of getting cattle to their Rockhampton meatworks in good condition,' Stan later recalled. 'The trip took six months with drovers on horseback.'

Stan spent two years testing ideas and repairing equipment on various Vestey cattle stations. He spent time learning about roadtrain operations with the experienced outback transport pioneer Kurt Johannsen in Alice Springs, and built a Diamond T prototype for Vestey similar to those Johannsen had been operating since World War II ended.

The information Stan gathered was presented to John Vestey on one of his visits to the Vesteys' station, Helen Springs. Management wanted a vehicle powerful enough to pull two or three trailers, thus significantly increasing the current load capacity. Drivers wanted sleeping cabs, good seats, ventilation and power-assisted steering.

The obvious financial choice would have been a Mack or International, but the British chairman of Vestey was not to be persuaded. He preferred to invest in the mother country. Despite several lucrative approaches, however, none of the major British manufacturers was interested in building a truck to the specifications demanded by Vestey, because of the limited market.

After discussing the logistics of such a unit with Stan, John Vestey took the information back to London and consulted several engineers, including the truck builder George Rotinoff, who ran a small manufacturing company in Slough, Buckinghamshire.

•

Rotinoff was born in Russia in 1903. His father, an Armenian engineer, worked in the construction industry in Russia and later in Britain after the Rotinoff family fled Russia in 1917 during the Bolshevik Revolution.

George Rotinoff joined his father's business in 1925 after completing his studies at Eton and Cambridge. In 1942 he began a company of his own, Rotinoff Construction, which was initially involved in coal mining. After World War II, the company began reconditioning, dismantling and restructuring Sherman Tanks and Diamond T tank transporters for heavy-duty civilian work.

As the surplus military resources dwindled, George turned his attention to building a heavy vehicle of his own, and in 1952 the Rotinoff truck concept was born. George had the experience to build an efficient, heavy-duty high-tonnage tractor that would compete well in the overseas market with the Thornycroft Mighty Antar.

After designing and building a prototype, trials were held in England, Denmark and Switzerland. Neither the British nor the Danes placed orders, so real production did not start until the Atlantic GR.7, with its supercharged 250 bhp (183 kW) six-cylinder Rolls-Royce diesel engine, was released in 1955, after an order was placed by the Swiss Army. This truck and its successor, the eight-cylinder Super Atlantic, were supplied to the Swiss and Iraqi armies and were also used in desert oil well haulage in the Middle East. The engine was massive; it had originally been designed for marine use.

Rotinoff had hoped the vehicle would appeal to the British Army, but it contracted Thornycroft to build the Mighty Antar instead. Rotinoff continued to supply the Swiss, who later went on to purchase the Super Atlantics as well.

The original Atlantic was fitted with a David Brown twelve-speed transmission with four main and three auxiliary gears. Later models had a 275 bhp (205 kW) C6.TFL Rolls-Royce turbocharged diesel and fifteen-speed transmission.

The next model was the Super Atlantic, built for even heavier applications. The Super Atlantic GR.7 was powered by a C8.TFL 988-cubic inch (16.2-litre) 'straight eight' Rolls-Royce turbo diesel, giving 335 bhp (246 kW).

It was the first vehicle to haul a load of more than 200 tonnes on British roads. These Atlantic models impressed Lord Vestey so much that he commissioned Rotinoff to build the two Viscounts in 1957.

Later models of the Super Atlantic produced 365 bhp (272 kW) of power. These were fitted with fifteen- or eighteen-speed transmissions and were capable of gross weights of up to 300 tonnes.

Rotinoff marketed the Viscount with the option of being fitted with a Rolls-Royce B.81.8P eight-cylinder gasoline engine rated at 220 bhp (161 kW) (designated the Viscount 64.GKS). One of these was built but was never sold. The 7.3-metre wheelbase GR.37/AU Viscount was a load-carrying drawbar tractor suitable for Australian roadtrain operations. The two that came to Australia were the only two produced.

When George Rotinoff died suddenly, on 2 May 1957, only 35 Rotinoffs had been built. The company continued to operate until 1960, when it changed its name to Lomount Vehicle & Engineering Ltd and went into more generalised work.

The two Rotinoff Viscounts, named 'Jackie' and 'Julie' on their arrival in Australia, are true rarities in the world of big trucks. The specifications of the Viscounts were very similar to the Atlantic and Super Atlantic models, but the wheelbase and chassis were especially lengthened to accommodate a cattle-crate body.

The two Viscounts were shipped to Australia in September 1957 and delivered to Freighter Industries in Sydney to be fitted with body work before travelling on to Melbourne to collect four self-tracking trailers based on a design by Kurt Johannsen.

Fitted with their new cattle-crate bodies and two 13.7-metre double-bogie trailers each, the twin Viscounts headed off on their long journey to Vestey's Maryville roadtrain base on Helen Springs Station, north of Tennant Creek in the Territory.

The Vestey organisation got its start in an odd way. In the early 1900s one of the Vestey brothers visited Shanghai and, surprised at how cheap eggs were, arranged to import thousands of eggs into Britain. Within a few years the family could afford to purchase its own shipping line.

Administration of the Northern Territory was handed to the federal government by South Australia in 1911 and, in 1912, after Dr J.A. Gilruth had been appointed the first administrator, the government legislated to allow perpetual leases for pastoral holdings in the Territory.

Gilruth invited Lord Vestey to invest in the local beef industry. By 1916, the family had acquired some 93,000 square kilometres of land in the Kimberley and the Northern Territory. In 1917 they opened a meatworks at Bullocky Point in Darwin to process their own beef cattle.

Gilruth's relationship with the Vestey family caused a lot of controversy in Darwin. Territorians were shocked at Gilruth's blatant favouritism of Vestey and public meetings were called demanding that Gilruth not be reappointed as administrator.

Apparently, Gilruth had offered the Commonwealth of Australia some £5 million to purchase the whole of the Northern Territory on behalf of a syndicate. It was widely believed in Darwin that he did so on behalf of the Vestey organisation, and strikes, riots and fights at public meetings resulted.

Gilruth stayed, but hostility towards his rule led, in 1918, to 1200 men marching through the streets of Darwin calling for his removal. The government's response was extreme: a gunboat was sent to Darwin to quell the unrest. In 1919, Darwin residents again called on the Commonwealth to replace Gilruth, and he left Darwin of his own accord a few months later.

Vesteys' Meatworks slaughtered 19,000 cattle in its first season, with another 22,000 in 1919. This was remarkable considering that each season lasted less than four months and the cattle were walked in, over thousands of kilometres, by drovers on horseback.

Vestey closed the meatworks in 1920, blaming difficulties with shipping the beef out. Many believed the closure was due to problems with unions, while others said it was because Vestey had lost control of the Territory now that Gilruth was gone.

Vestey continued to operate its various cattle properties and other businesses in Australia and later established meatworks at Rockhampton in Queensland and Wyndham in Western Australia.

By the late 1950s, Vestey had one of the biggest transport operations in Australia and, in 1957, they formed the Northern Cattle Transport Company to operate a new roadtrain base at Maryville. Helen Springs Station was a fattening property; cattle were walked in from properties all over the country and fattened before being sent to the meatworks for processing.

Initially, fattened cattle were walked across to Rockhampton for processing, a 1200-kilometre trip that could take up to six months. Later, cattle were transported by road from Helen Springs to the Rockhampton meatworks and, later still, cattle were trucked as far as the railhead at Camooweal and travelled by rail the rest of the journey.

From the time the two Rotinoffs arrived in 1957, they averaged more than 160,000 kilometres per year during each season, which is remarkable given the condition of the roads they travelled on. Driver comfort was paramount in the initial design and the Viscounts had double-insulated cabs, sliding doors, arm rests, adjustable cushioned seats and large sleeper booths.

They were state of the art at the time. Both the windscreen and the sliding doors were fitted with sliding windows, the extra-large sun visor was adjustable and there was a forced-air ventilation system in the cab. The Viscounts were worth about £40,000 each when purchased.

'The arrival of the Rotinoffs in Australia was greeted with much excitement,' Stan Mason later recalled. 'These two unusual London-built trucks were the undisputed kings of the road, at times pulling three trailers and therefore moving more head of cattle than Vestey had earlier even dared hope.'

While the Viscounts were designed for bitumen running, some of the roads they travelled were little better than virgin scrubland or wheel-rutted dried mud from the last Top End wet season.

Neil Pearson, the Rolls-Royce engineer responsible for the maintenance of the engines, reported that the trailers tracked 'magnificently'. Travelling in a full circle, the wheel tracks barely varied from the prime mover to the trailers.

Unfortunately, the magnificent trailer design and the modern comforts of the cab were eclipsed by some basic mechanical design faults. As had been shown before, trucks built in Britain did not cope well with the harsher operating environment in Australia.

The manifolds cracked because the Rotinoffs ran at full throttle for an average of eighteen hours at a time on a daily basis. This was later remedied by installing Meehanite iron manifolds.

The transmissions tended to overheat under harsh conditions. George Rotinoff had originally modified and installed Sherman tank transmissions, but these were soon replaced with Fuller transmissions. This also served to eliminate some of the tailshaft problems that were experienced. Changing tailshafts had previously been such a regular occurrence on the roadside that Jackie and Julie rarely left the base without spare tailshafts strapped to the top of each trailer.

One driver reckoned that he'd done it so often he could do it blindfolded and said it finally made him leave the job. 'It is no easy task to change a tailshaft in the dark on the side of the road on below-freezing winter nights, or when it's 40 degrees in the shade and the bloody bullocks piddle all over you. There's not too many big shady trees across the Barkly Highway!'

Most of the trips the Rotinoffs undertook were longer than 1500 kilometres. One of the longest runs was from Wave Hill to Mount Isa and back, a distance of 2648 kilometres.

Conditions were hard and the truck had to be adaptable to cope with alternating between bitumen running, driving on the muddy black soil plains of the Top End and driving on the dry, dusty, corrugated tracks of the Centre. Generally, most drivers said the trucks coped well once all the initial problems had been rectified.

Eric Prisgrove, manager of the Maryville Roadtrain Base, conducted an extensive repairs and maintenance program in 1959, and managed to keep the trucks in an operational condition.

Many of the drivers were drovers or came from interstate or overseas and had no skills in driving heavy vehicles or basic bush mechanics. Eric implemented set duty rosters and operating procedures and a few basic training initiatives. He always defended the Rotinoffs against criticism. 'During my term of management I had in my employment five drivers only, and I replaced only one driver in this time. Previous to this there had been approximately 36 drivers over the two years.

Once the novelty of driving the Rotinoffs wore off, the vehicles suffered a lot of mistreatment.

'Breakdowns prior to 1959 were manmade and not faults of design. One of the main causes of damage was that the Sherman tank gearboxes were synchronised throughout and the drivers were able to change down from high to low gear without using intermediate gears. This, of course, helped them stop, as the braking systems were in a bad state of disrepair.

'Another part of the problem was that they were being overdriven at 2100 rpm instead of the cruising rpm of 1800, which was the standard for most heavy-duty diesels at the time.

'The only trouble I had with the Rotinoff Viscounts was with a batch of defective prime-mover tyres, and the other a flat battery because the drivers stopped for a cuppa and left the trailer lights on.'

The Rotinoffs travelled an incredible 3.2 million kilometres before being retired. The average speed was 65 kilometres per hour if the road was good. The trailers grossed up to 60 tonnes and could transport 140 steers at a time on single decks.

English migrant Richie Whitehead managed to land a job driving for Vestey from the roadtrain base to the railhead in Camooweal. He drove Jackie and enjoyed the experience: 'The Rotinoffs were good rigs in their day with driver comforts including a sleeping berth, a really big deal in those days and a comfy driving seat with arm rests—would you believe it!' Richie remembered years later.

'One annoying problem with the Rotinoffs was when operating in overdrive it was likely to throw a tailshaft due to the tailshaft being about 12 foot [3.7 metres] long with no centre bearing. We carried a spare shaft on top of the crates and were forever changing them on the roadside.'

The drivers were paid £50 a month with keep, and the roadtrains worked 24 hours a day. The drivers had to maintain them under the direction of the engineer.

In an interview with Neil Puckeridge in 1995, Neil 'Bluey' O'Sullivan, who spent thirteen months driving Julie in 1957 and 1958, recalled that the seating gave an armchair ride because of its flash hydraulic construction.

'The turbocharged Rolls-Royce engine had no trouble reaching 60 miles per hour [nearly 100 kilometres per hour] and the power steering was magic,' Bluey recalled. 'Every three months the diff oil had to be changed because the grease we'd applied to the wheels had turned to liquid and overflowed the differentials.

'New tyres were always fitted to the drive and braking wheels but retreads were fitted to the trailing wheels. The trip from Helen Springs to Camooweal resulted in an average of four flats per trip. There was always a spare engine in the workshop but mostly, any major repairs were done by Rolls-Royce.'

Changing tyres was an occupational hazard, according to Bluey, who said cattle had no respect for people. It was not unusual, while changing a tyre, to find yourself getting a stinking hot urine shower, or worse! Drivers could try to shepherd the load away from any flat tyres, but it didn't always work as the trays were specially designed to shed animal waste.

When they carted fat cattle from Camooweal to the Mount Isa railhead, four Viscount loads equalled one railway load of cattle. Each prime mover pulled two trailers, and the steam train would then puff along its way with over 400 head of Vestey cattle.

Queensland laws were different from the Territory's and the roadtrains' length was illegal in Queensland, where 40 feet (12 metres) was the limit. The Rotinoff prime mover and body crate were more than that on their own.

At first the drivers were charged with being over length every time they presented their waybills to the Camooweal police. Later this stopped, perhaps after a few politicians were reminded that Vestey had invested millions in the base at Helen Springs and the Rockhampton meatworks.

The Rotinoffs even had radios fitted to the cabs, but most of the time they were out of range of any stations. The drivers made their own fun to break the monotony of these long trips, according to Bluey.

One practice frowned on by management was to transfer the spare driver to the lead unit by way of the front bumper. He would then clamber over the two trailers up to the prime movers and give the front driver a fright by banging on the cab or throwing water over him.

Bluey recalled that each roadtrain had the name of three of Vestey's stations painted on the door: Helen Springs, Willamaloo and Manbuloo.

Barry Clough has fond memories of the first time he saw a Rotinoff working. Barry's father, Ewen, was the first driver of the AEC Government Roadtrain in the 1930s, and Barry had spent his life on cattle stations and working in the trucking industry. In the early 1960s he took a job working for his mate Peter Lynch driving an old Commer.

'Bruce Douglas was the butcher in Alice Springs in those days and you couldn't get a killer anywhere near the Alice because of the drought. He organised to get two vans of fat cattle down from the Barkly region every fortnight to supply the town.

'I worked all over the place but my regular run was to do the fortnightly trip up to Burramurra Station and bring the cattle back to the Alice. We used to follow the sand dunes and it was hard going with a bent strap trailer, I can tell you. I never got out of third gear in that old Commer between there and the Alice.

'On one trip I was just coming over a ridge when I saw this thing just disappearing over another ridge in the distance and it was long, real long. I thought to myself, "Christ! Nobody told me there was a railway track out here!"

'It took me about an hour to catch up with it and I couldn't believe my eyes as I caught glimpses of the length of it, through the billowing dust, going around corners ahead of me. I just had to have a look at it.

'Determined to get past it I put the pedal to the metal and took off alongside. It seemed to take forever and I kept turning my head to look at the train and was dodging bloodwood trees and anthills and trying to see where I was going in the dust. It turned out to be one of the Rotinoffs towing the other, each with two trailers.

'I have never forgotten it, the whole of my life!'

In 1960, under Eric Prisgrove's supervision, 'Jackie' was tested with three trailers, making an overall length of 61 metres, with a weight of 120 tonnes and the capacity to carry 200 head of cattle.

'In early 1961,' Eric recalled, 'I got permission from the NT Works Department to tow three trailers with Jackie. Julie, during this time, towed only one trailer. This was a test to see if the prime mover could cope with the extra weight, which it did. This trial was carried out to see if it was necessary to order two extra trailers. When I left Vestey's employment later in the year Jackie was still towing three trailers.'

While it was decided not to introduce the triple trailer configuration as a standard procedure, Jackie had handled the extra weight and length better than expected and was often seen towing this configuration later.

In the days of single-lane roads, passing roadtrains was a problem for cars and other trucks. Not only did billowing clouds of dust prevent the driver from seeing what was travelling behind him, the incredible length of the roadtrain prevented the driver from hearing a car horn beeping from behind.

Vestey solved this by fitting microphones in each of the trailers so the sound carried forward to the driver, who could then pull over to the side of the road. This worked well unless the wires broke or dust clogged the microphones.

Vestey ceased operations in 1967 and sold off its trucks and trailers. Jackie was purchased by an ex-employee, George Appelbee, who first came across the Rotinoff Viscounts when he was employed as a bookkeeper for the Vesteys at Halls Creek, Western Australia. At the time, Jackie was working out of Manbuloo Station, Katherine. She had been fitted with a platform body and was used to service Vestey stations.

Jackie had been re-registered in Western Australia with the number HC473. This, coupled with her new tray back, caused many people over the years to think that a third Viscount had made it to Australia.

George was impressed with just how sturdy she was and, when he heard the Rotinoffs were for sale later on, he purchased Jackie for use in his newly established earthmoving and dam sinking business.

People were amazed at what George did with Jackie. With his caterpillar D8 dozer on the back he'd head off into the bush. The weight of the D8 is clearly evident with the bow in Jackie's chassis today, but George reported she handled it well and was happy with her performance.

'I would put a bulldozer on the back of the truck and then drive through everything, including creek beds, to get to the sites. The truck's performance was phenomenal. When it was on the run for Vestey Brothers it could pull three or four trailers loaded with up to 80 head of cattle each over the roughest conditions.'

Jackie was finally retired in 1975 and for many years sat idle in Quinns Rock, Western Australia.

Julie was purchased by the Johannsens, Kurt and son Lindsay, who used it to haul copper ore from their mine at Jervois to the smelting works in Mount Isa, as well as for a variety of other tasks over the years.

Julie was refitted with a tray body and towed two trailers, carrying copper ore in sacks and drums from the mine site to Mount Isa, a distance of around 500 kilometres.

Lindsay Johannsen said he was always happy with Julie's performance but when she started having mechanical problems she was parked up at Jervois and never operated again. Many years later, she was relocated to Alice Springs and stored at the Old Ghan Museum for safekeeping, in the hope of being restored one day.

The Road Transport Historical Society was formed in August 1992 when a group of road transport enthusiasts in Alice Springs decided it was time to get serious about preserving some of the road transport heritage in Central Australia.

Preserving vehicles like the Vestey Rotinoff Viscounts was a priority. One was in Alice Springs, but how many others were there? And where were they? The society knew that two had operated out of Maryville, but several people reported that a third Rotinoff, a tray truck, was registered in Western Australia and used as a stores and supply truck on Vestey's remote stations in the top of the state. They had photos of it!

All our contacts in London, along with all Rotinoff enthusiasts, were adamant that only two were ever exported to Australia. There were theories that a second-hand unit from Switzerland or the Middle East had been brought into the country at some stage.

An interview on ABC radio, in which I mentioned the search for the Rotinoffs, sparked many 'wild goose chases' across central and northern Australia. To complicate matters further, Julie had been renamed the 'Mighty Quinn' for a few years and some suggested that perhaps this truck was the third elusive Rotinoff.

This theory was easily dispelled and it soon became evident that there was no third truck. Vestey had actually fitted Jackie with a platform and operated her out of Halls Creek as a supply truck for a short period before selling her to George Appelbee. The 'Mighty Quinn' was actually Julie in disguise.

In 2002, after much discussion, George Appelbee decided to donate the truck to the National Road Transport Hall of Fame. The champagne corks popped and the beer flowed when Jackie the Rotinoff finally returned to Central Australia later that year.

She was in a sad and sorry state of disrepair and badly rusted out, but several drums of spare parts, which came with her, proved invaluable in the restoration program.

So, both trucks turned up at the National Road Transport Hall of Fame in Alice Springs ten years apart, thanks to their owners recognising their significance and donating them to the museum quite separately.

The Rotinoff Viscount roadtrains are two of the most impressive trucks to ever come to Australia. Their historical significance to the development of the outback makes them worthy of inclusion in the National Road Transport Hall of Fame.

THE ROTINOFF VISCOUNT ROADTRAIN: SPECIFICATIONS

General data

Chassis weight: 21,800 lb (9900 kg)

Gross combination rating: 135,000 lb (61,200 kg)

Wheelbase: 24 ft (7.3 m)

Maximum speed: 47 mph (75 km/h) @ 2100 rpm

Overall length of prime mover: 40 ft (12.1 m)

Width over tyres: 8 ft (2.4 m)

Roadtrain combination length: 145 ft (44.2 m)

Triple configuration: 200 ft (60.1 m)

Engine

Rolls-Royce C6SFL, four-stroke, six-cylinder diesel engine giving 250 bhp (183 kW) at 2100 rpm. Torque 710 lb (322 kg) @ 1300 rpm. Compression ratio 14.0 to 1

Brakes

S cam air with ratchet handbrake acting on the rear axle

Clutch

18-in (46-cm), single-plate dry clutch

Fuel system

Triple filters in series

Cooling system

Copper fin and tube radiator. Six-blade 24-in (61-cm) diameter fan

Tyres

11 × 20 single front

Steering

Hydraulic power-operated

Chassis

Heavy-duty alloy steel, double-skinned 12 in (30 cm) deep

Gearbox

Six-speed overdrive synchromesh with auxiliary three-speed synchromesh (Sherman tank)

Rear bogie

Kirkstall rear end

THE ROLLS-ROYCE PERSPECTIVE

Neil Pearson, managing director of Rolls-Royce, Australia, was interviewed about the Rotinoffs by Jack Maddock in May 1980.

I was involved with them from when they first arrived in Sydney; the prime movers, that is. They landed in Sydney and then came to Melbourne to have the trailers made. There was no work done on them then [the trucks]. They were fully imported.

I was with Rolls-Royce, never with Rotinoffs. We were only ever involved from an engine point of view.

It was the highest-rated engine we had then, horsepower per cylinder: 275 horsepower out of six in those days, 2100 with a mechanical supercharge. It had a Rootes blower made by Sir George Godfrey. We used both CAV and Simms pumps. CAV was the best fuel pump but the Simms governor was better. It pulled down on speed so you didn't have a smoke problem.

It was one of the most reliable engines. In its early days it had a lot of problems. It was this engine that was developed in Euclids. This is where it started its life at that rating—in the big Euclid dump trucks.

There were the usual problems with high-rated engines: line erosion and cooling system temperature problems. Nothing terrible to overcome. It was the first step up from the Vickers tractor engine, which was rated at 180 hp [134 kW] at 1800.

This one suddenly jumped to 275 [205] at 2100. It was a hell of a boost. The supercharger took about 30 horsepower out of it, that's the advantage of the turbocharger—no loss of power.

The only aluminium used was in the cooling pipes and connections and the sump. The rest was all cast iron—the heads, the block and the wheel case.

I went out when they were doing the tests on the trailers. This was mainly a tracking test. They wanted to make certain that with the three trailers on it they were going to track well because of the condition of some of the roads these trucks were going to travel on.

It was magnificent how the trailers tracked. They were put in a big circle and the wheel tracks hardly varied from the trailers to the prime mover. They tracked beautifully into the prime mover.

John Vestey came out for the delivery run. He drove one of them. They drove right through Alice Springs by road. I only heard this report from John Vestey when he came back. He said he arrived in Alice Springs in the spare driver's seat with his feet on the dash holding it on because everything rattled off on the truck from Adelaide. It had to be reassembled when it got there. No one expected the road to be in that sort of condition, it was a hell of a track.

The Viscount was never meant to be an off-road vehicle. It was a highway vehicle. The road it ran on was mainly bitumen, across the Barkly Tablelands. They drove the cattle in on the hoof to Maryville and held them there to fatten them up. They came in from Wave Hill and places like that before they'd roadtrain them to Camooweal to the railhead. The idea was to get them to the abattoirs in Rockhampton in good condition.

The next time I got involved up there was when Rotinoffs sent their works manager, a chap called Crook. He came out from England to look at the transmission problems. We stripped the transmission in the Maryville workshop and it really was a magnificent piece of gear. The gearbox was close to the road, fairly low with lots of shafts in it.

Rotinoff had obviously never had experience in working with this sort of heat. The gearboxes had been heating up so badly the shafts were blue, and on the lot of them the bearings were frozen on and you couldn't get them out.

We said if they were going to continue using these boxes they could fit a heat exchanger, an oil cooler box, and we could pipe it into the engine cooling system, but the works manager didn't agree. He reckoned there was nothing wrong with the gearboxes.

We went out and did some tests and got 170 degrees Fahrenheit on the road surface. It was never resolved except that eventually Vestey pulled those gearboxes out and put Roadrangers in. From then on, they had no more troubles. This got them over their gearbox problems and eased the tailshaft angles. Being a shorter, smaller box it straightened out the tailshaft.

After they'd been running for a while up there they ran into trouble with the exhaust manifolds; they couldn't keep them on. I went up [to Helen Springs] to find out why. It was the first run I did with them, loaded from Maryville to Camooweal.

Our absolute peak rating for that engine was a one-hour rating. What was happening was that they were leaving Maryville fully loaded with the throttle full wide open and it sat there for twelve hours straight. The manifolds were a little above white heat. They were just a glowing mass. The cast iron couldn't take it; they kept cracking and breaking up. We fixed this problem by fitting Meehanite manifolds. It was all that was needed.

The gearbox was, I understand, a Sherman tank transmission and it was a great big cumbersome thing. It had about five shafts in it and impossible tailshaft angles. They used to have to carry a spare tailshaft strapped to the top of each trailer so they could change it on the road.

With 60 cattle, if they had a breakdown, they only had a four-hour limit. After that they just had to let the cattle go because they couldn't water them.

Vestey had built this station for them, about 90 miles [145 kilometres] north of Tennant Creek. It was built solely for the Rotinoffs and they employed a station manager and built him a residence. It was a beautifully built base with workshops and full maintenance facilities.

THE DROVERS' VIEW

Scotty Watson was a drover of note in the Northern Territory and for many years drove large herds of cattle between various Vestey properties in Queensland and the Northern Territory. It was not uncommon to move mobs of up to 2000 head of cattle and be on the job for six months at a time. He recalls the drovers' reactions to the Rotinoffs:

When Buntine's 'Knocker' and Kurt Johannsen's Diamond T started to cart a few cattle around, us drovers didn't worry too much. We thought our jobs were safe and the trucks carting cattle already, well, we really thought of them as little more than nuisances. Besides, they were welcome to the little stuff; our money was in moving large mobs over large distances. As far as taking this work off us and carting cattle by truck through the scrub we travelled, no bloody way!

I'd heard talk about Vestey's big Rotinoffs before they arrived. How ridiculous were those Pommy bastards thinking they could move big mobs in those things? Was I in for a shock. I just couldn't believe my eyes when I first seen one.

I was at Newcastle Waters walking a mob of 1300 through from Wave Hill to Helen Springs when one of those jolly green giants pulled in. I called them that because I reckoned it was a myth, you know, them being able to cart cattle and all that.

I couldn't believe the size of it. It was massive and the driver, he was pretty cocky about this being my last job on the hoof. As it turned out he was pretty right. I did a few more little jobs but most of the big mobs were moved by truck from then on. It put a lot of us blokes out of a job!

Some of them got jobs driving trucks, but I liked the idea of having a job with walk-on, walk-off freight, so I started driving coaches and did a bit of work in the tourist industry after that.

GEORGE ROTINOFF AND THE NUMBER SEVEN

Although of Russian descent, George Rotinoff was an English gentleman right down to his tweed cap, jacket and big cigar.

A widower who lived with his daughter and a nanny in fashionable Gerrards Cross, Buckinghamshire, George was a charming man on first-name terms with all his staff. He kept track of every detail of new developments and was responsible for a lot of the vehicle design.

He had a thing about the number seven. Seven always featured somewhere in the company's products. The serial numbers of all his trucks featured the number seven. The Atlantic models, for example, had the serial number GR7 and the Viscounts had the serial number GR77.

His two cars sported personalised numberplates featuring the number seven. His Rolls-Royce Wraith was registered GR71 and his Bentley Continental was GR77, the same as the serial number of the Viscount model.

His staff felt it ironic that he died in 1957.

IT'S NOT LIKE ON TV

KINGSLEY FOREMAN

Sadly, traffic accidents occur everywhere in Australia and there are often serious truck accidents way out in the outback.

People have a macabre interest in fatal outback crashes and often ask about the details of such accidents from the point of view of those, like myself, who were sent to tow the crashed trucks back to the city. It's a natural curiosity, I guess; people want to know how such things are handled and what it's like to be involved.

It was not unusual, when I worked for Richmond Heavy Towing in the 1980s, for us to travel 500 or 600 miles, one way, just to get to the site of a truck accident.

Every accident is different, of course, but there are some things that are common to each case. One thing that makes a big difference to the circumstances of a serious truck accident is whether or not it is a 'single truck accident'. This may occur when a driver falls asleep at the wheel, goes off the road and rolls the truck, often killing himself but not involving others.

During my time salvaging trucks at this type of accident, it was common for the police not to send an ambulance or a van for the body. We'd just leave the body in the truck and tow the wreck back to the police compound in Adelaide and it was there they'd remove the truck driver's body.

If there was more than one truck involved, they always sent up a team from the major crash task force and a van for the bodies. In the case of a head-on smash between two tractor-trailers you'd start to see pieces of fibreglass from the truck bodies long before you'd see the actual wreck. It's really surprising just how far the fibreglass can travel from an accident.

When you arrive at the site of the accident the whole road is blocked off. The local police direct the traffic off onto a detour or, if that's not possible, onto the dirt shoulder of the road. The main highway is only about 20 feet wide and that includes the lanes for traffic heading in both directions.

By the time we'd arrive, any injured people would have been taken to the nearest hospital, which in the outback was often hundreds of miles away, by the light aircraft of the Royal Flying Doctor Service, which covers the thousands of square miles of outback Australia.

The local police just block a section of the main highway where the accident is and the plane lands on the highway to ferry the injured to hospital. As well as the local police, the local Volunteer Fire Service are usually there as well, and sometimes even the State Emergency Service, if there is a local brigade.

A gruesome practicality is that the bodies are left behind until after the investigation has been concluded. The first thing you notice is that all the trained service staff are walking around looking at the ground. They have to do this so they don't step on any body parts.

In a section of road where there has been a fatal accident you will see paint marks made by the police indicating where the vehicles were, and you also see painted rings that indicate where bodies or body parts were.

It's really not much like the fatal scenes portrayed on TV. You don't usually see severed limbs and body parts, as the force of the impact mostly leaves very little that is substantial.

After the major crash investigators have taken their photos and made their measurements, they pick up what they can of the bodies of the crash victims and place the parts of each victim into plastic bags, so that all the parts of one body are in the same bag. Then the local fire service hose off the road and the police give the OK to start the recovery work.

Another thing that most truck rollovers have in common is that, because the trucks fall on their side or roof, there is a large amount of engine oil all over the spot, and hundreds of gallons of fuel as well, so you are sometimes working in ankle-deep slush.

The first thing we would do, while the truck is on its side, is to remove the drive shaft so no damage is done to the drive train during towing. Then we'd check out the air system to see if we can use it with the tow truck.

It is not unusual for an accident to break the air lines or to rip off the air tanks or even just the air taps. If the wrecked truck cannot hold air, the brakes have to be released by hand.

Many people don't understand that when you put your foot on the brake pedal it releases air and the brakes come on. If the wrecked truck cannot hold air the brakes are on, and they have to be released before anyone can tow it away. There are several ways of doing this. I always preferred just to release the bolt on the slack adjuster. It is a lot quicker than winding it off. Once that's done it's time to put the truck back on its wheels.

Air bags have been trialled for this operation but, to tell you the truth, my opinion is that they are hopeless and not worth the time and effort.

We always used four chains. Two would go on the tractor, one on the front axle and the other one on the last rear axle, both as high as possible off the ground. The other two chains we'd use on the trailer, one on the last axle and the other up near the leg support. When these were in place we'd position the rear of our tow truck in the middle of the tractor-trailer, then connect the ends of the four chains to the big pulling winch on the back of the tow truck.

When all was ready for the big pull, someone would sit in the tow truck with one foot hard on the brakes and use the other foot to give it plenty of revs to work the winch.

Sometimes, if it was a heavy wreck, we'd have to chain the tow truck to another tractor-trailer to anchor it down. Once the wreck was upright again, we'd hitch the tow truck onto the front and tow the wreck back to the city.

NOT ON A SIXPENCE

CHERYL VAN DER VELDEN

You can't stop a big rig on a sixpence,
If only the car drivers knew,
With such a long load you gotta have room
It takes just a gear change or two . . .

If I come along to a crossing
Before you walk out when you choose,
Just think for a bit—if I *have* to pull up,
Imagine the revs that I lose!

Then, when I drive along in my Kenworth,
I see all the cars weave and duck.
They think it's all fun but it isn't for me,
I just can't do that in my truck.

When you drive along all the back roads
And see the dead animals there,
Don't think for a minute that we didn't wish
That we could just give 'em a scare . . .

'Cos we can't stop a big rig on a sixpence,
We need a fair distance for that
As we see roos coming we just grit our teeth
And hope that we don't hear a . . . splat!

As we roll along all the highways
And look out our window at you,
Just give us a wave—not the finger,
We're doin' what we have to do.

We cart all the grain for your brekky,
We cart all the milk for your tea,
We cart all the fruit for your fam'ly,
We even cart fish from the sea.

So, when you drive along in your auto
And you pull in *front* of a truck
Just think of what's pushing behind it,
Or BOTH of us might need some luck.

'Cos you can't stop a big rig on a sixpence
And when you don't know what you've done,
We have to decide how to miss you
And that's when we tend to have fun.

Of course there's some cowboys among us
And sometimes we owe it to you,
But just try to think of us kindly—
It's a hell of a job that we do.

EASTER MONDAY 1995

SHARON HOURN

We woke early; the kids were excited to be going in the truck with their daddy, Darren, better known as Cracker.

Being a truck driver's kids can be tough when you're small. Khaleb was only a year old and Tamika was just two. Although Darren was often away, he had formed a bond with Tamika and she worshipped her daddy. Darren would ring whenever he was able and Tamika would get on the phone and say, 'Me go, Daddy . . . me go.'

She loved going with her dad in the truck and occasionally she even went on trips with Darren on her own. When she was allowed to go with him she'd wait at the front door for him to arrive back from loading up. I'd get a quick kiss and they'd be off.

•

It was 6.30 a.m. when we left home.

The first job was to load the B-double with sheep. The sheep had to be loaded directly out of a paddock and it was bitterly cold. I stayed in the truck with Khaleb and Tamika while Darren loaded with the driver of the second truck, a bloke called Phil, who I'd met just that morning.

We were held up for longer than usual—after loading the truck had two flat tyres—and by the time Darren changed them time was getting away.

We followed Phil, who thought it was a good idea to stop for an early lunch. It seemed to be getting colder as the day went on, so we were glad to get into the cafe and order lunch.

Khaleb ran amok while we had lunch. He was a noisy kid when he put his mind to it and he seemed so full of life that day after the cold morning and the early start. It was a nice friendly lunch and, as we all sat together and ate, we made arrangements to go to Phil's place for a barbecue tea when we got back home later that day.

Soon we were on our way again, with Phil leading the way in his B-double. We followed along and I talked to him on the UHF, finalising details for our barbecue later that day.

Tamika and Khaleb were in the bunk of Darren's B-double. Tamika was playing with her favourite doll. She adored that doll; if you kissed it on the forehead it talked to you. In fact it was able to say 120 different things. Khaleb was overdosing on lollies and getting tired. I could see he was getting sleepy. I always called him 'Man-o' and he was my precious little 'Man-o' then, as I put him on my lap and gave him his bottle.

Khaleb loved to be cuddled to sleep and I was busy doing just that when Tamika tapped my arm and informed me that she wanted a cuddle, too.

I said, 'Let Mummy get Man-o to sleep and then I'll cuddle you.'

She was a good kid and always so patient. She just moved forward and sat on the fridge between Darren and me.

As I cuddled Khaleb to sleep I glanced at my watch. I remember quite distinctly that it was 11.05 a.m. and we were going up a hill. The road at that point was under repair; there was a lot of loose gravel and a lot of dust.

Darren shook his head and told me to look in his mirror. When I did I could see a car was trying to overtake us, but the driver evidently thought better of it and soon pulled back in.

We topped the hill and started our descent. We had travelled this road hundreds of times and I knew there was a narrow bridge at the bottom of the hill we were going down.

Suddenly Darren broke the silence. 'Look at this idiot!' he exclaimed.

I looked and, sure enough, there was that same car trying to overtake us again. The car was only half on the road. There was not enough road to pass properly, and when I looked ahead I could see the bridge.

I looked back in the mirror and the car appeared to be in the same spot, half off the road attempting to overtake a B-double going downhill. Khaleb suddenly stopped dozing and sat up. Darren swore as he moved the truck over further and further to allow the car the extra room it needed.

I watched that car finally go past us and go onto the bridge but, at the same time, I realised that the truck seemed to be leaning . . . and then it was falling.

I grabbed my son, and wrapped my arms around him firmly. I found my voice from somewhere and remember saying aloud, 'Please, God . . . not like this.'

I looked at Darren and told him I loved him, and then I shut my eyes.

•

I could hear Darren calling me.

I opened my eyes and realised I couldn't move. It was pitch black and something incredibly heavy was crushing me. I called out to Darren. I somehow knew that he heard me but he couldn't see me.

I could hear Darren throwing things. Then I could hear people talking. I couldn't call out again . . . I was having trouble breathing. I could feel my nose was bleeding and there was something so heavy, so very heavy, on me.

I couldn't understand why it was so dark.

I heard Darren, he was yelling for people to help him find me. I heard him say, 'Someone ring an ambulance.' I don't know how much time passed.

Then a man was talking to me. He was asking my name and asking who else was with us. As my mind began to function I remembered my kids, Man-o and Tamika. I remember thinking, 'Tamika must be with Darren.' But where was Man-o?

I realised that my arms were pinned underneath me. It was dark because I was lying face down and I could not move.

Man-o was underneath me. I was on top of him,

I squeezed my stomach in as tight as I could, but there was no movement. No sound. I tried with all my might to pull my arms out but I was trapped; the only part of me that I could move was my head.

Suddenly I could feel that I was going to be sick. I started vomiting. I remember thinking at that moment that if I panicked I would die. I knew I could choke on my own vomit and blood.

Trapped in the darkness I prayed. I asked God to watch over Darren. I asked God if he could make the ambulance hurry, and I asked him to please let me black out.

After what seemed like hours I sensed someone there with me. It was a rescue worker and I asked him what time it was. He told me it was 2.30 p.m. At that moment I felt the panic rising again. I knew I had been trapped for three hours and I had no idea where Darren and Tamika were. In that time in the darkness I'd already gone through three oxygen bottles that had been taped to a stick and poked down through a hole in the floor of the truck.

I understood by now that I had been thrown down an embankment and the truck had rolled on top of me. The rescue workers were unsure how to get me out without crushing me further, so they had decided to cut the truck apart piece by piece.

The truck weighed 42 tonnes, and it had a full load of sheep. There was no way of pulling the truck back up the embankment.

The pain seemed unbearable, and in that time I'd prayed again and again, 'Please, God, just let me sleep.'

Not long after the rescue worker talked to me I heard another voice close by saying, 'Talk to me . . . talk to me.'

Then the people above started shouting to each other, 'One's alive! There is still one alive!'

I tried to tell them that it was just Tamika's talking doll, but they couldn't hear my whisper over their excited yelling.

Finally someone asked which child was talking.

Waves of agony passed through as I said again, 'It's a doll.' I knew then that Tamika was gone also.

Why did the doll start talking just then? It had been trapped with me and something was pressing against it, so it should have been talking all along, or at least until the batteries went flat.

I often wondered if God had a hand in that, to keep me holding on.

Four and a half hours after the truck went over, I felt myself being dragged through the burrs and dirt from under the truck and I could finally see daylight. I was moving along the ground on my belly, someone was pulling me by my ankles.

It was then that I saw my son.

No one in their worst nightmares will ever know the anguish I felt at that moment. I could see my baby lying there and I tried to reach out and grab him, but I was being dragged in the opposite direction.

I arrived at Yass Hospital about 4.10 p.m. I was wrapped in heated blankets. I was in a neck brace and strapped down so I couldn't move.

I asked a nurse, 'Where are my babies?'

She told me that they had been brought to the hospital and I begged her to let me see them.

She left and returned a few moments later holding my little girl wrapped in a white hospital blanket.

The nurse leaned down so I could see my Tamika's face. I was strapped down. I couldn't move or hold my own baby. The nurse placed Tamika's face next to mine and I kissed her little cheek; she was so cold. Tears flooded my eyes, and my heart ached for her life that was gone.

The nurse left and returned a few minutes later with Khaleb.

She repeated the process as before—as did I. I told my little Man-o how sorry I was. I felt sure I had killed him.

I desperately wanted to warm my kids, hold them and breathe life back into them, but I knew it was useless.

Not long after, I was airlifted to Canberra in a critical condition. I still had no idea where Darren was. I was still conscious when I was placed in the intensive care ward in Canberra.

I remember the moment Darren walked in. My aching body was flooded with emotion and I thanked God for saving him.

•

The next few months are still sketchy in my mind. I was heavily sedated much of the time and underwent several major operations, blood transfusions and skin grafts. Gangrene had set in on my left thigh and I had crushed several vertebrae in my back. Of course I also had many cuts and bruises.

Darren was told I would never walk again. The doctors also told him it was a miracle I was alive and that I had the cold weather to thank for saving my leg. According to the best medical opinion I should be a quadriplegic, as the bones in my spine were crushed and were piercing my spinal cord.

After the gangrene was removed there were multiple skin grafts. I had an operation in which 150 staples were inserted to hold my bones in place.

On Mother's Day 1995, I was told that I had an infection and they would have to redo the whole operation. That was my lowest point. I wanted to give up.

•

After that it got even harder.

I was released from hospital after three months, but I was still unable to care for myself. I had to wear a hard plastic back brace day and night and my leg had to be dressed daily. I was unable to walk, so I was totally dependent on Darren for everything.

Although it certainly took a long time for me to heal physically, the heart will never heal fully. The heartache and sorrow never goes, it is just tucked away under the surface.

I have been through all the anger, the disbelief, the unbearable sorrow, the hurt, the feeling that my heart has been ripped out of my chest and the dark cold loneliness of despair.

I have been through the 'Why me? Why my babies?' emotions, over and over.

I have had to look at two empty rooms with empty beds and toys on the floor, just as they were left.

I have cried on my kids' empty pillows with my heart aching for the missing cuddles.

There has been a lot of helplessness and emptiness.

I have felt every possible emotion a person can feel.

I truly believe that you have to keep looking for the positives. My kids were not assaulted or murdered, they were not kidnapped, and they did not disappear one day never to be seen again.

When you lose your kids like this you have to try to focus on any one positive thing. Maybe the fact that you told them you loved them or that you kissed their little cheeks goodnight so often is somewhere to start.

And of course . . . it's OK to cry.

THE SILVER SHED

RAY GILLELAND (THE NULLARBOR KID)

Late in 1956 I had arrived in Perth with a load of refrigerators. After unloading I pulled into Moylins' warehouse yard in Roe Street. We used Moylins as an agent for getting loads and I walked into the office to see what was going on. I was looking for a load to go east, but there was nothing doing.

It looked like a lost week or two in the Subiaco Hotel. Loading back east was always scarce. Sometimes there were a few cars, or whale oil or timber. Anything was better than rattling back empty, which shook the truck to pieces.

I'd hopped out of my truck, leaving my driver's door open, and as I wandered back out to the truck I saw one of the young storemen sitting in my driving seat pretending to drive like a little kid.

He saw me coming and, just before he jumped down, he noticed my 25.20 Winchester rifle, which was lying on the sleeping bunk. The rifle had been covered by a blanket but the blanket had become dislodged.

He grabbed the rifle and jumped down to the ground as I approached, and he started working the lever action, which would slide a bullet into the breach ready for firing. Like a lot of people without firearms knowledge, he had his index finger crooked so that, as he slammed shut the lever action, he automatically pulled the trigger.

All this happened very quickly and before I could stop him.

The bullet zipped past my right side too close for comfort and went straight into the open door of one of the bond stores and buried itself in a pile of cartons packed with tinned sardines that had just arrived from overseas. The noise of the gunshot in the enclosed courtyard was very loud and frightened the hell out of him. The near-miss frightened the hell out of me too.

He immediately threw the rifle back into the sleeper bunk and took off around the front of my truck and disappeared.

I was still some distance from the cabin of my truck when the boss rushed out to the door behind me and yelled, 'What the bloody hell was that?'

I looked back over my shoulder and called, 'Must be out in the street,' and kept walking.

The boss couldn't see anyone in the yard and went back inside, shaking his head.

Out of curiosity I walked over to the shed where the rifle had been pointing when it was fired and was joined by the 'gunfighter'.

'You dumb bastard, you nearly killed me,' I growled at him.

'I know. I'm sorry, mate, it scared the hell out of me too,' he said. 'That's why I ran. Do you think the boss knows what happened?' he asked, looking over his shoulder.

'No, you're safe,' I told him. 'He went back inside.'

'Wonder where the bullet went,' he mused.

'That's bloody obvious,' I said, pointing to a stack of cartons, one of which was slowly oozing oil from a small round hole about head high.

The gunfighter ran across to the stack and pulled the carton out in order to swap it for the one behind. But that one also had a hole in it and so did the next and the next.

He frantically rearranged the stack so that the damaged cartons were all to the rear and all looked normal. There was nothing he could do about the fishy smell that started to be very noticeable.

'By the way,' I said quietly, 'never get up in my cabin again and never, ever touch someone's rifle unless it's handed to you. Understand?'

'Yeah,' he said. 'I'm sorry.'

With that I took off for the pub, glad to get out of there in one piece. That shed stank of sardines for a long, long time, especially when it rained.

It was just a few days later that I had a call from Moylins to come down to the yard, as they might have a load to go east if I was interested.

At that time there was a shipping strike in Perth and Moylins had been asked to supply someone to transport an urgent consignment from Perth to Melbourne as soon as possible.

'What's the load?' I asked loudly.

Moylins' boss looked at me and quickly crossed the floor to shut the office door. Then he said, very softly, 'It's silver bullion.'

'Yeah, yeah,' I replied, 'and pigs might fly.'

'No,' he assured me, 'I'm serious . . . silver bullion from the Perth Mint to the Melbourne Mint.'

'You're joking!'

'No, I'm not bloody well joking and keep your voice down,' he whispered. 'It's all hush-hush, never been done before. This will be the first time.'

I stood staring at him, but in my mind's eye I was picturing an armed escort, probably a car with armed guards and maybe one in the cabin with me. Who could say no to that? What an adventure.

'Well, this is something out of the box,' I mused.

'Melbourne Mint is in urgent need of some silver for coin minting,' he went on. 'They are short and Perth has plenty. Getting it there in a hurry is the problem. It usually goes by ship. Somebody upstairs came up with this idea as the shipping strike looks like continuing for a while yet.'

I smiled, thinking of all these armed guards for company. Wow, one side of Australia to the other, over 2000 miles, and never been done before.

'I'm game!' I said. I left it to Moylins to work out the details of weight, cost, insurance, freight rate and so on.

It was decided that one of the new-style shipping containers would be the most suitable way of carrying the silver. Those containers were just starting to make an impact on the shipping of goods and were not known much outside the shipping industry. Moylins could arrange for it to be dropped off at the wharf in Port Melbourne after unloading. It sounded OK by me.

As it all had to be hush-hush we needed a 'cover story'. I was to go to the wharf and pick up a container for Moylins, supposedly to 'load for overseas and be delivered back to the wharf after the strike was over'. That would account for why an empty container was taken from the wharf.

The next day I picked up the container without any fuss and went back to the pub. It was a plain silvery-grey colour without any signwriting on it. There were no other drivers in town from the east, so no one knew what I was up to.

Next morning, promptly at 9 a.m., I pulled up outside the Perth Mint as instructed. Two men in grey dustcoats came out and stopped the traffic and the trams and I drove across the road and reversed in through two big iron gates and up into an inner courtyard blocked off from the road.

The two dust-coated mint employees shut the gates behind me as I reversed up. Then they came into the inner courtyard and each withdrew a large pistol from their right-hand pocket. I remembered then that I'd thought it strange when they walked out onto the road waving at the traffic with one hand with the other in their pocket. Now I knew why.

I jumped up and opened the two rear doors of the container as two more mint employees wheeled out a sort of tray on wheels with some silver ingots on it. Two more men climbed onto the truck and I was motioned aside with a wave of the hand by the foreman or whoever he was. Evidently they would do all the handling. I was to keep count with the boss as they went on.

Everything went smoothly, the trolley coming and going with the ingots, which were gently laid on the floor of the container till the tally was complete. The doors were shut and padlocked and then a lead seal was inserted through the door handle and stopper and it was sealed shut with the Perth Mint seal.

'Now, here is a phone number for the mint in Melbourne,' the foreman told me. 'Ring them when you are an hour away and they will be waiting for you. It's in William Street. Don't tell anyone what you have. As far as anyone is concerned it's an empty container going back to the east coast. Sign this list and we will post it to the Melbourne Mint.'

I signed for the ingots, he put the list into an envelope and I had to sign my name across the seal on the envelope.

'That won't be touched till you arrive in Melbourne and open it yourself,' he said as he handed me a piece of paper with a Melbourne telephone number on it.

Hardly a word had been spoken the whole time I was there. There was no skylarking; it was all terribly serious.

I turned to the foreman. 'Who's going with me?' I asked.

'What do you mean?'

'Armed guards,' I said. 'How many will there be? A carload? Or just one with me in the truck?'

The foreman stared at me blankly. 'Where did you get that idea from?' he asked. 'The mint is not supplying armed guards. Once you're out the gate it's all yours. We have no more responsibility; it's on your truck so it's your problem to get it to the gates of the Melbourne Mint.'

That stopped me in my tracks. 'Oh . . . Well, do I send a telegram to you or the Melbourne Mint for a progress report on how I'm going?'

'No,' he said, 'you don't send telegrams or make phone calls to anyone. Not anyone, do you understand? You're on your own. Just make the one call one hour out from delivery stating your arrival time outside the Melbourne Mint gate. That's all.'

I looked at him, still blankly trying to take all this in and suddenly realising what I had got myself into.

As the two guards put their coats back on and slipped their pistols into their pocket, one quietly said, 'Do you carry a gun, driver?'

'Yes, I do actually,' I said, picturing my 25.20 Winchester rifle and my .45 Colt pistol under the mattress in my sleeping bunk, but my mind was still spinning with all these new revelations. I'm doing this all alone, no armed guards . . . nothing.

'Good,' he said, and gave me a quick smile. 'Hope you don't need it, but good luck.'

That was when it actually struck me what I was in for and the enormous responsibility I had till I reached the Melbourne Mint. Was I really in any danger?

I thought to myself, 'Well, Ray, you do have over £100,000 on board!'

In those bygone days, banks would be robbed for five or ten thousand pounds, and these ingots could be melted down. No serial numbers for a robber to worry about.

I began to imagine rough characters with leather aprons peering through goggles as they poured molten silver into moulds for jewellery or some such thing and selling them in pubs or somewhere. I had visions of me being left for dead in the outback. I could see the newspaper headlines: 'Truckie Loses Gun Battle with Desperados'.

Bloody hell.

I slowly shook my head and my heart skipped a beat as I thought, 'What the hell have I got myself into now?' I felt like yelling, 'Take it all off! I'm not going! It's not fair, this isn't what I thought it was going to be!'

Then I calmed down and thought, 'Oh, bugger 'em. I'll do it. It's too late now . . . make the best of it.'

'Just hang on a minute,' I said as they opened the gates and stopped the traffic again. I jumped up into the cabin and promptly pulled my rifle from under the sleeping bunk and laid it on top of the bunk. I felt better then. 'OK, I'm off,' I said as I trundled out into the Perth sunshine, swung a left and drove off down the road.

I remember thinking to myself, 'Is it really happening?' I looked around the cabin. I had no paperwork, nothing to say what I was carrying. I glanced at the rifle on the bunk.

'It's not a dream,' I said to myself, looking in the rear-vision mirror. 'That container *is* there and it ain't empty, believe me!'

The thought gave me a sort of brief shudder.

•

For the first few hours out of Perth I watched every car that overtook me, wondering if it was a carrying a gang of bullion thieves.

It was very difficult to watch like that as the little rear-view mirror attached to the top of the door vibrated, which meant I had to lean out and hold the edge steady with my right hand to stop it shaking so I could actually see what was behind me. This became very tiresome, I can tell you.

Fortunately, once I was out in the bush there were fewer cars to watch. There was never much traffic on the 400 miles from Perth to Kalgoorlie but, after some time, I noticed a big blue Hudson sedan, which came up very fast and then sat behind me for no reason. It could have passed me very easily—they were big and powerful cars. Next time I could look it had pulled to the side of the road and stopped.

The first time I didn't take much notice, but then up it came again and tucked in behind me and again pulled over and stopped.

'Hmmmm,' I thought, 'that's strange.'

The third time I really began to worry, as once he caught up and sat behind me, two other cars overtook both of us. That's when I felt with my left hand for the comforting wooden stock of my rifle. I was fairly sure by then that the people in the Hudson were up to no good. I was so nervous that I felt under the mattress of the bunk for the extra comforting touch of my .45 Colt pistol.

Then, without warning, the Hudson sped past me, followed by another car, which had caught up with it. Both were going very fast. I could see there were several people in the car but exactly who they were I couldn't tell.

'Now what?' I thought. But they continued very fast and I soon lost sight of them both.

I relaxed a little and had a swig of flat lemonade, lit a cigarette and let the heart rate get back to normal.

It was then I had a heart-to-heart talk with myself: 'Wake up to yourself, Ray, no one knows what you're carrying, so just relax. You've seen too many gangster movies.'

No sooner had my heartbeat settled down to near normal, however, than it was racing again! I came over a little rise and came face to face with the big blue Hudson, half on and half off the road. There was no one else in sight. There was no sign of the other car as I peered ahead down the road and then quickly into the rear-vision mirror. There was just the big blue Hudson and some people standing around the car and looking my way.

'This is it!' I thought. 'This is definitely trouble.'

I took another quick glance behind and moved to the wrong side of the road and gave a long blast on my air-horn and kept going full speed, which in that truck was 45 miles per hour. At the same time I grabbed the .45 pistol with my left hand and pulled on the air-horn again, steering only with my right hand.

As I whipped past, glaring at the car, I had time to see Dad jump around the front of the car off the road and Mum holding a little toddler bent over and being sick into the grass near the passenger door. It looked like Grandma climbing into the back seat holding on to her purse.

I quickly returned to the right side of the road and looked into the rear-vision mirror in time to see Dad shaking his fist at me.

The kid was obviously car sick every few miles.

'So much for hijackers,' I thought as I put the pistol away. I lit another cigarette, giggling nervously and feeling like a fool. It seemed time to have another little heart-to-heart with myself about too much imagination. I told myself, 'You're an idiot, just shut up and drive.'

I decided to press on till I was tired and park in the middle of a little town somewhere for a sleep, preferably near the police station.

Back east, 'near a police station' was the last place I would want to park, but no one knew me over here. I was a law-abiding citizen working for the Commonwealth government, even though it would be hard to prove it.

I stopped in Merredin under a streetlight, locked all the doors and went to sleep with my pistol under my pillow.

I awoke next morning, wondering where to eat; as I climbed down from the cab, I could see a roughly dressed man leaning on the trailer staring at the back doors of the container.

'Morning,' he said.

I nodded.

'What's that thing?' he asked, pointing to the container.

'Ummm . . . it's a shipping container.'

'Make a good shed on the farm,' was the reply. 'Where can I buy one?'

'Don't think you can,' I said.

'Oh, well,' he said, 'it looks nice and strong and easy to move . . . pity. What's in it?'

'It's empty.'

'Why does it have a padlock on it?'

'Don't know.'

'Don't know much, do you?' he said as he gave a wave and walked off.

'Get stuffed . . .' I thought to myself. I suddenly realised I should get out of there right away.

I climbed back in, pressed the starter button, warmed it up, built up the air pressure for the brakes and took off. I had a gulp of flat lemonade and lit a cigarette. I wasn't liking this trip at all. I twiddled with the radio knob . . . nothing, so I switched it off in disgust.

I got something to eat at Southern Cross, which was only 60 miles down the track, but there were more people wanting to know what the tin shed was on the back of my truck and where could they buy one? Was I delivering to a farm somewhere? Could they have a look inside? All they got from me were grumbles and dirty looks.

It had been decided in Perth that, for this trip back east, arrangements would be made with the Commonwealth Railways to piggyback my truck over the worst part of the Nullarbor Plain, from Kalgoorlie to Port Augusta. This was a fairly new idea at the time.

All the way to Coolgardie and Kalgoorlie, wherever I stopped, I had the usual curiosity. 'Where can I buy one of those tin sheds?' Bloody hell. Instead of going unnoticed I was like a travelling circus, attracting people whenever I stopped. It felt as if I had a neon sign blinking on and off on top of the cabin saying, 'Look at me . . . look at me!'

In Coolgardie a couple of kids were playing around, jumping on and off the trailer behind the shed. When I shooed them off they yelled at me, 'We weren't doing nothing to your old truck . . . what are you got in there, gold or sumpthin?'

One farmer was even up on top trying to open the doors before I saw him.

'Get down off there!' I yelled at him. 'Piss off!'

Don't think he didn't give me a mouthful of abuse.

I don't think I would make a very good undercover man, somehow. It was actually a relief to drive up on the flat-top rail carriage and watch the truck get tied down.

'Well, if anything happens to it now,' I thought, 'it's not my fault. It's the railway's responsibility till Port Augusta.'

Nothing happened to it.

As soon as I unloaded her at Port Augusta I took off east, having decided to go through the back roads to Kapunda and Murray Bridge and then through the 100 miles of Little Desert to Bordertown.

At about 2 a.m. I decided to stop and check my tyres. I was getting sleepy anyway and Tintinara, a little hamlet out in the middle of nowhere, was coming up soon. I pulled over onto a wide gravel section under the one light outside the pub but well off the road. I turned off the motor and jumped to the ground.

Just as my feet hit the ground there was a deafening explosion and I was peppered with what felt like shotgun pellets from my head to my feet. My left ear stung like crazy and I could feel blood dripping onto my neck. I immediately fell to the ground and lay perfectly still, wondering if I had been shot and, if so, why? Was it hijackers finally come for the silver ingots?

Why had they waited so long? I wondered.

Then I realised that my guns were in the cabin, and my back and legs were stinging like mad.

Should I make a run for it?

Where do I make for? The cabin and my pistol? Or just out into the darkness?

All this raced through my mind at a thousand miles an hour, but then something else intruded to push those thoughts away.

What was that smell? That smell like hot rubber?

I knew that smell.

I carefully looked under my left arm, without moving my head too much in case I was shot again.

I could see heat fumes coming off the inside tyre and I could also see that it had blown a hole in itself right at the base where it made contact with the road. The tyre was obviously overheated and damaged and it had burst when I stopped the truck and the dead weight rested on the tyre. The loose blue metal gravel had sprayed all over me.

I slowly sat up and rested my arms on my knees. I gave a long sigh, closed my eyes for a brief second and once again waited for my heart rate to drop back to normal. I'd been too long living on my nerves this trip and I just wanted to be in Melbourne sometime the next day and get it over with, but I was so tired.

As I changed the wheel I kept muttering to myself, 'Never again. Cars, whale oil, anything, but bugger the mint and their silver bullion. Go through this again . . . never!'

Tired as I was I pressed on, but by about 4 a.m. I knew I had to have a nap. As I drove through the black night it seemed that a man on a bicycle was pedalling hard to keep in front of me and then, suddenly, he would disappear under the front of the truck and I would jerk awake.

That was when it was time to stop.

Along this section of road there were a few railway crossings where the road turned sharply across the rail track and then turned sharply again to continue parallel to the rail line.

All vehicles had to slow down to nearly walking pace to manoeuvre through these S-bends and it was safe to park next to the fence in the grass after crossing the line. That way you avoided being run into by speeding and sleepy drivers.

I pulled in next to the fence, switched off, put my head on my pillow on the steering wheel and 'zap', I was gone . . . asleep.

Sometime later I was disturbed by something. Without lifting my head I opened my eyes slowly and looked out into the darkness through the lower front windscreen. I could see two little round lights in the sky moving across my vision. Without moving my head, my eyes followed these two lights that were coming closer to me in a sort of roundabout way. There also seemed to be a sort of vibration in the air. What was it?

The lights appeared to be flying low in the sky . . . like a space ship . . . . A space ship? . . . A SPACE SHIP!

My next thought was that maybe they wanted silver bullion to melt down for something important to them.

I lifted my head and stared . . . they were definitely coming closer. And I could hear a booming noise.

I jumped up and grabbed the Winchester rifle. I opened the door and jumped to the ground, at the same time levering a bullet into the breach and automatically pushing the safety catch. I had no idea what on earth I was going to do, but I was going to do something.

Then, as I swung around for another look, I realised that the deep booming noise had now become a loud throb! It was not a space ship but a diesel train approaching down the track towards me. The bright headlights swung around onto me as the train straightened for its run through the crossing only a couple of feet away.

I hadn't realised that I had been holding my breath. I let out a huge sigh of relief and leaned the rifle against the bumper bar of the truck.

The booming became louder and louder and the intense white light filled my whole vision; I felt like a rabbit in a spot-light. My heart skipped a beat as, for a horrible second or two, I thought, 'Did I park on the crossing? I know I was sleepy, could I have rolled onto the rails in my sleep? Where are the rails?'

I started to run around the truck, bent over with my eyes glued to the ground looking for the rails. As I reached the fence side of the truck there was an almighty roar and the double-engine diesel goods train thundered by a few feet away inside the fence. It was so close I could nearly touch it, the round portholes of the engine throwing a bright glow over me.

I slithered to the ground and sat there, completely done in. It was only then that I started to laugh. I laughed and laughed, probably hysterically. Imagine being so stupid as to think I could park on a railway line.

Next day, as I was driving into Melbourne, I swore I would never tell anyone about my 'space ship' experience.

•

I duly rang the mint number and arrived on time. It was almost the same as in Perth. There were grey dustcoats again, but more of them this time. Again they stopped traffic with hands in pockets and I reversed into an inner courtyard. The seal was checked and broken open, the doors were opened and the ingots all unloaded. No problem.

As the last one was handed down, the foreman ordered that six ingots be loaded into their little black unmarked panel van. Two armed guards were to go with it to Dandenong. That struck me as very funny. I had carried over ten times that amount 2000 miles from one side of Australia to the other and no one was at all interested in what might have happened to me.

I shook my head and laughed and said I was off and we went through the rigmarole of stopping all traffic both ways again for quite a distance from the gate. I felt very important as I drove out of the Melbourne Mint, aware of the stares from all the passengers on the stationary trams. I just couldn't help myself, I just had to give a couple of blasts on the air-horn and I smiled as the sound echoed around the city buildings and all the tram passengers flinched.

At Port Melbourne they were curious about me bringing an empty container all the way across Australia from Perth. I told them I'd had it filled with silver bullion on a very secret 'hush-hush' job for the Melbourne Mint.

'What a load of bullshit, you cheeky young bastard!' they said. 'Piss off!'

I went straight to the Waterside Hotel . . . and got drunk.

Writing this is the first time I have ever told this story to anybody. Don't bother telling anybody else, though, they won't believe you either.

It's true. I did carry the first overland load of silver bullion from Perth to Melbourne and I have been told that only two or three loads were ever sent that way.

The adventures and misadventures that happened on that trip were mostly due to lack of sleep and extreme nervousness. It was all in my mind, but it was real to me.

In 2004 I spoke to Perth Mint historian Anthea Harris, who checked all the old files and archives and verified the year and value of the consignment. It was something not even she was aware of, and it had all happened just on 50 years before.

THE BIG LOAD

FRANK DANIEL

In 1968 I was transporting grain from the Riverina district into Sydney via the Hume Highway. The most popular meal stop on the highway at that time was Bimbo's Roadhouse at Bargo, midway between Mittagong and Campbelltown.

I was having breakfast at Bimbo's one morning with another truck driver, a good mate of mine, when I related a story I'd read in the *Daily Telegraph* a few days before.

The story was about the manufacture of a very large bank-vault door by an engineering firm in Newtown. This door was so large that, when finished, it posed a problem in transferring it from the workshop to the semi-trailer, which was waiting to carry it to a new bank building in the city. A Coles Crane was brought in to lift the heavy door and that's when the trouble started. The crane wouldn't fit through the factory door and, to make matters worse, the vault door, inside the factory, was larger than the factory entrance. This didn't pose a problem for the engineers. They simply removed the front wall of the corrugated-iron building and a portion of the gabled roof and one of the roof trusses. This enabled the crane driver to make a direct lift from above the workshop; a few minor adjustments and the door was lifted skyward out of the shed and slewed onto the waiting truck and trailer.

My mate didn't appear to have much faith in my story and the harder I tried to convince him that I wasn't telling him a yarn, the less he believed me.

I told him that there was an actual photograph in the paper, and that I would prove it to him. I burrowed through a pile of old newspapers in the dining room, but blow me down, there was not a single copy of that particular issue of the *Tele* to win my argument.

Three or four days later I was having a meal at Bimbo's when my mate walked in and joined me at the table.

'I saw the biggest load that I've ever seen in my life yesterday,' he began. 'It was massive. 'There was two big fat coppers driving two of them new Mini Cooper S pursuit cars, one on each side of the centre line, with lights flashing on the roof of each car and their hazard lights winking and blinking. Coming behind them,' he went on, 'was a bloody great big Brambles Mack R-700 carrying a 15-tonne concrete block of ballast. It had a stiff-arm hooked to the bullbar of another big Bull-dog Mack, which was hooked up to a four-axle dolly which in turn was towing an eight-axle wide-spread low-loader.'

I was more than impressed.

He went on. 'Another whopping great Mack R-700 with a 15-tonne block of ballast was coming behind with a similar stiff-arm set-up and was pushing as hard as it could to help the two prime movers up the front. On each side of this big turnout were three more motorcycle cops with lights flashing and keeping the traffic at a safe distance off the road.'

This yarn was getting the better of me as he continued. 'Now! Coming up behind this whole shebang was two more big fat coppers in Mini Coopers, with lights flashing, one each side of the centre line.' Here he paused for a few seconds and then said, 'It was the biggest load I ever saw in my life!'

I was amazed. It didn't take me too long to bite!

'What were they carrying on the low-loader?'

He gave me a good hard look and replied slowly, 'The combination for that safe you saw the other day!'

MACK MAKE 'EM TOUGH

KINGSLEY FOREMAN

Here's an example of how tough US-made trucks are.

The truck was a Mack Superliner that Richmond Heavy Towing had bought second-hand in the late 1970s, just to do jobs repossessing trailers for our regular customers.

The very first day it was in service, before we'd had time to check out the new purchase properly, I had to do a job repossessing a trailer for one of our regular clients. When I got to the address I found the trailer easily enough, but it was loaded with old cars that had been flattened and were ready to go to the scrap dealer. The repossession agent was with me and he made a few calls and arranged for me to drive down to the scrap dealer and unload the trailer before we impounded it. So off I went, down to the scrap dealer, at Gillman near Port Adelaide.

I arrived at Gillman and drove onto the weighbridge. They worked out how much scrap there was and I drove over to their magnetic crane, where they unloaded the crushed cars from the trailer.

I left the scrap dealer and was heading back to our holding yard at Richmond with the trailer when the warning bell on the Mack started to ring like crazy. The water temperature gauge was reading 220 degrees Fahrenheit, so I drove into the yard and left the Mack to cool down.

I went straight to the boss and said, 'Bob, you'd better look at the Mack, it's overheating.'

'No worries,' Bob said. 'I'll take care of it.' Then he added, 'Oh, now you're back there's a job for you in one of the tilt-trays. Can you do a car tow?'

I went off to do the car tow and later that afternoon, as it was getting dark, PJ called me up to the phone room as he often did and said, 'Got a job for you.'

There had been a truck accident out near Lameroo, a small town 240 miles east of Adelaide. A tractor-trailer truck had been involved in a head-on accident with a car. Luckily it didn't go over on its side, but the turntable had been ripped off the tractor and PJ wanted me to take the Mack to bring back the trailer while another driver, Ron, would take the firm's Kenworth tow truck to bring back the prime mover.

'Did the boss fix the Mack?' I asked PJ.

'He had a good look at it and couldn't find anything wrong with it,' PJ replied. 'He said it must be just a faulty sensor. I'm sorry but you'll just have to put up with it until this job is finished.'

So I followed Ron, who was driving the Kenworth, all the way to Lameroo with the warning bell ringing in my ears. When we got to the accident scene the truck was on its wheels;

the trailer was a stainless-steel milk tanker. Before we'd arrived they'd drained all the milk out onto the ground. One of the air couplings was broken off, so I could get air in to release the brakes but I couldn't use them. I would have to haul it back without brakes. So, while Ron hooked up the prime mover, I grabbed a big hammer and gave the king-pin on the trailer a good hit to make sure that it was OK to use.

That was all OK, but we were then told that it was not going back to Adelaide at all. It was now going straight to Royan's Truck Repairs in Melbourne.

When you drive tow trucks you never know what you will be doing next. Now, instead of driving 240 miles back home to Adelaide, we had to go over 500 miles further away from home to Melbourne.

When I'd dealt with the trailer I took a look at the truck I was driving and saw that the Mack had steam spurting out of the radiator cap! It appeared that the boss had been wrong about the problem being a faulty gauge. So, there we were—240 miles from Adelaide and over 500 miles to go—and my truck was spurting steam out of the radiator! Nothing for it but to let it cool down while we went to the local roadhouse about 5 miles away to have a feed.

When we got back to the Mack, Ron and I went all over it looking for the cause of the problem. Eventually we found the culprit. There was a tiny hole in the hose between the heads. We used a piece of hose from the wreck that Ron was towing to fix it. It was a simple job and soon we were ready to roll on to Melbourne.

I had driven that Mack with no water for 240 miles. It didn't crack the head and it ran like a dream the whole way with the warning bell screaming. Now, that's what I call a tough truck!

It ran like a dream all the way to Melbourne, too. But it had water in the radiator for that trip.

YOU AIN'T GOT NO PIGS

FRANK DANIEL

In 1975 I had a bit of a spell from the trucking game and, having just completed a three-month-long droving trip with my mate Slatter, we found ourselves working as builders' labourers in my hometown of Canowindra. We were working for a couple of local contractors and our main task was digging the foundations for houses, laying reinforcement mesh, mixing cement and general buggering about.

We were digging the foundations for a new residence in Charlotte Street one day when we were approached by a well-known character and former local footballer of renown, Ned Carroll. Ned was a mate of ours and a beaut sort of a bloke who spent all his life doing good turns for others and expecting little if anything in return. A very charitable bloke was Ned, but this day he wanted a favour.

Ned had a dozen large white sows that he wanted delivered to the local market from his farm, 'Gunnadoo', there and then! Straight away! That day with no delay! He'd forgotten to order a carrier to do the job and was now in a bit of a pickle, which was typical of Ned.

My motto was 'ever-ready' and I saw no reason why I couldn't help him out. It was only a 'five-minute job', as Ned put it, which meant it shouldn't take more than an hour or so at the most.

After minimal consultation with Slatter, we decided that he could carry on digging the trench and I could go and help Ned. If our boss asked where I was, Slatter would explain.

I owned a Ford F-350 truck with a horse float still under construction on the back. The float was almost complete and had been for the last two years at least, but lacked a full-width back door. This truck had been used for carting my horses around the rodeo circuit for a number of years and for hauling horses to and from various saleyards for Billy O'Connor.

As I mentioned, there was no door on the back of the float and you might keep this in mind, but don't get too far ahead of me!

I made my way out to 'Gunnadoo', and Ned and I loaded the pigs without too much trouble. Pigs can be hard to load onto trucks at times, but everything went along without a hitch.

How did we keep them in the back, I can hear you asking, without a door? I asked Ned the same question.

'Not a problem,' was what Ned always used to say, and today was no different.

We found some old reo mesh, which just so happened to be the right width to close in the tail of the float. It was just the right height too, so we wired it to every vantage point we could find, leaving about 18 inches of floor space to the rear. It was there that we sat my five-year-old German shepherd, Quinn.

'That'll fix 'em,' said Ned. 'You can only do the best you can with the tools you've got!'

He was happy, I was happy, the dog was happy and even the pigs looked content, so off to the saleyards we went.

Not wanting to upset my precious load, I proceeded with great caution down the deeply eroded driveway, straddling the deepest gutters to the best of my ability, then out through the deep drain at the front gate and on to the road.

'Not a problem!'

'Gunnadoo' is about a mile north of town and the saleyards were on the western side, a journey of some 2 miles at best. It was a very easy trip down through the town and I drove steadily, taking extra good care of my load. I knew Quinn would bluff them if they moved in his direction and I didn't want to put any pressure on the 'back gate'. I drove extra slowly and cautiously, so I reckoned we were all right.

The general procedure when wanting to unload at the agent's yards was to drive into the laneway and park behind the truck, or trucks, lined up for delivery and wait your turn. As each truck unloaded at the ramp and moved off, another took its place and we all moved up. As we waited for each truck to unload I was yarning to a few of the stockmen who worked for the local agent, discussing the price of pigs and so on, which was something I knew nothing about.

Soon it was my turn. The truck before me was moving out from the unloading ramp when a vehicle driven by an old bloke named Tony Dunmore entered the lane. Tony drove round my old jigger and proceeded to reverse into the ramp. I didn't know what to think about this; it wasn't like Tony to push in and I had to get back to Slatter and the building site as soon as possible.

I said to one of the yardmen, Old Mick, 'Hey, I thought it was my turn!'

'No worries, son,' said the bloke, 'just back in here to this low gate and you can let your pigs jump down. It won't hurt them and the truck will be much lower with its back wheels parked in the drain along the fence.'

That suited me, so I backed the old Ford into the gateway as directed.

As soon as I got down from the cabin I was aware that Tony Dunmore was moving towards me and I could see the confusion and disbelief on his face. He started apologising profusely for 'rounding me up'.

'Sorry, Frank,' he said. 'I didn't think you had any pigs. I couldn't see any as I passed you, sorry.'

Old Mick the yardman also had a funny look on his face. What was going on? They had me beat. I couldn't figure them out at all, so I moved around to the back of my vehicle.

When I looked inside the rear of the truck, all I had left was some bent-up reo mesh, a German shepherd dog with a blank look on his face and a lot of pig shit.

As Tony Dunmore put it, 'You ain't got no pigs, mate!'

Well, we all shared in the joke and had a good laugh at my expense, but I didn't hang around long to be laughed at. I bolted. I made a hasty retreat, backtracking to 'Gunnadoo' the way I had come, vainly searching for stray pigs along the way and sighting none.

Back at the farm, Ned was waiting, unfazed . . . and so were the pigs.

Ned just said, 'They all fell out at the gate when you were crossing the gutter, and they all ran home and back into the shed. I didn't even have to round them up! They must like it here!'

This yarn is still worth a good laugh in Canowindra. I'm still not sure how such a thing could happen.

It must have been the dog's fault!

DONE CARTIN'

FRANK DANIEL

This poem was written when Frank Daniel Transport closed, after 35 years' trucking, in 1998.

Tall tales of Grandpa hauling wool to Sydney far away,
Sparked adventure in my soul, I'd follow him some day.
Seeking dim horizons through the glimmering distant sheen,
Australia was the landscape, with me part of the scene.

Rear-view mirrors hold fond memories of places I have been;
The vastness of this country: hills and deserts in between.
Seasons came and seasons went, like the good folk that I met;
A million miles by thirty—thirst for a million yet.

Friends were there to meet me as I drove from state to state,
There wasn't any a town in which I didn't have a mate.
Blokes who told me stories of their histories wide and vast,
Swapping tale for tale in gratitude for the keeping of the past.

I'll miss the whining tyres; good friends along the road,
The scheduled life recorded in my log books, load by load.
Over-night between the cities, blaring lights across the plains,
Battling with the elements, the *'droughts and flooding rains'*.

Hassles with the highway cops and blueys in the mail.
'Scalies' from the RTA checking weights on measured scale.
The drovers with their hungry mobs, like visions from the past,
The waving arms of children hoping for an air-horn blast.

Times were good, times were hard; time never once stood still,
Fortunes came and fortunes went, all part of life's great thrill.
But now the years have slowed the urge to carry on much more,
The spell I've earned is mine to keep, and easy to endure.

My spirit of adventure says there are greener pastures still,
The banks have got their money back: I'll seek another thrill.
The time has come to spread my wings; no grief is there in
     parting,
I've no complaints, I've done my bit, I'm finished with the
     carting.

THIS TRUCKING LIFE

ROD HANNIFEY

Years ago interstate trucking was seen as an exotic and exciting profession by those for whom a long trip was an adventure or a holiday. In other words, it was wildly over-romanticised.

In those days, when life was simpler and fewer Australians travelled, truckies were seen as men who saw the country and lived a freewheeling lifestyle. Just imagine being your own boss and king of the road!

The truth, of course, is that a truckie's life was never that good. Many jobs look romantic and exciting from the outside. People who said we were our own bosses never knew the reality. And while it's easy to say we got to see a lot of the country, what we actually got to see was a lot of Australia's roads and we did it alone, spending a lot of time away from our families in the process, and it is still the same today.

We live in a mobile space that is office, kitchen and bedroom all rolled into one and that bedroom space is often 1 metre by 2 or less; the entire space is only a few square metres.

At least we don't have to travel far to work. On the other hand, we never stop commuting, doing thousands of kilometres to and from home every week.

I've been doing interstate in B-doubles, 25 metres long and averaging about 62 tonnes, for the last thirteen years, travelling around 2.5 million kilometres along the eastern seaboard between Melbourne and Mackay. In that time I've also done three trips to Perth, one up to Townsville and one to Darwin. On the Darwin trip I was pulling triples, three trailers, 53 metres long and over 110 tonnes gross weight.

Few nations in the world have these types of vehicles on their roads in the numbers that we do here in Australia, and yet there are hardly any Australians who properly understand the size and weight of these vehicles. Australian drivers are not taught to respect them and share the road with trucks. This is a serious flaw in our driver education schemes. While it is true that not all truckies are perfect, statistics indicate that more than 80 per cent of fatalities between cars and trucks result from the car driver being at fault.

The media are much more inclined to report tales of bad behaviour on the part of truck drivers, especially following a fatal crash—the truckie is often purported to be the one at fault.

Australian car drivers really do need more understanding and education about sharing the road with these larger vehicles. Better education would go a long way towards making our roads safer for all Australians, motorists and truckies alike.

It can be a lonely life for truckie wives and partners as well. They spend a lot of time hoping their partners are safe on the road. They also end up looking after the family pretty much on their own. Imagine being a truckie's wife, with your husband regularly away from home and, more often than not, far away. Not only are truckies away from home most nights, they are so far away that they are unable to come home on short notice in an emergency, be it real or imagined.

Even truckies who get home regularly find it hard to have a normal marriage or relationship. Too often when the truckie does get home, he is so tired all he needs is to recover to be ready to go and do it all again, in order to pay the bills and feed the family he so rarely has time with. It sometimes seems that every second truckie I talk to has had a relationship breakdown and has consequently become estranged from one long-term partner or more. Often these relationship breakdowns involve kids and mostly they are caused by the pressures of the job and the lifestyle.

Truckies are entrusted with a truck and trailer combination worth three-quarters of a million dollars or more and could be carrying a load worth that much or more again. They travel from one end of this large country to the other on less than perfect roads with insufficient, underdeveloped rest areas, which mostly have little or no shade and a few primitive toilets.

John Williamson's song 'The Truckie's Wife' has some lines that ring true. He says the truckie is often 'like an uncle who comes home with ice creams and toys' rather than a father.

My wife has put up with my lifestyle doing interstate hauls for thirteen years. Often I will go to work saying I should be home tomorrow, then later that day I'll call her to say I won't be home for a week as I'm off to Sydney and then on to Melbourne, or across to Perth, or somewhere other than home. My children often ask if I'll be home next Thursday or Friday for a school event or a birthday and all I can say is, 'I don't know where I will be tomorrow, let alone in three or four days' time or next week. Sorry, kids, but I will try.'

It hits home every time you miss one of those events. Sure, there are the odd occasions when other dads are at work and you can be the lone dad at a school event, but it's not often . . . and it isn't the same.

I'm not happy about the fact that my wife sometimes does not really want me in 'her' bed, when irregular early-morning starts and late-night finishes mean I disrupt the family's sleep. When I come home it seems that, by trying to be a good husband and father, I am trying to change all her schedules and interfere with how she looks after the kids. It seems I can't win on the domestic front. If I try to help or get involved I upset the routines, and yet if I don't try to help I am not playing my part in the children's lives.

I've learned to be very cautious about saying I'll be home for a school event or something else because I know how often I end up being redirected, or experiencing some sort of delay or breakdown. Even worse than not being there is promising to be there and then being delayed for any one of myriad reasons and arriving home two days later to face a disappointed child. Sometimes absence is the lesser of two evils; disappointment *and* absence being even worse.

No job is perfect. I sometimes get the impression that my wife thinks I have a good time chatting on the UHF radio and travelling to different places. The reality, of course, is that I have a difficult and demanding job and have to carry out my work efficiently and safely and comply with laws made by people who mostly sleep in their own beds and fly when they travel, or have someone drive them on the good roads between major cities.

Airline pilots are very respected and admired and they deserve all the credit and pay they get, but just consider the conditions and assistance they have as they travel the highways in the sky: a co-pilot, a navigator, cabin crew to make coffee, perfectly controlled and monitored runways. The other 'drivers' with whom they share the highways in the sky are all highly trained and monitored. We have none of that support and share the road with many who are unskilled and poorly trained but who still use the roads.

It has been said that the Australian economy now rides on the back of a prime mover. Yet Australia's truckies are not respected for the job they do or the time they spend away from their families and on the road so that you can have your food, fuel, furniture and every other thing you can see or touch. A truck delivers all these things at some time or place that suits a consumer or manufacturer or supplier. Many items may have been on a number of trucks to reach you.

I may not spend as much time as I'd like to with my wife and family but they are special and precious, and so are yours. So, please drive safely, respect the size and weight of large trucks and give us a wave occasionally. Truckies are human too.

A BRIEF HISTORY OF AUSTRALIAN ROAD TRANSPORT

LIZ MARTIN AND JIM HAYNES

Before the coming of the British in 1788, there was no form of transport in Australia except for what the British invaders called 'shanks's pony'.

In the colonial days the horse played an important role in transport as well as recreation and sport. Horseback, buggies, carriages and, later, coaches provided the main means of travel for passengers, while horses, bullocks and then camels provided the main means of hauling goods around the various colonies.

All inter-colonial travel was by coastal shipping, and inland river systems had paddleboats to carry both passengers and freight around sections of the outback.

Apart from horse-drawn vehicles and teamsters the only other forms of road transport in the late nineteenth century were the government-operated trains, trams and trolley buses, originally horse-drawn, then electric- and petrol-powered, and the humble bicycle and wheelbarrow.

The wheelbarrow was commonly used in the outback, where travellers, diggers and swaggies used them to push their life possessions in front of them as they trekked Australia in search of a new life. The wheelbarrow, in fact, was such a common mode of long-distance travel that for many years after the introduction of the stagecoach many Aborigines called any vehicle with wheels on it a 'wheelbarrow'.

The velocipede bicycle first appeared in Australia in October 1846, on the streets of Melbourne. The pennyfarthing appeared in Melbourne in 1875 where, three years later, Australia's first bicycle club was formed.

By the end of the century, the bicycle had became a common sight on the streets of most major Australian cities. Socialites and the well-to-do rode through parklands and along roadsides, much to the amusement of the general public.

The first bicycles in Australia had cumbersome wooden wheels and iron tyres. Initially the bicycle was used for social-ising and as a status symbol by professionals, but its many advantages over the horse were soon exploited for local mail deliveries and small parcel freight. This was particularly true in the petrol-rationing periods of both world wars when many people opted for the bicycle rather than horse-drawn wagons. A man with a bicycle was considered a much better employ-ment prospect when jobs were hard to come by. The added advantages of the bicycle were that it did not need petrol and it did not need to be stabled, groomed and fed. For those who could afford the initial outlay for the purchase of a bicycle, the quality of life was immediately improved.

The bicycle soon became a popular mode of transport in the bush. It was used to open up the lines of communication in remote settlements all over Australia, particularly in the rich goldfields of Western Australia.

Prior to the bicycle, Aboriginal runners carried messages between the settlements and cattle stations. The Aborigines referred to the letters as 'paper talk' or 'paper yabber'.

The early rural cyclist met with many problems. He had often to travel alongside the routes and roadways rather than on them because the ruts from bullock and horses' hooves made the roads impassable for cyclists.

Cyclists followed the railway lines, travelling on the ballast, or used the same outback routes as the camel trains, which travelled in single file and thus compacted the ground and pushed away loose stones. Teamsters and motor lorries could not use the narrow, winding tracks. The pads remained firm even in flooded conditions and many shearers, clergymen, fence patrols and kangaroo shooters used them to ride their bicycles through camel country. The camels, however, were not too impressed with the arrival of the bicycle and often took fright if an unexpected bicycle appeared from behind.

The first specially built cycle path in Australia was between Mulline and Menzies in Western Australia in 1898, and in 1899 the Yalgoo Roads Board tried to implement a five-shilling annual road tax on bicycle owners who used the route. The road tax proposal was met with much opposition from bicycle owners, who claimed that they did not cause as much road damage as the teamsters, who paid ten shillings a year. When we look at the taxation problems facing the transport industry today we realise that, while nothing stays exactly the same, very little changes.

The bicycle was also used extensively by shearers, who wanted to travel as quickly as possible from job to job in the shearing season without the problems of feeding and looking after a horse. The Australian shearer was paid per sheep shorn and timing was crucial.

By the 1890s, 200,000 Australians were riding bicycles.

The bicycle's decline began soon after the end of World War I. By then Australia was a relatively affluent country and some of her citizens could afford the luxury of the more comfortable horseless carriage.

At first, motorised transport was more of a novelty than a realistic method of transport. The Americans and Europeans were developing the petrol engine, while the British developed steam-driven vehicles. The first stationary steam engine arrived in Australia in 1813 and was used to power a flour mill in Sydney. The first railways were developed, sadly on different gauges in various colonies, in the 1850s.

Australia's first motorcycle was built by H. Knight-Heaton in 1893 and introduced to Australia in April 1896. A crowd of over 5000 people jammed George Street in Sydney to see a demonstration of a motorcycle powered by an Australian-built 3-hp (2.2-kW) internal combustion engine, which travelled at speeds of up to 40 miles (about 65 kilometres) per hour.

This motorcycle was probably Australia's first petrol-engined vehicle. The motorcycle gained much popularity with the public and for speedy transport and delivery services. While large companies used T Model Fords for their deliveries, smaller companies delivered their wares from box-type sidecars built onto the sides of motorbikes.

There is little information available on the first motor car to arrive in Australia. Some believe it was a 4.6-hp (3.4-kW) Benz brought to Melbourne in 1896 by the Tarrant Motor Company, while others claim it was a Bellee-London powered tricycle brought to Perth by French engineer A.G. Bargligi in 1898.

The very first commercial vehicle to land in Australia was a steam-powered French Chaboche imported by Sydney cycle dealer Mark Foy in 1902. At this time, the number of vehicle registrations in Australia numbered just over twenty.

Unfortunately, no one in Australia had any idea of how to maintain this vehicle and it had a very short life. However, the concept of motorised transport was growing and the first 'car yard' in Australia was established in 1903 when Duncan and Fraser established an Oldsmobile dealership in Adelaide.

In 1910 there were only 5000 vehicles in Australia. By 1923 Australia was ranked the sixth in the world for numbers of motor vehicles registered and by 1929 there were 475,000 cars, 88,000 motorbikes and around about 77,000 commercial vehicles and motor trucks.

COMMERCIAL ROAD TRANSPORT

As early as the 1860s Australians were looking for mechanical road transport suitable for hauling large loads of produce, wool and minerals from remote sites to railheads and ports. The bullock and horse teams served well enough if the weather was fine and the roads passable, but they were very slow and unreliable when it came to flooded rivers, steep mountain climbs or hundreds of kilometres of waterless desert. While the bullock was happy to graze, he needed regular watering.

In 1863 the Yudnamutana Mining Company in the Flinders Ranges of South Australia imported several steam traction engines, each hauling six wagons, to carry ore to Port Augusta and return with supplies.

The 'roadtrains' proved awkward and could not cope with the primitive road conditions in South Australia at the time. They were eventually retired and sold off as scrap metal and the idea of the roadtrain faded into obscurity for another 50 years.

In 1910 another South Australian, John Napier, imported a Daimler-Renard roadtrain to work in the Maree and Oodnadatta regions. This roadtrain was unique in that each of its trailers featured drive wheels. The central axle on each trailer was driven by a powered prop shaft in the prime mover which transferred power trailer by trailer to the last axle.

Another roadtrain was imported by Victorian engineer Ralph Falkiner in 1914. This electric roadtrain was 90 metres long, hauled ten trailers and weighed over 43 tonnes. The prime mover was powered by two 120-hp (89-kW) Austro-Daimler engines driving a dynamo, which in turn powered the electric motors on every axle on the unit. A total of 22 small 12.5-hp (9.3-kW) electric motors were fitted to the roadtrain, two under each trailer.

In effect, this massive unit was a 44-wheel drive. The prime mover did not pull the trailers; it merely controlled the direction and set the course for the trailers to follow while the engine car steered the whole train.

It was loaded with 60 tonnes of freight headed for a retailer in Wagga Wagga. As fate would have it, a crankshaft snapped and the freight had to be forwarded by rail. The electric roadtrain did several more trips, slightly more successfully, before it ended its days hauling gravel at Albion Quarries. It was finally put to rest in a storage shed in South Melbourne, where it was unfortunately destroyed by fire.

The Holt Manufacturing Company of California, forerunner of today's giant Caterpillar organisation, also developed a roadtrain, which was trialled in New South Wales in 1914. It managed to complete three runs from Bourke to Kallara Station, covering a distance of 182 kilometres in less than five days.

Australia also produced some of its own roadtrains. The Caldwell-Vale petrol-engined giants were produced from 1910 to 1914. Like others of the day, these were expensive to operate and had problems over rugged terrain, and their success was relatively short-lived. The Caldwell-Vale team produced about 50 agricultural and road tractors in its fifteen years of operation.

With World War I imminent, the development of the road-train took a back seat as governments and manufacturers turned their attentions to the war effort and the construction of military vehicles.

•

The first trucks in Australia were little more than motor cars with platforms sticking out behind them adapted from an assortment of chassis, engines and automobiles imported from other countries.

Semi-trailers first came into being in the early 1920s, and were mainly crude, unbraked homemade wooden-framed platforms hauled behind trucks. Some were modified bullock drays or wagons and even had the original wooden wheels.

Some of the first known examples were run by Bill Johns, who operated an A Model Ford between Albany and Perth on the west coast, and by brothers Les and Joe Kempton in Carnarvon, Western Australia, who used an AEC prime mover to haul a wooden-framed trailer. Another early wooden-framed model, claimed to be the first in Australia, was built by Charles Wilson of Daysdale, New South Wales.

One of the first commercial vehicles imported in any number was the T Model Ford, the 'Tin Lizzie'. Its 20-hp (15-kW) side-valve engine, two-speed planetary gears and high ground clearance made it the ideal choice for many outback applications and it certainly played a major part in popularising motor transport in Australia.

Ford first appeared in Australia in 1909 and by 1915 they were importing just under 2000 vehicles a month into the country. These vehicles arrived in passenger car or chassis-only form and local manufacturers and distributors added tray tops and bodies, in which form they were used for all sorts of passenger, commercial and rural operations. One of the first imported police cars, a T Model Ford, began service in Perth in 1911.

In 1924 Ford opened its Australian plant in Geelong and the first Australian-built Model T rolled off the production line.

By 1910 the motorised lorry or truck was appearing in the bush. Local operators had very little driving skill or mechanical knowledge and it was not until after World War I, when many ex-servicemen returned to Australia with newly acquired driving and maintenance skills, that road transport started to compete effectively with the horse, the rail and the few remaining river traders in Australia.

The growing popularity of motor vehicles caused problems for governments. Legislators introduced laws consistent with those passed by the British government of the day. The Victorian government introduced the Steam Roller and Traction Engine Act, which limited self-propelled vehicles to a speed of 4 miles (about 6 kilometres) per hour and stipulated that all horseless carriages be preceded on public roads by a man carrying a red flag.

W.J. Proctor, general manager of the Dunlop Rubber Company, has the distinction of being the only motorist to be convicted under the Steam Roller and Traction Engine Act, when in 1901 he was charged with frightening a racehorse while driving his De Dion motor car along Remington Street in Melbourne.

By 1906 laws were becoming a little more liberal and the South Australian Motor Vehicles Act of 1906 lifted the speed limit to 15 miles (24 kilometres) per hour, although it imposed many other restrictions. Even when governments realised there was a future in motorised transport, they constantly placed restrictions on the private enterprise sector so that their rail operations would remain viable.

Australia's first Motor Traffic Act was introduced in 1909. Until this time, vehicles were unregistered and no licences were required by drivers. Most states had by that time introduced speed limit legislation. Motorists were often apprehended by law enforcement officers on bicycles and horses if they travelled 'too fast'.

In 1909 R.J. Durance and his wife, Ivy, set up the first Ford agencies in Australia. They sold 1400 T Model Fords in their first year. By 1910 there were over 37,000 motorised trucks, cars and motorcycles registered in Australia, and later there was a huge influx of vehicles as a result of World War I.

While the road transport industry was becoming an established part of the Australian rural lifestyle, most companies operated a myriad of decrepit and crudely modified trucks. Profit margins were too small to allow investment in new vehicles and most financiers scoffed at the idea of lending money to truck purchasers.

In the late 1920s the Tin Lizzie had been joined by America's classic Chevrolet 25 Hundredweight, known locally as the Chev 4 or the 'Grasshopper' because of its semi-elliptical springs. Other motor vehicles such as the Overland Crossley, Morris Commercial and Bean also sold well, but it was the Fords and Chevs that ruled the road, particularly with the arrival of the 1928 A Model Ford and the big Chev 6. At this stage trucks were still fitted with wooden-framed cabins and sheeted with galvanised tin.

The first Mack, an AC model, arrived in Australia in 1919 and was used for bulk haulage by the Vacuum Oil Company in Sydney. The second arrived six weeks later, but it would be another 30 years before Mack would change the course of heavy transport history in Australia.

Australia's first purpose-built furniture removal van was a Mack. The 1924 AB model was put into service in 1928 by Thos Mills and Sons of Rose Bay, Sydney. It was retired 30 years later, having clocked up a million miles (1.6 million kilometres), in 1958.

The end of World War I had marked a turning point for road transport in Australia. Many returned ex-servicemen, who had been trained in heavy duty transport operations while in military service, put their new skills to work by buying army surplus trucks and going into business as carriers.

By the end of 1919, some 7000 trucks were registered Australia wide, with over 2500 of them in New South Wales alone. By 1929 Australia had over 100,000 registered trucks.

American trucks dominated this period. Fords, Dodges and Chevrolets ruled the road. Most trucks were fitted with open-sided cabs, solid tyres, and shift drive with separately mounted crash gearboxes. They had brakes on only two wheels, were barely capable of producing more than 1300 rpm and travelled at a top speed of around 12 miles (19 kilometres) per hour.

A general lack of mechanical knowledge and after-sales service meant that the simpler the engine, the more economical the vehicle would be, especially for outback operators. With fewer working parts to service and replace than the six cylinder, the four cylinder was considered the ultimate for outback trucking conditions.

Solid tyres were often ineffective in the bush, slipping on wet grass and causing traction problems. Tram rails were becoming more common in city and suburban streets and these proved a nightmare for solid-tyred vehicles. If tyres got stuck in the tramlines, the truck had to stay in them until it came to a set of points!

The introduction of pneumatic tyres in 1928 improved things greatly and lifted working speed to around 20 miles (32 kilometres) per hour. In the late 1920s governments introduced legislation penalising drivers of solid-tyred vehicles because of damage caused to road surfaces. If nothing else, the legislation provided the incentive for truck operators to upgrade their vehicles. The pneumatic tyre not only lasted longer, it actually improved fuel consumption because of reduced rolling resistance.

The third axle did not appear until 1923 and one of the first rigid 6 trucks to come to Australia was the British-made Caledon. The term 4x2 means the truck has four wheels, two in the front and two sets of duals in the rear, of which the rear two are driven. In the 6x4 there are two front wheels and four rear dual wheels, of which all four rear wheels are driven. In most instances 'wheel' means two tyres, as in dual tyres.

Australia saw the first of its Albion trucks and buses in the early 1920s. For the next 50 years they gained a reputation for reliability and quality. Albion was taken over by the Leyland Group in 1951, and by 1972 Albion's famous 'Sure as Sunrise' motto was gone and the sunburst logo disappeared under the Leyland marketing umbrella. Republic and Bean trucks also operated in Australia, but were not as common as the Albion.

By the mid-1930s the average size of trucks had increased and 3- to 5-tonners were a common sight. The light American Internationals were making inroads into the heavier freight market. Many operators of Internationals chose to repower their trucks with the reliable and more powerful Gardner diesel engines after World War II. The Gardner was considered to be the 'Rolls-Royce' of diesel engines in those days.

This era also saw the start of full implementation of the registration plate all over Australia. The New South Wales government first introduced porcelain enamel plates for horse-powered cabs, vans and buses as early as 1901, and general motor vehicle plates were first introduced in South Australia in 1906 and were law in Tasmania, Victoria and New South Wales by 1911, but Western Australians did not need plates until 1920.

Registration varied widely from state to state. New South Wales trucks had number plates prefixed with an 'L' (for lorry) up until 1937, South Australia has always used conventional motor vehicle plates on its heavy vehicles, while in Tasmania some vehicles were required to display an additional small plate identifying the vehicle type and use, and trucks and passenger vehicles in Western Australia had the letters HTRE on their plates.

At this time most of Australia's freight, both interstate and international, was carried by shipping lines, with trucks transporting goods from the shipping agents and handling baggage from the British passenger liners.

The Fremantle to Perth run was one of the most competitive and highly sought-after runs in Australia, and the port facilities in Melbourne and Sydney provided lucrative work. In South Australia steam boats and barges still carried freight on the Murray system, but the motor vehicle had mostly taken over from the bullock and camel teams in the more populated areas of the outback.

Things were changing as better trucks became available. Jack Lewis, who hauled building materials from Perth to Wiluna in the 1930s in a Morris 30 Hundredweight, found the going tough once he reached Greenmount Hill, so he would place the hand throttle full on, hop out of the truck to reduce the load and steer the truck while walking alongside.

Bill Roots, another Western Australian haulier, remembered that his truck was so slow and the tyre ruts so deep on the Albany to Esperance road that he used to wedge the hand throttle open and have a sleep. The truck had no option but to continue in the right direction. Bill recalled he only once came across an oncoming vehicle.

While much attention was given to engine technology, fuel consumption and loading capacity, the safety and comfort of the driver were not considered to be a priority at all. The traditional wooden, coach-built cabs were upgraded to steel and the windscreen replaced the canvas shroud wind dodger, but it was usually made of plain flat glass set in a wooden frame.

Side windows, doors and roofs were simply left off once they had shaken off and drivers often sat on wooden crates or kerosene tins, wrapped in an empty wool bale or cut-open tyre tube for protection from the weather. Our earliest trucking pioneers often suffered with sight and hearing problems as a result.

The 1930s saw the introduction of more sophisticated trucks like Diamond Ts and Internationals, which could carry twenty cattle and average 20 miles (32 kilometres) per hour.

The Diamond T first appeared in Australia in 1934. Available in two sizes, the 30 hundredweight with a wheelbase of 135 inches (3.4 metres) and the 2-tonner with a wheelbase of 158 inches (4 metres), and powered by a 27-hp (20-kW), six-cylinder Hercules engine, the Diamond T not only looked good, it functioned effectively.

The first trucks to be assembled in Australia with a high level of Australian content were the Dodge, Fargo and De Soto models manufactured by T.J. Richards and Sons. First established in Adelaide in late 1935, this company, later to become Chrysler Australia, built the first all-Australian truck cab. The Dodge was the best-known and most popular truck in the medium- to heavy-duty range in Australia, with the Dodge Canter and the later Fuso models being used in a wide variety of applications.

WORLD WAR II AND BEYOND

By 1939 there were over half a million cars, trucks and buses on Australian roads, but the onset of World War II effectively cut off the supply of British trucks to Australia. Most vehicles imported from the 1940s onwards were of American or Canadian origin.

Thousands of vehicles and heavy transports arrived in Australia with the US military when Australia became the Allied base for the Pacific War. Civilian vehicles were requisitioned for use in the Australian services. After the attack on Pearl Harbor, the only vehicles that were brought into Australia were on a 'lend lease' arrangement. These were usually the KS5 4-tonne International or the Chevrolet 1500 series 3-tonner.

From 1942 the heavier trucks, like the NR 6x4 Macks and the Diamond T tank transporters, arrived by the thousands, along with the US Army truck of the day, a standard GMC 212 powered by GMC 270-cubic inch (4.4-litre) engines.

The GMC 270 was one of the best engines of its time, capable of developing 106 gross hp (79-kW) at 3000 rpm and 222-lb/ft (300 Nm) torque at 1000. Thousands of such vehicles were purchased by civilian operators at war's end. The Transport Branch of the Munitions Department operated a fleet of 60 Brockway LHDs and, likewise, many of these found their way into civilian life after the war.

Maple Leafs, Ford and Chevrolet Blitzes and GMCs worked in the more populous areas, and the heavier Internationals, Federals, Diamond Ts and NR Macks settled into rugged outback applications. These ex-army vehicles taught Australian operators all about heavier and bigger trucks. The big British

Leylands, Fodens, AECs and Thornycrofts started to make their appearance on the Australian roads once the ex-military American trucks started to wear out.

In time, the Foden would become the undisputed king of the road in Australia, followed closely by Leylands, Super Comets, Super Hippo and Super Beaver models. AEC models, such as the Monarch, Matador, Mammoth and Lynx, and Regal trucks were also very popular and Thornycroft Nubian 6×6 fire engines were stationed at airports and fire stations right across the country.

Despite this British invasion, the Americans retained a foothold in Australia with the Mack, Ford and International ranges. The choice of trucks in Australia was enormous, with operators able to choose between the best of the British and American makes.

The 1950s saw the start of the road transport revolution in Australia. The historic *Hughes and Vale* case of 1954 had relaxed regulations pertaining to interstate travel and the restrictive and confusing laws of the individual states. Of the many thousands of operators who started carrying at the end of World War II, many now had well-established businesses and were a respected part of their local community.

The 1950s also saw the first step towards uniformity, when the Australian Motor Vehicles Standards Committee made recommendations to federal and state governments on standardising vehicle size, axle loads and weights.

The big development, as far as performance was concerned, was the availability of the Fuller Roadranger multi-speed transmission. For the first time, big engines could be kept operating at or near peak power rpm. Another development in the 1950s was the introduction of power steering, which alleviated the difficulty of steering heavy trucks.

A transport revolution in Australia was taking place, and UK and US manufacturers marketed aggressively, quickly adapting their ranges to suit Australian conditions. The Foden range, in particular, bore little resemblance to its British counterparts. The Fodens and Leylands are credited with opening up much of Australia, including the rich mineral resources of Western Australia.

Top of the Leyland range in Australia was the Mastiff 12-tonne, powered by a 180-hp (134-kW) Perkins eight-cylinder diesel engine. Top speed was around 85 kilometres per hour. The Leyland Hippos, Super Hippos and Buffaloes were also very popular trucks, as were the 4-tonne Terriers and the Boxers, Reivers and Super Comets of the small to medium range. One feature of the Leyland range that appealed to larger operators was that the cabs, including instrumentation, were completely interchangeable with all other Leyland models.

The legendary Commer is one of the unsung heroes of the Australian road transport industry. It was such a common sight on Australian roads that it was hardly given a second thought—that is, if it were not for the famous knocking sound that made it stand out from the rest.

The diesel-powered Commer had an unusual engine. It had three cylinders with opposed pistons that made their attachment to the crankshaft more complicated than most engines. The distinct knocking sound that could be heard for miles gave the truck its 'Knocker' nickname. The highways at the time were little more than narrow winding bush tracks, and work in the Australian outback was more arduous than the Commer had been built for. It was renowned for its habit of de-coking, or melting its pistons, as it struggled to complete the task at hand.

Drivers of Commers had to have a fairly extensive mechanical background to keep them going. The Perkins engine was soon the preferred option for power in Commers and the demise of the Commer Knocker in the 1970s marked the end of another era in Australia's road transport history.

In the mid-1950s operators began to look at the more efficient and powerful American Cummins engine. For some time Foden fitted its trucks with a Cummins engine and this combination was popular with heavy vehicle operators.

The big Fodens, fitted with 250-hp (186-kW) Cummins engines, offered a 100-tonne gross weight, which far exceeded anything else available in either the American or British marques. It guaranteed Foden would remain the undisputed king of the heavy hauliers for a while yet.

Smaller operators of the early 1960s began using Dodge and International trucks. The Dodge 760, fitted with a 360-cubic inch (5.9-litre) V8 petrol motor, was a popular vehicle on the eastern seaboard in single-drive, bogie-trailer applications. However, at 4 miles a gallon (70 litres per 100 kilometres) they were uneconomical to operate and were soon discarded with the arrival of diesel engines.

The most common option for a diesel-engined Dodge was the V8 Cummins. Similarly, the smaller International trucks, such as the C-Line 80, were fitted with Cummins diesel engines, although these were generally the smaller six-cylinder 160 Cummins.

As the mid-1950s approached, the Internationals and Macks were gaining a reputation for being faster and more versatile than the British trucks.

By the 1960s, Macks and Internationals were a common sight all around Australia. The classic B Model Mack and the International R190 Series were considered to be the 'milemakers' for the day, and most of Australia's older transport companies owe an important part of their success to these mighty 'big rigs'.

In the more populous states they were competing with Atkinsons, ERFs, Scammells and Mercedes-Benz. In the rugged outback regions of northern Queensland, the northern regions of Western Australia and the Northern Territory, their wide-spread acceptance marked the end of the Foden's dominance.

International K and L series were common on Australian roads, but it was the legendary International R190 Series that would go on to become Australia's most remembered International. The R190s were powered by petrol engines and this gave them the lead in speed, as diesel engines of the day were still slow to power.

The mighty R190 was just as much at home in roadtrain applications on gruelling Northern Territory runs as it was on the Hume Highway in Victoria. One drawback of the R190 was the heat inside the cab; many old-timers still refer to them affectionately as 'hot boxes'. The bigger and more powerful R200 series found its niche in the heavier tipping and quarrying industries.

The International 3070 series, specially designed for long-distance and heavy-haulage applications, was very popular in Australia. Powered by 320-hp (239-kW) Cummins 903 engines, all four models in the series were cab over trucks. The 3070 range featured a flat one-piece windshield and International's simple tilt system for pushing the cab out of the way to get at the engine.

In 1992, International Australia was taken over by European truck builders Iveco, part of the Fiat group. International still hold a large share of the Australian truck market and the new 525-hp (391-kW) Transtar 4700 series is gaining a reputation for handling the tough stuff in rugged applications.

The arrival of the B Model Mack finally established the Mack name as a leader in reliability and good value for money in the toughest conditions Australia had to offer. The B Model was first released in 1953 and by the early 1960s it reigned supreme in the outback. These trucks survived the many hardships of the outback that the British models found difficult. They brought new dimensions of speed, strength, comfort and reliability to the industry.

In the Northern Territory, roadtrain operators were able to double their speed from 27 kilometres per hour to around 55, and in the more populated areas in the southern and eastern states the B Model could pick up 60 tonnes of freight and cross the nation in quicker time than ever before. It was also successful in heavier off-road applications such as livestock and ore haulage.

The B61 was the backbone of Brambles' coal haulage operation and revolutionised heavy transport in Australia.

In 1966 Mack released its ground-breaking Maxidyne engine and Maxitorque transmission. Instead of ten- or fifteen-speed gearboxes the Mack now only required five gears. The R series and the later Superliners are also legends in the world of trucking.

Today, the Mack organisation is so large it churns out around 30,000 trucks every year, and it continues to hold the lion's share of the Australian market when it comes to heavy-duty and off-road applications.

Up until the Volvo takeover of Mack, a Mack truck was usually just that, a Mack. It was Mack from one end to the other, including engine, gearbox, diffs and suspension. Operators today can order a Mack with a different engine, usually a Cummins or Caterpillar. In days gone by it was easy to tell if the Mack was a pedigree by the colour of the dog on the grille. If it was chrome then the engine came from a competitor, but if the bulldog was gold then the truck was powered by a genuine 'pedigree' Mack engine.

The 1960s brought containerisation. This technology allowed cargo to be put into a standard-sized container and then shipped, trucked, railed or air-freighted to any part of the world. It revolutionised the road transport industry and led to new and previously unheard-of efficiency between transport modes.

The mid-1960s saw over 35 independent heavy truck manu-facturers marketing their product in Australia. Today, less than ten of those producers remain active here. This trend started in the late 1950s when the giant Leyland Motors organisation acquired many of its smaller competitors, including Albion, Scammell and AEC. Leyland later added Thornycroft, Guy, Austin and Morris to its list of acquisitions, and changed its name to the British Leyland Motor Corporation in 1968.

Chrysler UK took over Commer and Karrier from the Rootes Group and Seddon had become the largest independent truck manufacturer in Great Britain, having acquired Atkinson in 1971.

The American PACCAR organisation, famous for its Kenworth and Peterbuilt range, moved into the United Kingdom in 1980 and acquired the Foden of Britain company. Volvo bought out the White truck organisation and Mercedes-Benz acquired Freightliner. This European takeover of American marques culminated in 1990 with Renault's outright purchase of Mack in 1990.

Mercedes-Benz first made its appearance in Australia just before the turn of the century with the arrival of the Benz Velo car. From the early 1920s, Mercedes-Benz trucks played an active role in the farming industry and, in 1958, Mercedes-Benz made a serious commitment to this country through the incorporation of Mercedes-Benz Australia. Ever since, the three-pointed star has played a significant role in Aussie road transport.

The 1418 was a very popular truck and, to the amazement of many, built a reputation pulling double roadtrains from Adelaide to Darwin in the 1970s, when the road was dirt from Port Augusta. The dirt road continued to the Northern Territory border and a single lane of dilapidated World War II bitumen track went from there to Darwin. The standard directions on leaving Port Augusta were: 'Follow this road until you come to the next set of traffic lights and turn right'. The next set of lights was, of course, in Darwin, 2720 kilometres up the track.

Mercedes-Benz covers the light truck range right up to roadtrains and specialised off-road and heavy-duty trucks. Over 2000 Unimogs have been supplied to the armed forces since 1982 and most of Australia's public transport authorities use the Mercedes-Benz range of buses and coaches. The company also claims to hold the dominant share of the private bus market in

Australia. Sydney operates the world's largest Mercedes-Benz city bus fleet.

The 1970s probably saw more technological advances and performance improvements than any other period of motorised road transport in Australia, with truck manufacturers looking for the first time at aerodynamics and peak performance of engines. The big Americans such as Mack, Kenworth, Dodge, White and International were all the vogue in the 1960s and 1970s.

Kenworth was a relative latecomer to Australian road transport but soon proved itself well suited to Australian conditions. The first Kenworths arrived in 1962, although it wasn't until 1974 and the birth of the SAR that Kenworth took the lead in the heavy truck market. The 'S' stood for short, and the 'AR' for Australian Right Hand Drive.

The SAR was king of the road on the long hauls for quite a few years. The K120 series of cabovers proved to be popular with Australian operators, as did the W900 series. The SARs were usually fitted with Detroit or Cummins engines, and a fifteen-speed Fuller Roadranger transmission. Kenworth today enjoys a large share of the Australian market, its trucks being used in logging, interstate and roadtrain applications.

Other long-established manufacturers continue to be a part of the Australian scene.

Ford competes successfully in the medium- to heavy-duty truck range. Well-known Territory roadtrain operator Dean McBride operated a fleet of nine Ford LTL roadtrains on the gruelling Alice Springs to Darwin linehaul operation. Each truck hauled three trailers and travelled an average of 300,000 kilometres per annum on a non-stop turnaround of freight from the Alice Springs railhead.

The most familiar Whites to be seen on Australian roads were the long-nosed Road Boss generally powered by a 238-hp (177-kW) Detroit engine and the cabover Road Commander with a 6-71N Detroit engine. First introduced in 1972, the Road Commander, like the Road Boss, soon gained a reputation for reliability and toughness and they were widely used in many applications, although mainly on highway work rather than off-road.

Two trucks less commonly seen in Australia were the Oshkosh and the Fiat. The first Oshkosh arrived here in 1967, a 6×4 powered by a 225-bhp (168-kW) version of the Cat 1673 and fitted with a five-speed Fuller transmission and four-speed auxiliary box. The catchcry at the time was 'Oh My Gosh! It's an Oshkosh!'

The most common Fiats in Australia were the 170.35 powered by a 352-hp (263-kW) V8 engine and the smaller six-cylinder 170.26 model.

The first MAN chassis came to Australia in 1930. Later models were particularly popular in Tasmanian forests, where the freezing temperatures were no worse than the European conditions for which they were built. MAN moved into Australia with a degree of force in 1951, specialising in all-wheel-drive trucks in the medium to heavy range. This was also the year MAN released the world's first V8 diesel, and the trucks soon gained a reputation for being rugged and durable under even the most extreme conditions.

MAN gained much publicity when Danish adventurer Hans Tholstrup crossed Australia from east to west in a six-cylinder

280-hp (209-kW) MAN. The eleven-day trip covered over 6200 kilometres of some of the worst and most isolated country in the world, crossing the Great Victoria, Gibson and Simpson deserts. With a load of two tractors, petrol and food and beer supplies and no back-up vehicle, the MAN handled the trip with no major catastrophes. Tholstrup only had to call in help on one occasion when the truck sank into a deep waterhole at the Warburton Mission.

Scania entered the local truck market with a range of fully built-up vehicles imported from Sweden in 1971, and soon after started to assemble, market and service from its assembly plant near Melbourne. By 1978 the plant was producing 500 trucks a year and the company had a boost when transport tycoon Lindsay Fox, of Linfox, ordered 100 trucks. Scania are a major supplier of trucks to the fuel industry.

Volvo at one stage ranked number one in heavy truck sales in Australia. From the G and F model cabovers to the long-nosed N models, Volvo has always had plenty of dedicated fans in Australia. Initially Volvo concentrated its efforts on the medium truck range, not giving any serious consideration to the smaller or larger ends of the truck market. It wasn't until Lindsay Fox visited Sweden in 1987 and suggested it that Volvo decided to introduce its small F7 model to Australia.

With nearly 2000 trucks in the Linfox fleet, Volvo heeded Fox's advice and two FL6 trucks were sent to work on a trial basis in Linfox's beverage distribution fleet. Linfox subsequently ordered another seven FL6s and Volvo's small truck range has gained much popularity since. At the other end of the scale, the FH16 Globetrotter, released in 1995, is making a name for itself

THE BEST AUSTRALIAN TRUCKING STORIES

among the heaviest trucks on the road in triple configuration roadtrain applications.

Japanese manufacturers are relative newcomers to the Australian road transport scene. Initially memories of World War II meant many people were reluctant to purchase a Japanese vehicle, but eventually the affordability and simplicity of Japanese-made trucks made them an exceptionally attractive option for many small to medium truck buyers.

The reliability of Isuzu trucks was first realised in Australia in 1956 when they were chosen for use at the Australian Antarctic bases. By 1978 Isuzu outsold Bedfords, and today Isuzu operates from its own Australian plant in Dandenong, Victoria. The SBR and JCR models, in the 3- to 7-tonne range, and the medium-sized SPZ440 and VPR 290 are very popular with Australian drivers.

The Nissan UD range was first introduced into Australia in 1973, with the CK range and the CW40, CW45, CW51 models taking the medium truck market by storm in the 1970s and 1980s. The ten thousandth UD was sold in Australia in 1992.

The quality and efficiency of small- to medium-sized Japanese trucks has made them extremely popular. Seven out of every ten vehicles sold in this range in Australia are Japanese.

There has never been a truly Australian truck. The closest thing to an Aussie truck was the Leader. Leader Trucks Australia was established on the Darling Downs in Queensland as part of the Great Western Group by Cyril Anderson in 1972. The first of the Leaders were two tandem-drive twin-steer trucks for Blue Metal Industries. So successful were these two originals that the company subsequently bought another 60.

Leader found their niche in the heavy transport market with rigid 4x4 and 6x6 configurations for tray, tipper and agitator applications. Leader was the first manufacturer to fit Caterpillar engines to trucks, automatic transmission to diesel trucks in assembly and to offer disc brakes.

The company boasted that its components were 80 per cent genuine Australian with only the engine, transmission and steering box imported. By 1980 Leader had sold its thousandth truck in Australia and had also sold to New Zealand, South Africa, Hong Kong, China and Indonesia.

Cyril Anderson was no newcomer to the road transport industry. His involvement began in 1934 when he bought a 2-tonne Studebaker truck and started a carrying business between Brisbane and Toowoomba. Cyril Anderson Transport eventually became Western Transport and one of Australia's great transport stories.

Western Transport operated over 100 prime movers and 100 body trucks, and established Westco Motors and later Westco Truck Sales in Toowoomba. Leader went off the market for economic reasons in February 1983, by which time 1295 Leader trucks had been assembled and sold from the Toowoomba plant.

New standards for braking requirements were introduced in 1979, making our trucks as safe as any in the world. Emission testing has introduced amazingly high standards, and Australia has always been regarded as a testing ground by the best in the world.

Australian transport operators are now able to take their choice from the world's best. Take a quick look at any highway or bush road in Australia and you'll see a blend of Macks, Kenworths, Volvos, Internationals and Mercedes.

TAXES, BLOCKHEADS AND OTHER CONTROVERSIES

While the *Hughes and Vale* case was a significant turning point for the transport industry in Australia in the 1950s, the battle was not won.

In an attempt to overcome the loss of revenue which resulted from the *Hughes and Vale* case, New South Wales introduced the Roads Maintenance Contribution Act. Under this act, state-issued 'interstate plates' were exempt from state registration taxes, but a new tax was introduced for interstate vehicles using state roads and each driver had to file returns for each vehicle for each month and pay a tax which was a percentage per mile of gross vehicle weight. All other states then followed New South Wales in introducing similar systems and road taxes.

In New South Wales a record of all journeys had to be sent to the State Department of Transport, and hundreds of inspectors were employed to watch at certain strategic points along the roads and highways. These inspectors watched for interstate plates and noted down each vehicle's number plate as it passed. Their records were checked against every driver's monthly returns and fines applied if the inspectors' records did not match logbooks.

These laws were challenged, but the High Court ruled that the new taxes were valid. Even so, many found them iniquitous and the fight to have them changed continued for over 25 years.

In 1979, 3000 truck drivers staged blockages of major highways at over 30 strategic locations in Queensland, Victoria, New South Wales and South Australia to protest against what had become known generally as the 'tonne-mile taxes'. The most famous and iconic of these, at the Razorback, near Picton, New

South Wales, became known as the 'Razorback Blockade'. The huge publicity this generated galvanised the opposition to the road tax and highlighted the plight of the truckies.

Many high-profile politicians and community leaders and entertainers became involved, including Sydney radio personality John Laws. The tonne-mile tax was abolished shortly after the protests.

The victory against the road tax led to a demand for the road transport industry to be reformed. The list of proposed reforms included the establishment of advisory bodies to solve problems in the industry, equal pay for all drivers, licensing to control the number of trucks, and uniform weight and speed limits to be implemented across all states.

An interstate commission was set up and proposed two very important moves. Firstly, that significant changes be made to all vehicle charges and, secondly, that a national commission be created.

At the time, microeconomic reform was a central policy platform of the then Labor federal government. However, as many of Labor's high-priority areas, such as transport and electricity generation and distribution, were state responsibilities, the cooperation of all six states and two territories was needed. The reform the transport industry hoped for seemed a near-impossible task and a political minefield.

The state, territory and federal leaders assembled at a special Premiers' Conference in 1991. The breakthrough came when Premier Nick Greiner of New South Wales, a Liberal, famously gave bipartisan support to the reform process. The National Road Transport Commission was formally established by an inter-governmental agreement in 1992.

As rail transport is also governed by states and territories, a review in 2002 recommended that the National Road Transport Commission's role be expanded to include rail and intermodal transport. Road transport was finally to be given the same priority as railways. This mutual recognition led to the development of a national policy on key safety issues such as fatigue, testing for drugs and alcohol, and medical fitness. This legislation was significant as it meant that rail workers were subject to the same stringent conditions and regulations that truck drivers now faced.

Eventually there was equity in both regulations and recognition of the importance and legitimacy of road and rail transport and, in 2004, the National Road Transport Commission was formally renamed the National Transport Commission to accommodate the inclusion of rail and intermodal transport into its existing mandate.

PRESERVING OUR HERITAGE, REMEMBERING OUR DEAD

In recent times a few enthusiasts and historians have started to realise that our rich and important road transport heritage, so much a part of Australia's twentieth-century history, was rusting away and disappearing rapidly. Some of those who cared and understood started to attempt to preserve and restore some of the rarer and iconic vehicles. Many trucks from yesteryear which helped open up the outback were rusting away on rural properties and cattle stations.

In Alice Springs a public meeting in 1992 led to the formation of a community-based volunteer organisation which was dedicated to the preservation of Australia's unique road transport heritage. The Road Transport Historical Society Inc. was formed later the same year. This motivated group of volunteers, led by Liz Martin, began collecting vehicles, photos and memorabilia.

After much hard work, fundraising and lobbying, the National Road Transport Hall of Fame was officially opened just three years later, on 31 July 1995.

As a museum, the Hall of Fame is unique in the way it displays vehicles. Rather than showing restored vehicles in pristine condition, museum policy is to display vehicles as they were in their working lives, including any crude modifications and adaptations bush mechanics and engineers undertook out of necessity or to ensure the vehicles could perform in Australia's harsh working environment. The vehicles on display include fire engines, carters' vans and heavy machinery, as well as trucks.

This institution has another important function. Each year it inducts drivers into the Shell Rimula Hall of Fame, recording and preserving the details of their working lives and high-lighting the contribution that the road transport industry has made to Australia.

The 500 individual citations that form the Hall of Fame provide a record of the many decades of road transport history in all areas of Australia. More than this, they tell the story of Australia's development throughout the entire twentieth century and into the twenty-first.

Around the same time as people started to preserve the history, others were looking to do something in remembrance of those killed on the nation's roads while involved in their work as drivers. The first of these to gain national recognition was set up at Tarcutta, New South Wales, which had become the halfway change-over spot on the Hume Highway between Sydney and Melbourne.

There was already a memorial of sorts at Rocky's Service Station at Yass. Yass was bypassed in 1993 and the memorial was moved to Tarcutta, where a wall of remembrance was erected by a committee headed by Ron Pullen. Bruce Baird, Minister for Transport, opened the Tarcutta memorial in 1994.

Eventually Ron and a hard-working associate, Dianne Carroll, also set up Trans-Help, a charitable foundation to help those involved in road transport, which now owns the old nursing home at Tarcutta. The Tarcutta story is told elsewhere in this collection.

There are other memorials in New South Wales, at Tamworth, which commemorates those who lost their lives on the New England Highway, and at the end of the old Putty Road, for those who died along that stretch. At Tarcutta and Tamworth, drivers who have passed on but didn't die on the road are also remembered.

Gatton in Queensland has the Lights on the Hill Memorial. A huge gathering is held there to celebrate the trucking lifestyle every year in February.

TRUCKIES AND THEIR TRUCKS

One thing that remains common in Australia is the affection of truck drivers for their rigs. Most trucks have their names on the bug deflector, across the bonnet above the radiator, on the fuel tanks or on the doors. It is a requirement of law that the business name is clearly marked, but most trucks are also given a nickname.

Kurt Johannsen named his Diamond T, the first commercially operated cattle roadtrain in the world, 'Bertha'. Vestey Brothers' two Viscount Rotinoffs were immediately christened 'Jackie' and 'Julie' on their arrival in Australia. Noel Buntine, roadtrain legend of the Northern Territory, operated three B Model Macks named 'Power and Glory', 'High and Mighty' and 'Wild and Willing'.

Jim Lowrie's old green Commer Knocker was 'Green Bottle', and McBride Transport operated a fleet of Ford Louisville roadtrains each named after a Ford car, such as 'Mustang' and 'Fairlane'. The lone Mack CLR Elite in that fleet is named 'Mutt'.

This system was particularly valuable where companies ran large fleets of the same marque. Simply by giving the name of the truck, personnel at Mack Trucks, for example, would be able to identify the truck and source the required parts.

This innovative approach to vehicle identification has long been superseded by computerised and effective plant numbering systems in large fleets, but the tradition of naming trucks will no doubt be a part of Australian trucking for many years to come.